ADVANCE PRAISE FOR
AFTER ALL

"Neff's prose sparkles with period details and movie-worthy dialogue.... Fans of the first book [*Über Alles*, 2016], or those interested in the fragile geopolitics following the war, will enjoy this sequel...."

—*Kirkus Reviews*

"*After All* recounts the fast-moving pursuit of an escaped German general through South America, using his attractive songstress daughter as the live bait. You'll be hooked early and entertained throughout this well-written historical novel."

—Julian Terry, Motion Picture Director, Hollywood, California

"In Robert Arthur Neff's historical novel *After All*, intrigue and romance collide in post–World War II South America .... The integration of historical events ... breathes realism into a well-paced plot that's filled with intrigue .... The many international settings, from Soviet-threatened Prague to an Oktoberfest celebration in Blumenau, Brazil, give *After All* a thrilling atmosphere .... *After All* is a historical novel full of talented liars, alluring places, and plot points drawn from real life."

—Eileen Gonzales, *Clarion Foreword Review*

"Romance, revenge, and Rio create the perfect storm that will have you on the edge of your seat as you find yourself traveling back to an era and an exotic place so full of danger and intrigue, you won't want *After All* to ever end."

—John Livesay, TEDx speaker
and author of *Better Selling Through Storytelling*

"Educational yet riveting. Solid historical fiction with evident research and assimilation and a pleasant writing style make this an exceptionally good read. Weaving true history into a fictional tale of suspense, drama, intrigue, displacement, and other difficulties takes a special gift, which this author has."

—Jan Tangen, NetGalley 5-Star review

"Enjoying a new area of suspense in South America. The characters are well developed, as is the plot line. The author takes the reader into the 1940s postwar Brazil magnificently."

—Sue Johnson, NetGalley 5-Star review

"This sequel quickly brings readers who have not read *Über Alles* up to speed for each character—without being redundant or boring. As Neff previews the main characters, he builds in suspense to pique interest as to what is going to happen—it keeps you devoted to the read and makes it hard to put the book down."

—William Martin Edsel, Healthcare Executive (happily retired)
Pinehurst Surgical Clinic, Pinehurst, NC

"Oh . . . how I wanted it to go on and on . . . . I loved it . . . it was the perfect sequel to *Über Alles*."

—Amy Brinckerhoff, romance reader

"*After All* integrates love, spies, and personalities developing in different places simultaneously—all moving interactively toward a definitive ending. It describes the end of World War II and the beginning of the Cold War. It is a mystery and a history to be enjoyed."

—John Wiles, international traveler; managing partner,
B&W Sporting, LLC; and independent thinker

"The two books (*Über Alles* and *After All*) are the outline of a screenplay for a fantastic movie. (I'll volunteer as a technical consultant!) Hats off to author Robert Neff."

—Richard Pabst, CIA (retired)

"Robert Neff draws heavily from his experiences living and working in the culture he includes in his books. You are his pupil, but he allows you to become emotionally involved with the engaging lead characters. These two books (*Über Alles* and *After All*) offer so much to the reader that they should be well circulated to book groups and libraries across the country and abroad. They are night-table musts."

—John Brophy, *Cornell University Alumni Magazine*

[FROM *ÜBER ALLES*]

"An absolutely riveting account of the lives of two musical artists . . . in that decade when the Nazis sought to eradicate anyone they deemed racially impure or sexually deviant . . . . You won't be able to put it down."

—Maestro George Marriner Maull, Artistic Director
and Conductor of The Discovery Orchestra

"*Über Alles* is a well-constructed novel focused upon one of the pivotal eras of human history. It succeeds both as an engaging romantic tale and as a solid look back at World War II. Readers will be well rewarded."

—Gregory Coleman, President, BuzzFeed;
former president, *Reader's Digest*

"Finding a good read to wrap yourself around is tough these days. Writers feel compelled to pen twisted and bizarre plots. Nothing seems real; everything is sensational. So, when a book comes along with a true-to-life story that's so bold, so intriguing, and so well written as to hold a reader captive, it's rare. Such a book is *Über Alles*, by Rob Neff. His poignant love story/wartime thriller is set against the harrowing backdrop of Hitler's Germany. Neff's strong, dimensional characters come to life as they defy the power of the Nazis over the power of love. As someone who lived under the black storm cloud of World War II, Neff presents a singular vantage point that rings true. If you are prepared to vicariously travel back to World War II, if you are willing to tie your heart to a story that will fill—and break—it, if you want a book worthy of your valuable leisure time—then you must read *Über Alles*."

—Laurie Bogart Morrow, author, *The Hardscrabble Chronicles*

AFTER ALL

A Gathering Storm of Romance, Revenge, and Espionage in Postwar South America

Robert Arthur Neff

FOREWORD

World War II in Europe ended on Tuesday, May 8, 1945, when Reichspräsident Karl Dönitz, successor to deceased Nazi führer Adolf Hitler, signed documentation surrendering all of Germany's armed forces. It happened on US President Harry Truman's sixty-first birthday and only the twenty-seventh day of his presidency. He addressed the nation solemnly, dedicating the costly victory to the country's wartime leader, Franklin Roosevelt, and counseling a weary nation that "work, work, work" lay ahead for Americans before a just and lasting peace could be established.

The president's realistic assessment was set aside temporarily by a nation exhausted by wartime sacrifices and the loss of over 400,000 of its military personnel; a joyful national "street party" erupted from sea to shining sea as people celebrated VE Day and anticipated that VJ Day could not be far away. Three months later, that companion victory was achieved when atomic bombs decimated two Japanese cities and the Asian nation's wartime leaders concluded that further resistance risked total annihilation of their home islands.

Conditions within Europe were chaotic. Captured Allied troops were returned to their respective commands and the woeful survivors of scores of horrific concentration camps were freed from captivity. Surrendering German military personnel surged westward to avoid capture by the USSR; nevertheless, more than two million of them failed to escape that dire alternative. The victorious Allies began the task of staking out their respective control zones on the European continent, and this quickly produced awkward divisions of former nations and their leading cities. Even before the Allied victory could be savored fully, new animosities among those recent wartime allies surfaced and threatened the peace.

At Nuremberg, the trial of twenty-two principal Nazis was scheduled by their captors to begin only six months after VE Day, to be followed by twelve additional Nuremberg adjudications of accused wartime guilt by many more from the losing side. Even as this process was being readied, angry survivors from the cruel prisons and harsh ghettos were demanding a much wider net to ensnare countless additional Nazis and their collaborators who had visited misery upon helpless social outcasts during the six wartime years.

The United States, which had assembled a military force unparalleled in history and had executed a remarkable strategy for victory, was not well prepared for the war's aftermath.

General George C. Marshall authored a generous plan to provide the financial underpinning of postwar European economic recovery, but no one anticipated the political tug-of-war that erupted between communism and capitalist democracy for the loyalties of Europe. A US intelligence agency named the Office of Strategic Services (OSS) had been cobbled together hastily during wartime to meet the nation's need for information about its enemies, but the OSS was disbanded by a presidential executive order issued on September 20, 1945, and effective ten days later. The Central Intelligence Agency (CIA) was not created until two years later, on September 18, 1947, to provide a permanent intelligence arm protecting the nation's international interests. During the critical postwar hiatus, the United States was shorthanded in dealing with the newly emerging peacetime international intrigues.

The story related in *After All* begins during that two-year period, when it refocuses upon the lives of two young Germans whose wartime romance and tribulations were the subject of my historical novel entitled *Über Alles*. Dieter Meister was a barroom piano man who had been displaced from a Frankfurt music academy because he was the orphaned child of a Jewish mother. In Berlin he met Sofie von Seigler, the daughter of an important Wehrmacht general and his Jewish secretary. Sofie had been born during General von Seigler's pre–World War I deployment to Poland.

Although Dieter and Sofie were apolitical musicians, circumstances beyond their control had embroiled the two in the catastrophic Nazi conquest of Western Europe, and eventually they became hopelessly separated. At the conclusion of the story related in *Über Alles*, Dieter and Sofie had been reunited in Brazil. They viewed their new horizons hopefully—after all, they had endured history's most costly war—but residual shadows from that conflict soon darkened the skies of their bright new world.

—ROBERT ARTHUR NEFF

Neutral Brazil joined the Allies and declared war on the Axis powers in August 1942 after suffering heavy shipping losses to German U-boats marauding in the Atlantic Ocean.

DRAMATIS PERSONAE

———————

(Real persons appear in italic type;
created characters in roman type)

Sofie von Seigler – b. 1915. Daughter of Wehrmacht general
and Polish SWW operative; consort of Dieter Meister.
Sofie is a professional chanteuse known as "Sophia."

Dieter Meister – b. 1911. a.k.a. Dieter Havlik. Jewish piano
player, escaped from Theresienstadt Detention Camp, now
performing in Copacabana Palace Hotel, Rio de Janeiro,
Brazil.

Elsa Danzig b.1911. Polish SWW spy stationed in
Czechoslovakia. Participant in Dieter's escape from
Theresienstadt.

William Carney b. 1906. OSS operative in London who
searches for General Otto von Seigler.

Lilka Rudovska b. 1875. Exiled Polish SWW coordinator
overseeing continental operatives from London. Mother of
Sofie von Seigler.

Booker Pittman b. 1909. *Grandson of American educator Booker T. Washington. Became a prominent jazz musician and bandleader in Brazil, where he was known as "Buca."*

Simon Wiesenthal b. 1908. *Austrian Jewish holocaust survivor who dedicated his post-WWII life to pursuit and capture of Nazi war criminals.*

Francisco Matarazzo "Baby" Pignatari b. 1917. *Flamboyant Italian-Brazilian industrialist known for his daring behavior, good looks, excessive wealth, and succession of romantic affairs with some of the world's most beautiful women, in addition to having four wives.*

General Otto von Seigler b. 1890. Professional Wehrmacht officer; expert in matters of Polish banking system. Consort of Lilka Rudovska and father of Sofie von Seigler.

Octavio Oliveira b. 1901. Director of Security for Rio's Copacabana Palace Hotel.

Farouk bin Ahmed Fuad b.1920. *King of Egypt 1936-52. Playboy. Frequent visitor to the Copacabana Palace Hotel in Rio de Janeiro, Brazil.*

Dr. Maxmilian Ullrich b. 1902. Prague Branch Manager, Bank Julius Baer.

Lola Morais b. 1908. Vocalist with the Booker Pittman Orchestra.

Maria Eva Duarte de Peron b. 1919. *a.k.a. "Evita." Popular First Lady of Argentina from 1946 until her death in 1952 at age 33.*

Juan Domingo Peron b. 1895. Quintessential Argentine military and political figure. President of Argentina 1946-55 and 1973-74.

Branka, b. 1909. Wartime Polish SWW stringer in Lisbon who becomes General von Seigler's companion and escapes to Brazil with him.

Joe English b. 1906. OSS associate of William Carney in London who later becomes an operative in the new CIA.

Magda b. 1912. SWW partner of Elsa Danzig in Prague who resigns after Poland's defeat and emigrates to Chicago USA.

Chefe Suarez b. 1892. Police Chief in Blumenau, Catarina State, Brazil, where one of the world's largest Oktoberfest Festivals is observed annually.

Jerome Doyle b. 1910. Chief of FBI's Special Intelligence Service in South America. The Service operated secretly under cover of a corporation named "Importers and Exporters Service Company," headquartered on the 43rd floor of 30 Rockefeller Plaza in New York City.

Lucia DeSimone b. 1918. Language teacher at Joinville University in Brazil, who tutors General von Seigler and Branka (a.k.a. Kurt and Gerda Hahn) in the Portuguese language at their remote fazenda in Catarina State.

PROLOGUE

Saturday, 12 May 1945
Copacabana Palace Hotel
Avenida Atlântica
Rio de Janeiro, Brazil

My dear Elsa,

This letter is long overdue, but until we learned of the Allied victory in Europe on Tuesday, I could not safely send it. As it is, I am not using your name on the envelope, but only the box number at Praha Hlavní Nádraží Station which you gave to me. I hope you will acknowledge your receipt. Just use the hotel name above and indicate that it is for the "Piano Man." Elsa, I believe that I have been born twice. First at Dr. Hoch's Konservatorium in Frankfurt, on 20 June 1911, when an elderly Jewish physician used his forceps to ease me from the body of a young music student named Eva Rosenberg. She was destined to perish in the Great Influenza Pandemic before my eighth birthday. I was born the second time on a roadside outside the Theresienstadt Detention Camp near Prague, on 6 March 1943, when you and the big Gypsy fellow pulled my moribund body from a large garbage can filled with putrid fish entrails. You both risked your lives to free me, and then you nursed me back to some semblance of health and delivered me to the next link in my escape path.

That journey took me to Lisbon, where I became a supernumerary crewman on a freighter bound for Brazil. Once here, with an introduction and endorsement provided by my former (Portuguese) manager at the Fischerstube in Berlin, I became the "Piano Man" in the lounge bar and restaurant of Brazil's most famous luxury hotel. You can imagine the change in my life! For over three years I had wallowed in the filth and sickness of Theresienstadt—and had survived only by providing piano music for the guards and billeted military. I also cleaned their dining areas, latrines, and kitchen, and augmented my meager meals with leftover scraps salvaged from their dirty plates. Then, in only a few weeks, I was miraculously transformed into a well-paid, well-fed entertainer in an overpriced luxury hotel, observing the eccentricities and foibles of the world's "celebrities." I had truly been born again, and you were the midwife!

I will always remember how you cleaned and dressed the sores on my body and massaged my limbs each day until I could move about on my own. You bathed me as if I were a child and encouraged me to eat and read and speak and think like a free person again. Most important, you sheltered a fugitive at the risk of your own freedom— perhaps even your life.

Elsa, of course I know that you were a professional gatherer of intelligence working in enemy-held territory. I also realize that your work was generally performed as part of an "escort service" where your charms could loosen the tongues of occupying military and businessmen. It was depersonalizing and undoubtedly humiliating for you. In the last moments we shared, I reassured you that "you are not a whore— you are a warrior," and more than ever I know how true that was. With the war now ended, I want to reverse our roles and help you to be born again—and I have already put this in place—so you cannot say "no" to me.

A year ago, at a place called Bretton Woods in the USA state of New Hampshire, the finance people from many Allied countries set the base for postwar business and trade. They agreed on exchange rates that are now in effect. I have most of a Swiss Franc account— which was set up by a friend who you know, to help my escape— sitting untouched with Bank Julius Baer. I have instructed them to release the contents to you, using the name by which I know you, plus the date on which you freed me, expressed as dd/mm/yyyy. The account's assets, at the Bretton Woods exchange rate, will provide you with about 19,000 US dollars. I am told that dollars are the desired postwar currency and that you should be able to acquire a cozy apartment almost anywhere in Europe with that amount.

You are a talented and charming woman, but we are both approaching our 35th birthdays now, and it is time for us both to emerge from the chrysalis stage into our newborn selves. You made that possible for me, and now I can partially return the favor—so do not deny me that.

With warmest affection and unbounded gratitude,

D.

1

Sofie Goes To Work

Doctor Fritz Kaufman, her favorite vocal coach at Berlin's Humboldt University, had once lectured a sullen, young Sofie von Seigler that the quality of a vocal performance is frequently predetermined by the singer's attitude when she arrives on stage. Sofie had at first rejected the advice—as she did many untested suggestions—but with added experience, her teacher's observation had become an integral part of Sofie's performance preparation. And so, on a cloudless Rio de Janeiro morning in 1945, the lithe singer emerged from the entrance to her Ipanema beachfront apartment building on Rua Francisco Otaviano and hurried three blocks eastward to Copacabana Beach, where she paused to remove her sandals, then began shuffling northward through the fine sand along the margin of Avenida Atlântica toward the iconic Copacabana Palace Hotel. At 11:30 a.m., she and Dieter "the Piano Man" would begin entertaining sophisticated midday diners in the exclusive Bar do Copa, where they had become popular over a two-year engagement.

Sofie loved her daily strolls close by the ocean, and having passed this way on so many similar mornings she now looked forward to frequent greetings from vendors, body surfers, sand artists, and even tourists who recognized the popular chanteuse known as "Sophia." Lately her most boisterous daily greetings had emanated from a crew of hard hats, draped on the face of a seaside building under construction. The first to see her this morning shouted, "*Olá*, Sophia—come up here and sing to us," which was followed by a chorus of hoots and whistles, then a plaintive, "Sophia, *I love* you! Marry me!" There were more howls and extended arms from a dozen smiling workers to magnify the greeting. Sofie devoured their attention and returned it with waves, blown kisses, and finally a few twirls in the sand which caused her skirt to billow upward, intentionally revealing her long, tanned legs. That was the salutation they had wanted, and with one final chorus of hoots and whistles, they turned back to their work.

The same routine would be repeated tomorrow, but for now it sent her on her way, smiling broadly and humming some of the melodies she knew her audience would request in another hour. Bless you, Doctor Kaufman, she thought. I wonder if you are still back there in Berlin.

At the Copacabana Palace she was promoted enthusiastically as "The International Vocalist, Sophia" and her credits listed prior appearances in London, Paris, and Prague—many with the famous Django Reinhardt Hot Jazz Club du France. Her poster photograph showed the windblown blonde hair now so appreciated by those construction workers, and in the image she was shown wearing an outrageous, revealing electric-blue gown— daring even by Rio's loosened postwar standards.

Sofie's Swiss passport and Brazilian *cédula*—on file at the hotel—identified her as Sofia Havlik, domiciliary of Neufchatel, Switzerland/ female /married/ born 1915. Her accompanist was duly recorded as being Dieter Havlik, also of Neufchatel—a male born in 1911. Their employer's assumption was that Sofie and Dieter were a couple who had emigrated from Europe during World War II, seeking to build new careers in the thriving Brazilian capital city.

Both passports were excellent forgeries, but in 1945 Brazil there was no perceived need to delve further into immigrant European identities—the two musicians had professional talents to support themselves, which was attested by their ability to fill most of the tables in the Bar do Copa five days and two evenings weekly. That was enough.

Sofie entered the hotel lobby and crossed its broad, polished floor to the closed doorway of the Bar do Copa. She was certain that Dieter would already be inside, tinkering with the room's beautiful Bechstein piano; it had been commandeered the previous evening by one Luis Varona, an energetic Brazilian pianist who was known for his heavy Afro-Cuban jazz innovations (and profuse sweating during performances). The meticulous Dieter would insist upon tuning and cleaning the instrument before blending it with Sofie's—Sophia's—sophisticated delivery.

She appreciated that, of course, but often found herself troubled by Dieter's compulsions, because she knew well that for more than three years he had survived only by laboring over a decrepit and dirty piano as a prisoner in the Nazis' infamous Theresienstadt Detention Camp near Prague. That damaged piano had been his major ally in a daily battle for life until he could implement an ingenious escape plan, which ultimately set him free. Sofie often wondered whether Dieter's current insistence upon artistic perfection was the product of those horrible years—or was it confirmation of his commitment to offer unflawed accompaniment for the love of his life?

She waved at Dieter from the doorway, then turned to proceed to the elevator bank and upward to a cramped room on the sixth floor, which the hotel's management provided for their convenience. Room 626 was on the Copacabana Palace's "ugly side," facing away from the ocean and toward some commercial buildings and the dire poverty of flimsy favela shacks clinging to the hillside. It wasn't a room that could be rented commercially. There was rarely a reason to raise the shade that covered the room's only window, because there was nothing to see—even in "the world's most beautiful urban setting."

Room 626 did have a spacious cedar-lined closet, suitable for storing their performance clothing, and a single sleeping couch, which was welcoming after two or three hours of standing, smiling, posing, and spinning out overly familiar melodies. There was also a small dresser with a companion chair and a clear, lighted makeup mirror, where Sofie could apply the final touches necessary to achieve the dazzling Sophia. The room's only other amenities were a lumpy lounge chair that had long ago graced the lobby, with a basic reading lamp by its side. Even without style, Room 626 was very accommodating for the young couple because it allowed them to disappear quickly after performances, rather than having to travel back immediately to their Ipanema apartment.

Before Sofie could enter the open lift door, an attendant from the reception desk called her name and beckoned her back to the lobby. "This came for you last night, senhora," she said, pushing a tan commercial envelope across the counter. It had only the hand-printed name "Sofia Havlik" on its outside—there was no sender information or postage to identify its origin.

Sofie examined it briefly, then asked the clerk, "Do you know who delivered it?" The answer was a shrug, followed by, "No, senhora, I didn't come on until 7:00 a.m.—maybe you could ask Carlos tonight. He was here, I think." With that, the clerk turned her attention to a hotel guest and Sofie glanced at her watch. It was already time to dress for their midday show, so she ascended to Room 626 and tossed the envelope into the well-used chair. "Maybe something from those crazy construction guys," she mumbled to no one, as she started gathering her hair into a pile of loose, blonde curls. For now, her concerns were all about the next performance.

2

〰

Dieter "The Piano Man"

Dieter Havlik had hailed a cab to take him to the Copacabana Palace at eight thirty that morning; he was carrying a short stack of "cheat sheets" for new ballads he planned to integrate into Sophia's repertoire. Musical tastes evolved quickly among the international patrons of the Copacabana Palace, and successful performers had to demonstrate their awareness of what was new and topical. The celebrated Buca Pittman Orchestra had been featured in the hotel's main ballroom over the weekend, and Dieter had heard that "Buca" was mixing his familiar jazz rhythms with some new samba flourishes pilfered from the ubiquitous Ipanema beach performers. He had thought that might be a way to add variety to Sophia's repertoire, too.

Buca's real name was Booker; he had been named for his famous grandfather, Booker T. Washington, but that didn't mean a whole lot to musicians. More impressive to Dieter was the fact that Buca had played clarinet and saxophone with the likes of Louis Armstrong and Count Basie in the United States before moving to Brazil in 1937. When Dieter mentioned his admiration for Buca to the hotel manager, he had been offered the chance to meet Buca over morning coffee with the manager today. However, forty minutes after the suggested time, Dieter was still sitting alone with a cooling *cafezinho*, hoping that the promise was not hollow—or "peta," as the locals would call it.

Since his arrival in Rio in March 1943, Dieter's life had been centered in the Copacabana Palace. During the first months of his freedom—after escaping from Theresienstadt and crossing the Atlantic as a smuggled seaman—Dieter had been guilt-ridden. He knew that his cellmates, Jura Havlik and Adam Wodzinski, might never again know freedom's blessings. On a hundred nights since his arrival in Rio, Dieter's sleep had been shattered by images of huddling with those two captured physicians under "Old Jacob's Coat," a parting favor from another internee as he was being shipped off to Auschwitz-Birkenau to die. On other nights he would dream of cleaning speckles of blood from Jura's clothing in order to avoid the guards' conclusion that Jura's advancing consumption now needed "special care" at that extermination camp in Poland. So—today he should be cursing a broken coffee date amid the lavish setting of the Bar do Copa? Not likely, he thought—no, not likely at all.

Dieter carried his tepid beverage across the room to the elaborate Bechstein and began dabbing at its ivory keys with his moistened napkin. He always carried a small bottle of white vinegar mixed with water to performances and meticulously addressed any stains from sweat, spittle, liquor, tobacco, or whatever might have sullied the Schreger lines of the porous ivory keys. As his nightmares were, this was an involuntary holdover from Dieter's Theresienstadt years.

When the door opened and Sofie waved, letting him know she had arrived, the furrows of disappointment vanished instantly from Dieter's face. She could always work that magic. From their first encounter, he had found her mixture of brash confidence and vulnerable femininity to be a remarkable tonic, and when the war drove them far apart, Dieter had viewed that separation as his greatest hardship. The miracle of their being reunited so far from Germany was like a favorite song he could retrieve and play mentally, and for two years they had coasted on this good fortune without the need to plan beyond the next day's musical selections. True freedom, for them, included the absence of deadlines.

He understood that now, with the war ended, there would inevitably be a requirement to address some "avoided" issues. Dieter knew that Sofie was concerned about the considerable fortune she held at Switzerland's Bank Julius Baer in a numbered account created for her by her father during the peak years of Nazi hegemony. She did not want to know its source, but of course she understood that it vastly exceeded the salary of even a high-ranking Wehrmacht officer. Approaching age thirty, the tall Sofie was still a head-turner, and her voice had acquired a singular maturity. But how long would even a well-received routine in a luxury hotel satisfy her artistic appetite? And then, what of her parents? Her father was living anonymously somewhere in Brazil's interior, and her mother had recently retired from a career in Polish SWW intelligence. Should either be invited back into her life? Or, more important, into their lives?

Once again, Dieter set those deferred issues aside and penciled a new encore selection into today's performance—he decided it would be Jerome Kern's "All The Things You Are." What could describe better his feelings for Sofie than Kern's genius lyrics? She had, for nearly four years, been Dieter's "promised kiss of springtime" that helped him through the lonely winters of internment in Theresienstadt.

3

***

A Cryptic Message

After performing in the Bar do Copacabana for two and a half hours, both looked forward to some privacy in Room 626, where Sophia could remove her makeup and revert to being just Sofie, and Dieter could stretch his legs and read a German magazine in the shabby chair. They closed the door with obvious pleasure and moved to their respective corners of the room.

"What's this?" Dieter asked, holding up the forgotten envelope resting in his chair.

"Don't know. Dropped at the desk last night—no time to look at it when I got here. Hand it to me, *Schatzi*, and I'll open it now."

Sofie picked through the contents for a few minutes while Dieter closed his eyes and leaned back quietly. Finally he sat up and inquired, "So?"

"Strange," she countered. "It's a bunch of pages from a US Army report of some kind. It's dated 8 July 1945 and seems to be information extracted from Russian and Red Cross reports regarding the eighteen thousand Theresienstadt prisoners liberated on May 8. Then there are lots of names and notations in some sort of alphabetical groupings."

"*All* eighteen thousand names? It doesn't look big enough for . . ."

"No, no. Only some pages with names beginning with *H* and *M*—why would that be . . . ?"

Dieter moved quickly to her side and took the pages, running his finger along the alphabetically sequenced *H* names and looking for *Havlik*. He had never dared hope that Jura could survive more than a few weeks after his own escape, and the notion that he might have been liberated two years later seemed out of the question, but then, Juraslav Havlik was a physician—as was his cellmate, Adam Wodzinski—and doctors could occasionally do remarkable things to prolong life. Even more important, Jura was Sofie's much older half brother, who had hidden them in his Prague clinic when they fled Berlin in 1939.

But his search for *Havlik* proved fruitless, and Dieter put the pages down, more confused than before.

"There are these pages, too, Dieter," Sofie offered tenderly, sensing his obvious disappointment over failing to find what he was searching for. She handed him more sheets of paper with listings of *M* surnames among the liberated prisoners, and he half-heartedly passed through them until his expression froze and he pointed at a highlighted name. "Look at this!"

MEISTER, Dieter/ Berlin GR/ age about 34 / ambulatory

Both stared at the entry in disbelief.

*

"Liebling—you were long gone from there in May, 1945—so how could you be liberated then?"

"No, Sofie—the point is that Dieter *Meister* was *never* in that place. When I was captured crossing into Poland on September 1,

1939, I carried a bogus Swiss passport which identified me as Dieter *Havlik*. Havlik, not Meister—and Swiss, not German. There are no Havliks on that list. Not your half brother, Jura, and not Dieter Havlik, the name I was using! Nobody named Havlik!"

"But didn't that Gestapo Colonel who apprehended you want you because you were Dieter Meister—from Germany— with a Jewish mother—involved with the daughter of a Wehrmacht General? Didn't he want to leverage that information to his advantage? I thought . . . "

"Yes, yes—but he wasn't sure immediately how to use the information, so he kept it secret when they caught me at the border, and then he just let Jura and me decay in Theresienstadt. We expected to be called out every day and interrogated, but nothing ever happened. Much later, we learned the Colonel had been shot and killed soon after our capture, and we concluded that my real identity died with him. I don't think that he—Colonel Gunther—ever told anybody that he had captured Dieter Meister."

"You were an enigma to them," she smiled, "and they just couldn't catch you. That one Gestapo accountant followed us in Prague for weeks, and I tried to get Father to have him transferred. Remember?"

"Mmmm. Yes. Jurgen Deitz was his name. He drove us crazy. That *scheisskopf* Gunther had him killed and made it look like an accident so he—Colonel Gunther—would be the only one with the Dieter Meister card to play. That's just before we fled from Prague— but you were already gone. It was Jura and me, plus the two Polish girls from Gdańsk. They were SWW spies, you know."

"Yes—Magda and Elsa. I wonder where they are now? Probably old and fat."

"That's not fair—they were pretty when they got dressed up.

And smart, too. You know Elsa was part of the rescue operation when I slipped away from Theresienstadt. She and the big Gypsy fellow picked up the garbage can I was hiding in, and then she took good care of me until I got my strength back."

"I'm sure she took excellent care of you! When we were all hiding in the Havlik Clinic, she watched you like you were dessert."

"Back to these lists. The cover page is on US Army stationery, and the two attachments are taken from the report by Russian liberators and the Red Cross overseers. Right? Somebody wanted you to see my real name on there and do something when you found it. What?"

"Aren't you forgetting, Schatzi, that you weren't *there* when they opened the camp? Neither Dieter Meister nor Dieter Havlik could be liberated if there wasn't somebody there saying that's who he was."

"So . . . ?"

"So either some other prisoner gave them your name or someone else added your name to the list for a purpose—without there being any such liberated prisoner at all. "

"I'll tell you what we should do. We should figure this out logically. First, let's each make a list—separately—of all the people we can think of who ever knew that someone named Dieter Meister was imprisoned in Theresienstadt. Then let's go down those names and try to imagine why each might want to bring that to your—or our—attention. Right now I am baffled. Maybe we can come up with some obvious reason for delivering this to you."

Sofie gave a dismissive shrug of her shoulders and said, "Okay— give me a sheet of paper and a pencil and I'll put names down as I think of them. Puzzling, isn't it? I'll also ask Carlos, the night deskman, if he has any recollection of the person who dropped it off. It might be easier to work backward from that, don't you think?"

❧

Twenty-four hours later they again sat in Room 626 after a busy luncheon performance and Sofie unfolded the small piece of stationery she had been carrying and jotting names upon since their earlier discussion of the enigmatic prisoner lists.

"Okay, Piano Man," she began, trying to keep the matter from seeming overly worrisome. "Your list will probably have all of these, too. Of course my mother, Lilka, knows your real identity—and her SWW contacts in Prague, fat Magda and fat Elsa, were with you when you all had to flee. Right? My half brother, Dr. Jura Havlik, knew, too, but you think he died in Theresienstadt. Colonel Gunther and that cockroach, Deitz, knew, but they are dead, too. My father and his adjutant, Major Kolb, had a role in your flight to Lisbon and the boat trip to Brazil from there.

"And you know that my father and Branka, the former Lisbon SWW resident, are a couple now—so she knows. So, I count six live people who know that Dieter Meister was the identity of a Theresienstadt prisoner who managed to escape before the camp was liberated."

"Yes, I have those six," Dieter replied, as he unfolded his own paper and flattened it on the arm of his chair. "You forgot Herr Stinnes who provided passage on his freighter for me, and later for you, to travel across the ocean. What do you think?"

"Well, he was father's childhood friend and he certainly knew our identities—but he really doesn't delve deeply into facts about his passengers. He just collects outrageous fees and turns his head. There were a lot of affluent Jews and Nazis who got away from

Europe as anonymously as possible, and Stinnes was a good conduit. I would put a question mark by that name."

"Okay, well, here's one you wouldn't think of. Remember that I lived with the Portuguese fellow who managed the Fischerstube—where I played piano in Berlin and where you first saw me?"

"How could I not? You were the love of his life and he tried to keep me from getting to know you. He told me you were a Jew and I'd get in trouble if we were friends."

"I guess you do remember him—his name was Miguel—well, his family owns a hotel in Lisbon. I finally confronted him about his treachery—you know, telling the police about us—and he was contrite. His family and the Guinle family, the owners of the Copacabana, are longtime friends, and he got me my first audition here over two years ago. It was a form of apology, I think, and it helped me a lot. I didn't know at the time that I'd see you again. But Miguel knows my whole story . . ." Dieter's words trailed off as he wondered whether he might again have put Sofie into some kind of jeopardy unwittingly.

"So we have—what? Eight names of people who might possess enough knowledge to direct that information to me in Rio. But we still have no reason why anyone would *want* to do that. How do we follow that path? Should we try to communicate to all eight an 'acknowledgment' of our receipt? I'm still apprehensive."

"Me, too."

"Oh, I just thought of another—that Adam—Adam Wadzinski—the other doctor in the prison cell with you and Jura. Could he have lived until the place was liberated? You don't talk much about Adam, but you three shared the same cell a long time, Dieter. Should we add Adam to the list?"

"Sure—we should start with everybody then eliminate some if we can. Adam and Jura knew one another from medical school in Poland—they became very close there. Adam came from a good family in Posen, and he played classics well on the piano. In Theresienstadt that was his value, and he managed to avoid some of the harsher treatment because they needed his performances at times. They used him as they did all of the musicians—to show outsiders that we were happy 'temporary detainees,' still able to practice our art in 'The Village Hitler Gave to the Jews.' Such a fraud—and how gullible those outsiders were!

"I suppose he could have lived. That makes our list nine, right?"

4

70 *Grosvenor Street, London / OSS Headquarters. Late Spring 1945.*

One of the room's occupants wore a US Army Major's tunic and the other a recently crafted Seville Row business suit, and both spoke the English language with the distinctly American "rough edges" which had invaded London's Mayfair District as World War II raged on the Continent. The Americans' embassy was nearby at One Grosvenor Square, as was the building which had become the London headquarters for US five-star General Dwight David Eisenhower, who commanded the victorious joint Allied forces. But #70 Grosvenor had no nameplate to define its mission, and few people passing by suspected that America's nascent efforts at Continental espionage were centered there. It was OSS Headquarters.

In 1942, the colorful and sometimes outrageous Major General "Wild Bill" Donovan had overseen creation of the Office of Strategic Services at the request of his Columbia Law School classmate, Franklin D. Roosevelt. Wild Bill continued to direct the new spying operation from his suite in the exclusive

Connaught Hotel, two blocks away on Carlos Place. By 1945, Wild Bill's OSS had aggregated over 11,000 men and women worldwide, including the two now chatting at #70. But back in Washington, the powerful FBI Director, J. Edgar Hoover, was advising America's new president, Harry Truman, that the wartime OSS should be allowed to dissolve, leaving the FBI unchallenged as the country's only postwar intelligence agency.

The civilian-clothed man crossed one well-creased pants leg over the other and leaned forward conspiratorially toward his coffee-sipping listener. "You know, Joe, the British have long done this sort of thing, and their MI6 service is respected by their military as well as by the British Parliament. They have recruited top talent and have funded them well. We are learning a lot from the Brits, but we don't want to become totally dependent on them, either. They distrust the Russians and don't tell them squat, while our brass have been directed to cozy up and work together with the Soviets. Same thing with the French—the Brits have had their doubts about them for years, and we romanticize."

"Okay, I get that, Carney, but what about the lady we're talking to today—Lilka Whatsername? How does she figure in our work?"

"Ah—there's the rub, Joe. She has been a part of the best espionage network in Europe, and they don't even have a damned country anymore!"

"The Poles, right?"

"Right! Remember, those poor bastards have had Russians, Austrians, and Germans all invading and beating up on them forever. They have developed tentacles all over Europe gathering survival info for a long time, and even though Hitler went through their army like a dose of salts, they still were able to find out a lot and to prepare for it. They can blend and they can speak languages better than MI6 guys, and—get this—they sometimes use pretty girls to loosen tongues. Sorta like Mata Hari, you know?"

"So, this Lilka is a seductress?"

"Hell, no! She's a Polish grandma type, with wrinkles and a missing tooth on one side. But she has been the mother hen to an effective network, and she has continued to direct them as part of the Polish government-in-exile. They're over on Eaton Place— near here. After Wild Bill brought me over, I started checking some of our informants with Lilka, and damned if she didn't have a folder on every one! OSS is gonna be phased out soon, and there will someday be a kind of central intelligence department or office to pick up the pieces. When that happens, you guys will have a shitload of digging to do, and I think she could be useful. Okay? Got it?"

❧

Their guest, Lilka, joined them minutes later and asked immediately if she might have some hot tea with milk. She was in no hurry to launch into social niceties, and she stirred, sipped, and smiled pleasantly before the first words were exchanged. When she did begin, it was direct and to the point.

"You're getting a late start to create any postwar value within the current OSS intelligence operation. But my guess is that peacetime will produce even greater needs. There's going to be a wrestling match among the old Allies over control in Europe, and it will involve digging into the internal politics of a dozen countries. You Americans always conclude that the fight is over when the shooting stops, and then you go home and leave a vacuum. That's when you most need good intelligence—to avoid giving away all of what you have fought to preserve.

"The other error I foresee is your conclusion that you can just insert inexperienced operatives into troubled areas with minimal language proficiency and a shortwave radio and gather useful intelligence. That only works in the movies. Good spy corps must be sown, cultivated, and nurtured over time. Otherwise they shout 'amateur' to seasoned operatives, and they are soon inundated in worthless, misleading information—their efforts can be truly counterproductive. Do you understand my point?"

The military man responded, somewhat shocked at the derogatory directness of the old woman. After all, he was representing the strongest nation on earth, and she was exiled from a defeated, occupied country. Still, he tried to soften his words. "Madame, we have won this war in Europe and we want to secure a lasting peace. You point out what we already know about the shortcomings of our intelligence-gathering machinery, but that doesn't advance our mission, does it? How would you suggest that we acquire the intelligence capability we will need to return Europe to healthy peacetime status?"

"Buy it!" was the reflexive response. "Choose the best of what is in place now and set your organization up to receive and evaluate the information flow those seasoned assets produce. Others can help you to identify the best-placed people and they can put your staff into contact with any people you believe can help you. Some may be ideologues, who will work only for their own governments, but most espionage professionals become more like businesspeople in the wake of a war, when their primary concern becomes their own hide."

"They can be bought, you're saying," the blue suit interjected.

"Not their souls or their loyalties," she countered. "But many of them have toiled for years, and some have endured hardship, deprivation, and danger. Few are comfortably off. Their major salable products are the knowledge and contacts they have cultivated. As the Continent puts itself together again, they know there is a market for them, and your money is as good as anyone else's. Don't ask them to do morally corrupt things, but pick their brains as you try to make Europe work again."

"How about you, Lilka—would you consider associating with a new employer?"

"Thank you Mr. Carney. That is flattering, but I am one of those ideologues," she smiled as she returned her teacup to its saucer and rose to leave. "However, if you do decide to employ the services of some established professionals on the Continent, I believe I may be helpful in your selection process."

When she had left, the two Americans looked at one another in disbelief. They were beginning to understand the magnitude of the problems ahead as well as the disadvantages they faced on a Continent ravaged by war and fulminating with intrigue.

"Anyone else coming in today to remind us how unprepared we are?" the military officer quipped. "Do you think everyone is onto our shortcomings as she is?"

"No, I don't," the man named Carney responded, "but unless we get going pretty soon on a permanent intelligence agency with real professionals processing information from reliable sources, we're going to be crapped on and lied to by every dipstick political leader in postwar Europe. And it can't be done by some soft-handed cocktail sipper in Washington, either—we need field operatives making timely judgments where the problems are. Oh, yeah—I do want to talk to one more guy today. You'll love this.

"This one's not from any organized team. He's like Madame Defarge—keeping a list of people who need to be tracked down and punished. I can't really figure him out, because his story changes from time to time. But we do know that he was a prisoner in Mauthausen when it was liberated, and a lot of his family members—they're Jews—were slaughtered, gassed, starved, you name it, by the Nazis. He says there are hundreds of criminal Nazis slipping away and blending into the general population—in Germany but also in other countries where they can start over. We are only grabbing the big names for Nuremberg, or so he says, and he wants to go after *all* of them."

"Who's Madame Defarge? Where does she fit in? You lost me."

"She was a character in that book about the French Revolution, and she was knitting a blanket or something, with a code for all of the people they were going to hunt down and kill. She's famous—you should read more. Anyhow, that's what this Wiesenthal reminds me of. He has his list of Germans and other Nazis he wants us to help him find and punish. He can tell you who were the brutal killers in the camps, but he also knows who stole everything from a lot of Jews and he wants revenge so it won't happen again. I think we should give him thirty minutes and hear what he has to say. Okay, Joe?"

5

––––––––––

Buca at the Copa

Friday was their most demanding workday. Sophia had both a midday and an evening show on Fridays, and that day was usually marked by the arrival of the more discerning weekend crowd, who expected that the higher room rates in effect would assure them the very best foods, libations, and entertainment. Sofie and Dieter liked to introduce new material to the weekend audiences, so they combed the popular entertainment publications from abroad, trying to catch trends and share popular, current sounds with their audiences. The combination of new material and more-demanding listeners was the Friday profile; Sophia even saved her most flattering gowns, makeup, and hairdos for *Sexta-Feria*, as the locals called it.

When the long day was over, the two performers liked to share Ramos Fizzes at a remote table in the bar before shedding their performance identities in Room 626 and then proceeding to their more comfortable home for the night.

Sofie had already kicked off her high heels and Dieter had loosened his bow tie when the handsome man walked to their corner table. He was tan-skinned, with a Gable-style mustache, and Sofie judged him to be about forty. Dieter knew immediately that it was Booker Pittman, and he was on his feet quickly with his hand extended when the man offered, "I'm Buca. We were supposed to have coffee together a couple of days ago, but something came up. Sorry about that, but you know musicians—mine are no different." He had addressed them in American English, rather than Brazilian Portuguese, and Dieter concluded that Buca thought that would be easier for Europeans. Sofie spoke English well, and she immediately smiled and invited him to sit.

"I caught your third set tonight—really enjoyed your work. So did the crowd. Great voice projection. I was 'way in the back of the room, and it carried perfectly. Nice mixture of material, too—do you do your own arrangements, Mr. Havlik?"

"I'm Dieter—Mr. Havlik was my father," was the quick, smiling reply. "Yes, I know Sophia's range and quality points pretty well, and I try to highlight them. She also has excellent sense of pitch, so we throw in occasional key changes which aren't in the sheets—it personalizes her delivery." After he had said it, Dieter thought that the response may have sounded too possessive, but after all, he wanted to establish his role in Sophia's popularity, didn't he? "Thank you for coming to hear us, Mr. Pittman. We are admirers of your work and will try to hear you sometime during the weekend."

"Booker," was the quick counter. "I understand that you don't do any Saturday shows, so you probably keep that day for yourselves, but I'd like to have them hold a table for you at our 9:00 p.m. appearance tomorrow and ask you to be my guests. And there's one other thing. Miss Sophia, I know that you haven't sung with an orchestra since you were in London, but I'd enjoy having you sing one or two numbers with my big band—just as an experiment. You pick the songs you're comfortable with and I'll keep my boys from being too loud—boisterous, eh?"

She got the pun and smiled. "That's generous, Booker, but you're right. We do save Saturdays for ourselves. Let us think about this and get back to you in the morning. Agreed, Lieblingsmensch?" The question was directed to Dieter, who admired her quick response as well as the term of endearment. He approved the answer with a smile and a nod. In minutes the three had left the room, but Sofie and Dieter knew they would be accepting the invitation and not strolling along the beach to some small eatery on Saturday night.

The talented American musician Booker Pittman moved to Brazil in 1937, where he was called "Buca." His band was considered the best in South America. Musidisc label; photographer unknown.

Once they reached Room 626, Sofie and Dieter flopped on the small bed and stretched like tired athletes. Fridays really were the most demanding days of their week, and this one had gone well. Dieter switched to a sitting position after flexing his hands and extending his arms, then he turned toward a smiling Sofie and asked, "Do you have the patience to look at our nine names again and see if we can make any sense of that?"

Her reaction was unexpected—an annoyed silence. Sofie stood and began unsnapping and unbuttoning her sleek performing gown, sliding it down over her hips to the floor. She transferred it to a hanger in the closet and finally turned to face Dieter, the light from his reading lamp highlighting her statuesque lines. "Do I look as if I want to decode some list tonight? Do you really believe that, after five hours of singing and getting an invitation to appear with the best orchestra in Rio, I am chafing at the bit to solve a puzzle? Right now, I would prefer to cuddle with a sexy piano player and get a little crazy, then go to sleep until I wake up, eat a big plate of *feijoada*, and wash it down with lots of *caipirinha*. Does that make sense late on a Friday night, Schatzi?"

Dieter turned the light off and opened the room's single window so that the breeze and Rio's night sounds could embrace them. The folded piece of paper he had been holding floated to the floor and remained there.

6

***

Wiesenthal

The man named Carney touched his fingertips together and looked at the military officer he called Joe. He was not sure that Joe understood the reason for their last interview of the afternoon—the chat with a freed Jewish concentration camp survivor named Wiesenthal.

The thirty-seven-year-old man who entered the OSS offices that day was about six feet tall, but he was gaunt, which created the impression that he was taller. His hair had thinned noticeably and he had a neatly trimmed mustache beneath his long, narrow nose. His eyes were the dominant feature of a tired face; they were large and intelligent and seemed to be evaluating every person and object in the room.

The worn leather valise he supported with both hands was filled to capacity, and the curled edges of several pages protruded beneath the unbuckled flap. He placed it upon a library table with the care of someone transporting a sleeping child, then turned toward the two OSS men and spoke in a soft but scolding voice.

"If you Americans are truly interested in visiting justice upon the thieves, torturers, and murderers who have ravaged Europe for a decade, these files will help identify many who should not be allowed to slip away unpunished."

Joe spoke first. "You've been in a Nazi camp and got sprung by the Ruskies, right?"

"No, sir. I was a prisoner in Mauthausen-Gusen. That's near Linz. The Americans freed us on May fifth this year. But that was only my last camp. There were three others before Mauthausen. From 1941, when my wife and I were sent to Janowska for me to do railroad work, I was moved around among many locations."

"And they kept you together?"

"No, sir. Before long, she was taken away to another place— she worked on radios, and that was a valuable skill. It kept her alive."

"What did you do? Something kept you alive, too."

"Of course. I had training in engineering and architecture. They were skills the Nazis needed, and we were treated better than most of the prisoners. Still, there were many times when I was painfully hungry, and just staying alive became my first thought. You know, I weighed less than one hundred pounds when we were liberated. The Americans weighed me; that's how I know. Many of my family members perished or just disappeared. The same with Cyla's family—Cyla is my wife. Between us we can account for ninety relatives who are gone."

"You said 'Cyla *is* my wife'—she lived through it all?"

"Thanks God, we are reunited. Yes, yes. She is with me again and we are both gathering strength. We are among the most blessed, which is why I implore you to use your best efforts to help avenge the less fortunate and to encourage those of us who are starting over."

Carney leaned forward until his eyes were focused directly into those of the gaunt, tired-looking Wiesenthal, but he didn't speak immediately. His fingertips were touching so that his hands described a small, open globe, and he drew several deep breaths and let them escape slowly. Finally he seemed ready to put his thoughts into words.

"Mr. Wiesenthal, five years ago the prevailing sentiment in our country was that it had been only twenty brief years since we last mobilized and sent our youth to Europe to scratch out a bloody victory in 'The War to End All Wars.' Yes, that's what they called it—'The War to End All Wars.' When it was over, we buried our dead and resumed building our relatively young nation, which was separated from Old World politics and intrigues by broad oceans on both sides. Post–World War I Americans cherished that separation and their independence as never before, and we binged upon our growing prosperity and a new brand of discovery.

"Unfortunately, Europe and Asia wouldn't let us enjoy the fruits of victory for long. They didn't manage their economies well and soon plunged the world into financial chaos. If that wasn't bad enough, many of them gravitated toward dictatorial leaders with insane ambitions, and old hatreds came bubbling to the surface all over Europe and Asia. Americans wanted nothing to do with this new menu of problems. Instead, we put together a grand World's Fair in New York and invited people from around the world to come and see the future. The prevailing sentiment in our country favored staying out of foreign entanglements and rebuilding our strength and prosperity.

"But, little by little, we realized that a true 'World War' was brewing, and that at some point we would be forced to choose between sides and even become participants. Strangely, there were loyalties to both sides—well, perhaps not so strangely when you remember that immigrants from both sides had become components of our nation. Mr. Churchill was probably the better salesman, and we became progressively tilted toward the interests of the Allies, and finally, we no longer had a choice when the Axis powers attacked us. We mobilized and went all out for four years, sustaining huge losses in the process, and finally, we were able to rejoice on VE Day—not long ago. The country's mentality has already reverted to isolation. Get out. Get back to 'normal' at home.

"Of course you know that sequence, but I had to lay it out in connection with your visit here today. Most Americans are bent upon their return to building cars, playing baseball, going to school, painting their houses—all of those inward-directed tasks they left behind in 1941. Our new president is going to wrap up the OSS this year, and when it is gone, it's going to be difficult for us to become involved in the pursuit of escaped enemies beyond those who have already been captured and slated for prosecution by Robert Jackson at Nuremberg."

Now it was the sad-eyed Wiesenthal who paused before attempting to present his brief to the two American OSS officials. He sensed that it might be his best opportunity to gain support from this ally, and he wanted to link his personal cause to their mission. He lifted the worn valise he had earlier carried into the room, and the protruding sheets of paper sent a silent message of prolonged and dedicated effort by the recently freed man.

Then he began, in a nearly inaudible voice, "Gentlemen, I understand that Europe's ancient hostilities have twice drawn your country into costly wars, and that it might be unpopular now to commit your resources to the capture of enemies who did not surrender themselves. But I ask you to imagine yourselves in the position of many liberated people here, who have been reduced to poverty and deprived of loved ones by felons who are walking free.

You want these wronged people to dedicate themselves to the tasks of restoring their infrastructure and businesses while the very people who deprived them of so much go unpunished. Can you see the difficulty in that? Can you understand why I believe you should take an interest in my collected information?"

"Why don't you give us one example from your accumulated accounts and tell us how OSS—or whatever successor organization evolves—could help to restore something to some oppressed group?" offered the man named Carney. His military counterpart nodded in approval, and Wiesenthal opened the valise and extracted a single file folder from the welter of documents.

7

———

Reflections After Midnight

Their duplex apartment at 18 Rua Francisco Otaviano was among the nicest anywhere on Ipanema Beach in 1945. The upper level comprised a spacious bedroom, with two attached closets and twin baths, plus an open terrace nearly twenty meters above the level of the beach and the Atlantic Ocean. Sofie had found the apartment soon after her arrival in Rio and had purchased it herself without any help from Dieter; she had surprised him with the completed project, decorated and furnished elegantly. Even though Dieter's employment and gratuities at the Copacabana Palace compensated him very well, he had viewed the duplex as being unreasonably luxurious for a musician's home, so he had been careful not to invite his few friends to visit him there. Sofie understood his reluctance and so she also had avoided showing their home to others.

Now Dieter sat on that open terrace above the gentle waves, smoking a cigarette and reflecting upon all that had happened during the past twenty-four hours. It was three thirty on Sunday morning—one of the few times when Rio could be nearly silent. Sofie had not moved since collapsing onto their bed an hour ago.

Her shoes, gown, and undergarments were scattered across the bedroom floor, and gentle humming sounds accompanied her deep sleep. In the soft moonlight filtering into their bedroom, Dieter could see her tanned skin contrasted with a tangle of pure white sheets and pillows. He was alone with his thoughts.

Saturday night at the Copacabana Palace had exceeded their expectations. Buca had provided an excellent table, and the staff—who were delighted that their fellow employees were in the Saturday night audience—had treated them like visiting royalty. The room had been packed, at least partially, because of the presence of Francisco "Baby" Pignatari, the twenty-eight-year-old Brazilian playboy/businessman who was known for his outrageous lifestyle and free-spending extravagance. Baby's party filled two large tables and seemed to attract other visitors from all corners of the room. Sofie and Dieter had watched with amusement as the handsome, two-meter-tall Italian/Brazilian kissed hands, ogled cleavage, and sometimes drowned out the music with bursts of his laughter.

It had been nearly eleven o'clock when the suave Buca tapped on his open microphone, then held up a hand to quiet the large room. "You have been such an excellent audience tonight, that the Buca Pittman Orchestra has decided to reward you with a special appearance by one of the Copacabana Palace's most popular performers—the talented and beautiful Sophia, whom you can hear several times weekly in the Bar do Copa. Please welcome her—Sophia!"

Sofie—Sophia—had received a polite smattering of applause from the room, which remained focused mainly upon Baby and his constant stream of table hoppers while she accepted the microphone from Buca and was bathed in her favorite pale-blue spotlight. Then, even in a room loaded with some of Rio's most attractive people, Dieter had sensed the shift of attention to the elegant Sophia, who stood confidently surveying the room until it became surreally quiet.

"A few years ago, I was privileged to open the International Lounge in Prague's Majestic Plaza Hotel, and I selected this version of an old American favorite to introduce myself to that audience. It was sung originally by a very young Judy Garland to the iconic Clark Gable at an MGM studio party celebrating his thirty-ninth birthday. It described the thoughts of a stage-struck teen hopelessly in love with a movie star. It also sums up my feelings for this vibrant city, which has become my home in the New World. I hope you'll enjoy Judy's—and my—rendition of James Monaco's 'You Made Me Love You.'" Dieter had known at once that Sophia was about to conquer the room.

As soon as he heard the rich background that strings and woodwinds provided to her mellow voice, Dieter knew that Sofie would be able to coax more nuanced feelings from the familiar lyrics, and he had closed his eyes to appreciate it fully. Now, alone in the pre-dawn stillness, he understood the message of that moment for him: a special talent like hers should not be smothered in a small venue, boxed in by the limitations of a piano accompaniment. If there were opportunities for Sofie to appear with a fine orchestra, Dieter had to encourage her to grasp them.

The audience had not been content with hearing only two samples of Sophia's magic, and they had demanded an encore—and then another. At 11:30, she had finally extended her arms and lowered her head in a grateful bow, then allowed the pale-blue spotlight to lead her back to Dieter and their table. Moments later, one of the ubiquitous flower vendors from the Avenida Atlântica appeared at the main entrance to the ballroom and proceeded to carry his entire armload of white roses to her table.

They were delivered with an engraved business card which read *Laminacao Nacional S. A./ Francisco Matarazzo Pignatari, Diretor Presidente*. On the reverse side was a simple hand-written message: *Bravo! From Baby*.

Many in the room recognized immediately the extravagant gesture of the country's most colorful titan, and immediately the name *Sophia* joined the legion of beautiful women connected in their minds to Baby Pignatari. Dieter had directed her glance toward the tables where Baby was holding court, and she had blown an air kiss in his direction, but the two never drew closer than that. At least—not that evening.

At 4:00 a.m. Dieter snuffed out his third cigarette and stepped inside the moonlit bedroom. He pulled a coverlet over the purring Sofie and noiselessly slipped in beside her. Their easy, unstructured life had taken on many new considerations that evening, and as he glanced one last time at the beautiful woman and plush setting, Dieter sensed that there could be serious challenges to their happiness in the months ahead.

8

—————

Simon's Folder

"You know, of course, that Poland has, for generations, had to protect itself from hostile neighbors. On all sides there were constant plots and plans to take over portions of the isolated nation. Being a buffer country in a way made Poland stronger—the country's intelligence-gathering capability enabled it to fend off some threats before they materialized fully—but nevertheless, portions of the country were regularly moving in and out of Polish control. In 1938, something happened which the Western countries hadn't foreseen. Germany and the USSR worked out a nonaggression agreement in which each acknowledged that the other had a 'sphere of interest' that would be respected. It was called The Molotov-Ribbentrop Pact—those were the two foreign ministers who put it together—and Stalin and Hitler both agreed it was a good thing."

At that point the gaunt man stopped speaking to assess whether the two OSS officers were interested and paying attention. Carney tapped his fingertips together impatiently and interjected, "Yes, we know that history, but the Pact didn't last—Hitler broke into Poland on his own timetable, and Stalin grabbed some areas in the east right away. Pretty soon they were fighting each other. How does this have anything to do with tracking down escaped Nazis?"

"Good—bear with me please, just a little longer. Remember what I said about Polish intelligence people giving advance warning? Well, when things began unwinding in 1939, the top people at Narodowy Bank Polski—the Polish central bank— decided to take defensive measures to protect the country's gold reserves. They wanted to get them out of the country and into safe custody before either the Germans or the Russians could confiscate them. Poland had a lot of bullion, gentlemen—a lot! Remember, I worked as a forced laborer in the railroads for the Nazis, and there were whispered stories everywhere about trains carrying gold away from Warsaw toward the south. The Nazis were already grabbing the gold in the bank in Danzig, and the bank officials thought they could get most of the reserves out through Romania and around by sea to safety in France."

"That's where it gets complicated," Carney interrupted, "because France was already shaky, and our sources said that the gold was instead taken to French West Africa—to Dakar—on a French warship, where it could be hidden from the Nazis. Our people got involved, too, because the exiled Poles wanted the gold to be redirected to Canada or the U.S., where it would be even safer. I don't think anyone is sure what happened once Hitler walked through Poland and took aim at the Low Countries and France. But I'm still not seeing a war criminal on the loose. What's the connection, Mr. Wiesenthal?"

"Ah. That's this folder, Mr. Carney. It is a dossier on a Wehrmacht general named Otto von Seigler. Not a well-known fellow, but for a time he was very much in the news in Germany. The Oster Conspiracy on Hitler's life—which failed, of course—

was concocted by individuals under General von Seigler's command. For a time it was speculated that von Seigler would be executed, but suddenly he was back in favor. Why? Because as a young officer he had been posted in Poland and working with the Polish banking system under the Pilsudski government. He spoke fluent Polish and even had a daughter born there to a Jew woman. His knowledge of Poland and its banking system was too much of an asset to be wasted when Hitler launched into that country in 1939. Göring vouched for von Seigler—they were friends—and the general acquitted himself brilliantly. It was Hitler's most impressive conquest in terms of maximum efficiency and minimal losses."

Joe finally joined the conversation. "So—whatever happened to the good general? I never heard his name—was he captured, or killed, or what?"

"He vanished! He took an R&R week in Lisbon, and poof! He was gone. Never returned to his home or his office in Berlin. His aide disappeared at the same time, and so did a Polish SWW operative—a woman named Branka—who was stationed in Lisbon. Some say that a lot of that Polish gold reserve became untraceable at just about that time, too, and they point to von Seigler as the mastermind who diverted it."

"So, are you telling us that he's down in the Algarve somewhere with a gorgeous Polish spy-lady and a truckload of gold—and the OSS can be validated by capturing and returning him?" Joe quipped without attempting to mute the sarcasm in his question. At once he realized that he had insulted the informant gratuitously and that Carney was looking at him with a raised, disapproving brow. "Really, Wiesenthal—how do you see our role in this intriguing situation?" It was an attempt at a softer expression of the futility of chasing long-gone persons in the tumultuous period immediately following cease-fire.

"Do you remember that I mentioned a daughter born in Poland to von Seigler and a Jewish woman? She was a graduate student studying music in Berlin—Sofie is her name—when the Oster Conspiracy was uncovered in 1938. Sofie was living with her father and serving as his hostess for official gatherings, and she was a favorite of the actress Emmy Sonnemann, Hermann Göring's wife. Even though von Seigler was not complicit in the assassination plot, the fact that he had a Jewish consort and half-Jewish daughter could have been used to his great disadvantage. Sofie, the daughter, left school and dropped out of sight. But later—calling herself 'Sophia' and claiming to be Swiss—she became popular in Prague and Paris and London as a vocalist. It was rumored that she was protected by a secret-police bodyguard—named Meister—assigned by Göring himself. "

"Why would she need that protection?" Joe queried. "Who would want to harm her?

"I don't really know, but that Meister became almost a folk hero. They said that he killed some Gestapo goons in Prague—and later their Gestapo commandant—and maybe even Heydrich himself! He could have been caught and held in Theresienstadt for a while, but apparently slipped away from there, too. I've heard Meister stories in more than one camp, but nobody seems to know where he came from or where he went. The Gypsies even talk about him as a kind of ghost, but then say he's real."

"Okay, go back to the daughter. Where is she? Do we know?"

"I'm not sure, but my informants are telling me that she may have been in Brazil for the last couple of years, singing in a hotel in Rio. She'd be about thirty years old now and probably not calling herself Sofie von Seigler any longer. It wouldn't be too difficult to determine—and I have an idea how we could bait her and find out for sure."

"And then what? Do you think she has contact with her father? And why would she tell anybody if she does? Sounds like a long shot to me—what do you think, Carney?"

"Dunno. Interesting. Hmmm . . . let's think this through."

9

The Tour

Rio's Sunday mornings were beautiful in their spring season—September and October. The mild winter had passed; trees and flowers along the Avenida Atlântica approached their finest, and strollers could watch the white, curling waves carry body surfers for long distances toward the flat beaches. Small coffee shops set tables and chairs outside where customers could sip dark Cerrado coffee and devour tasty *pão de queijo* cheese scones while engaging in quiet conversations. It was a favorite ritual for Sofie and Dieter to begin their spring Sundays and plan the week ahead in that relaxed atmosphere. But after their night as Buca's guests in the Copacabana ballroom, they had less time for desultory conversation and settled quickly into a review of the evening and what it might portend.

"You were excellent, you know. Everything came together so well—the acoustics, lighting, song selections, and your appearance. *Ausgezeichnet*, Sofie! I think there were at least three hundred in the room, and I didn't hear any conversations or dining noises taking away from the music. Everyone cued on you, Sofie—everyone."

"That's sweet, Schatzi, but you know that much of the electricity in the room was from Baby Pignatari's presence. People always know that there will be eccentric things happening around him, and when he paused to listen to the orchestra and me, so did the room. When he had that street fellow deliver all those roses, people thought something big was going on right in front of them. Made it really easy for me—and I loved it!"

"The only sad part was that—without trying to—your appearance and voice were compared to Lola's, and she suffered in the comparison. I could see the resentment in her face from the time the blue spotlight first found you. She sat off to the left of the orchestra and looked miserable. Did you know that? You weren't facing in that direction so you probably didn't—but she was unhappy, especially when the flowers were carried in and the audience made such a fuss."

"You know, Lola's pregnant, Dieter. She's going to have to step away from the band soon because she's showing already, and Buca won't take her on tour next month. I feel bad if my singing got more attention, but she would have the same problem with or without me. Buca's audiences expect jazzy arrangements and exciting vocals, and it's hard to deliver glamour in a maternity dress. We both know that he was auditioning me last night, and if there's an offer to include us in that tour, we will have to decide fairly quickly whether to take it. So—any thoughts?"

"I thought about it so much last night that it woke me up and I went out on the terrace and had a couple of smokes under the stars."

"You did? Didn't know you got up. I must have been sleeping hard. What did you conclude? Anything you feel like sharing in the morning light?"

"Well, if the opportunity is there, you must grasp it. Staying in one spot for too long—as a performer—doesn't help you to grow, and it also limits the variety of audiences who get to know your work. I understand that Buca's tour starts in BA, then moves to Montevideo, then Porto Alegre and up to Catarina for Oktoberfest, and finally to Santos and São Paulo. There will probably be recordings and even filming of some performances, and those will reach even more people. You don't ever achieve that kind of—well—geometric projection by remaining in a single locale, even a great place like Bar do Copa. Don't you agree?"

"Oktoberfest in Catarina?"

"You don't know about that, Schatzi? German farmers emigrated to the south of Brazil a century ago when things got bad at home—they also went to the middle of the United States. One fellow named Blumenau started a community along the Rio Itajaí-Açu, and it grew and grew northward to another place named Pomerode, and that whole region looks like Bavaria, and everybody speaks German and is Lutheran—well, mostly, I'm told. Both world wars have attracted more Germans to the area. There's a big music pavilion there, and Buca will swing up that way coming north. I'm sure that a vocalist who can handle German lyrics would be well received. It gets lots of publicity in Catarina, and German people travel there from all over the state."

"Dieter—you know that's the state where my father has relatives, and it's possible that he and Branka are somewhere there, too. After we came here, I got one of his postal cards from an island called Florianópolis—it wasn't signed, but I knew the hand. It was his. It just said things were well and the ocean was beautiful. Nothing more. Just a little code message like those we used during the war. Just saying he was well—and water pictures are our way of saying that there are no perceived dangers."

"Florianópolis is the capital city of Catarina state—it's small and mostly on an island. It's midway between BA and Rio, and probably was useful because of that location for travelers and boats, you know. A postal card from there could mean anything, but I doubt that Germans wanting to fit in would choose to live there. The German immigrants are all inland, as I was describing. Up in the hills with their *fincas* and European-style villages. That's where all of the Oktoberfest celebrants gather and probably where Buca will have his gig.

"Hmmm—what's your 'code' for danger, if water means all's clear?"

"Oh, any mention of a grandmother or of fire. Poppy and I started that when I first moved to Berlin from Kraków, when I was sixteen. It was fascinating, after Poland, to be the daughter of a Wehrmacht officer, and we became so close and had so many little secrets and rituals that were just ours. When he entertained, he let me be hostess of his gatherings, and we would sit for hours afterward and talk about the guests. Sometimes he would look over at me during dinner and roll his eyes, and I would know what he was saying. And we had our 'rescue me' code, where dabbing a handkerchief on the forehead or cheek was a call for help—you know—get me away from this person! Afterward, we would have little glasses of Bauer's pear schnapps over ice and be totally silly laughing about some of the ridiculous people we had entertained. I think I was his little island of happiness as things began to deteriorate in Germany, and he was always my strong fortress. Dieter, you know that there are so many accounts of horrible people doing horrible things during the war—and I know that they are true—but Poppy is a good person. I love him and am proud to be his daughter. Am I making sense, Dieter? Am I?"

The ardent man across from her took both her hands in his and kissed her fingertips. "I understand conflicted emotions better than most people," he replied carefully, " . . . and I expect that each of us may be torn between alternative loyalties and loves. We must always feel free to air our thoughts and to bare our emotions as successive challenges arise.

"Today our shared focus is a tour as vocalist with Brazil's best orchestra, and I am going to insist that you grasp that opportunity and exploit all of its possibilities, Sofie. You must never have to look back and wonder what might have been."

Tears floated across her eyes and down her cheeks. "Dieter, I love you. Thank you, thank you, thank you! It will be an adventure for both of us, and when the tour is over I'll really know whether I have the qualities of a top vocalist. So when I see Buca tomorrow—if he offers a contract for the tour—I'll tell him we are interested in negotiating the terms, right?"

"No, Sofie, not 'we': this is about you and your talent, and having me tagging along on the tour defeats the whole purpose. I'll help you with the contract, but you are the performer, and I would be perceived as a barrier between you and the musicians and between you and your audiences. I'll stay behind and keep things here in order until you return. Tell Buca that you are ready to take your voice on the road and that you'll be giving the tour your undivided commitment."

Two partly filled *copos de cafe* remained on the small table by the sea as the couple walked away slowly, contemplating their first separation since being reunited in Rio more than two years earlier. Sofie turned her head toward Dieter and whispered, "It means I may be away from you for as long as ten weeks. That will be a sacrifice for both of us, but you'll be in my thoughts every day."

10

Otto von Seigler

"Joe—did you get a report back from X-2 on our missing general, that von Seigler?"

"Yeah, and it really poses a bunch of questions for us if we are looking to find the guy and hope that it can lead to any material benefits for Wiesenthal's folks. Here's the basic stuff: Professional military from before World War I. He was a top student at Offizierschule and studied banking and finance. Learned Polish at Bundeswehr, and it notes he could read and write well in the language. When he was twenty-four, he was posted to Kraków and was the German financial liaison with the local banking community there. Spent more than two years in that work, and during that time he apparently moved in with the secretary/interpreter the Pilsudski Poles had assigned to watch him.

"They had a daughter named Zofia Lena von Seigler in 1915, and when she was only six weeks old Otto was recalled to Berlin and assigned to Wehrmacht Staff—director of foreign banking. Then he apparently got some battlefield exposure and distinguished himself as a strategist and planner. He was decorated for his leadership in defeating the Russian advances into Galicia in '17, but after that he isn't mentioned much through the balance of World War I.

"There is an entry that in 1918 he assigned his military death benefits to his daughter, Zofia Lena, and listed her address as being a hotel owned by her 'guardian,' Liv Zimmerman, in Kraków. This Zimmerman apparently married Zofia's mother about that time in a civil ceremony, but there's no indication that he ever adopted the girl.

"The next time there's anything meaningful about old Otto, he's a mid-level Wehrmacht general with close ties to Göring in Berlin, and he's got a big house on Wilhelmstrasse where he lives alone. There's no dirt on the guy, but his lifestyle has really stepped up, and he brings Zofia Lena to live in Berlin with him and attend private schools there. She is enrolled as Sofie von Seigler and she goes on to study music at Humboldt University in Berlin but still lives with her father.

"Then in September 1938—when the daughter is twenty-three—all hell breaks loose! That Abwehr Colonel Hans Oster almost pulls off a coup to murder Hitler, but some of the plotters back down at the last minute and it fails. Now—get this—Colonel Oster's superior is—guess who? Our man von Seigler! So he's put under house detention and is investigated because the plot was hatched somewhere within his command. The half-Jewish daughter slips away to Prague and later shows up in Paris. This is just before the Nazis invade Poland. So, von Seigler suddenly becomes valuable again, and Göring absolves him from any blame in the Oster Conspiracy. And he does a hell of a good job in implementing the orderly takeover of the Polish banking system and financial management of that conquered area.

"Here's the conundrum. Even though our general is back in

good standing, apparently the daughter never returns to live with him. There's a note in the file that she had a kind of omnibus "Letter of Safe Passage" from Göring, and he may even have assigned a bodyguard for her, too. That fellow is kind of a mystery, and there's no info on where he came from or whatever happened to him. But—now, get this—apparently some low-ranking Gestapo accountant in Prague observes him with Zofia and smells a rat, and he goes over his superior's head direct to Gestapo Headquarters in Berlin with questions about the guy, and names him as Corporal Dieter Meister!"

"Do we know anything more about the Gestapo accountant or how Berlin reacted? That would have been a gross violation of Gestapo protocol, Joe. Himmler didn't tolerate crap like that; that's why the Gestapo was so efficient and so feared."

"Yeah, well, get this, Carney—the file has a notation that the curious Gestapo accountant, his local Gestapo boss, and two special Gestapo agents sent to Prague to learn more about this Meister *all* died there mysteriously—within a few weeks of one another. And the note questions whether any of this is also related to the 1942 murder of Heydrich, the Reischsprotektor—overseer—of that Bohemia and Moravia region. 'Hangman' Reinhard Heydrich they called him. Remember?"

"Oh, hell, yeah. He was brutal. Everyone in that area of Czechoslovakia hated his guts, and when he was rubbed out they celebrated openly. Hitler retaliated and destroyed two whole towns, Lidice and Ležáky, because of their alleged complicity. I don't know anything about Meister's involvement, but that ambush of Heydrich was orchestrated by some Czech resistance guys who were trained right here in England and smuggled back into Prague. What else?"

"There's one more thing. There's a note that in April 1943

somebody pulled off an escape from the Theresienstadt concentration camp near Prague. That was almost impossible. You'd need help from outside and it would take physical stamina, which prisoners in those places didn't generally have. Remember Wiesenthal telling us that he weighed less than a hundred pounds when he was freed? They all worked their butts off and lived on about six hundred calories a day, and most of them were sick and never treated. They were damned near skeletons. Well, the guardhouse scuttlebutt was that the escaped prisoner was named Dieter Meister—the same name as the guy they said earlier was protecting Zofia or Sofie—or whatever her name was.

"Somebody added that tidbit to the von Seigler folder, as if there was a connection. I'm wondering whether somebody higher up helped Meister escape because they didn't want him where he could be questioned—know what I mean?"

"And the daughter—Zofia or Sofie—she was out in plain sight all through the war?"

"Well, yeah, pretty much. She sang in a hotel in Prague for a little while and then left there around the time that the four Gestapo guys turned up dead. Later on she sang in Paris with Django Reinhardt, the Gypsy jazz guitar player who was given immunity by the German military—to let him keep performing all through the war years. Then she was in London singing with a band. And now there's an FBI Special Intelligence Service report that she has been singing in Brazil for a couple of years."

"Brazil? Do we have any OSS people in Brazil who could check this out?"

"Are you kidding? Hell, no! Don't you remember that J. Edgar put the kibosh on OSS right away? He went straight to Roosevelt and made sure that OSS never had any presence in the Western hemisphere—it's all exclusive FBI territory—and they have people scattered all over South America. Roosevelt used them to monitor German naval movements in the South Atlantic and also to try and watch the dictators down there who might want to help exiled Nazis. FBI guys know that OSS will be shut down soon, and they won't risk their careers doing something J. Edgar doesn't like. Y'know what I mean?"

"So, Joe—how do we follow up on a singer in Brazil to find out who and where her father is, if we don't have any associates there to do some spadework? You have any ideas?"

"Maybe."

11

Avenida Atlântica

It was another hectic Friday as good weather and bigger weekend crowds converged onto Copacabana, Leblon, and Ipanema's beaches. Dieter noted how much more revealing women's clothing had become as silks and nylons returned to postwar use—and how they adhered provocatively to bodies—and how few undergarments were now being worn by women in Rio. Even those women from better families now smoked and drank openly, as their vocal ranges seemed to climb higher and louder. He found himself wondering whether the same postwar trends would settle in across the Atlantic, where Continental standards had once been drawn so much tighter. He was sitting at a table on Avenida Atlântica mulling these trivial thoughts and awaiting Sofie with the good news that they would be welcomed to resume their residence in the Bar du Copa after her tour with Buca.

He ground out the glowing end of his cigarette in the small ashtray on his table as he saw Sofie at a distance on the walkway, picking her way through the crowd. He thought to himself how graceful and clean her movements appeared and how often people seated at other sidewalk tables fixed their gazes on her and then followed her progress, even as they spoke to others. What was it that she projected that made her stand out that way? Now she was leaning over a railing, waving at a sand sculptor who had created a credible facsimile of the Notre Dame Cathedral using only a flat stick, a bucket of ocean water, and a large pile of beach sand. Admirers of his work regularly tossed coins onto a sheet spread in front of the sculpture, but Dieter could see that Sofie was extending paper money and motioning him to come and receive it. Suddenly a waft of breeze caught her diaphanous skirt from behind and blew it high over her shoulders. Those who had been stealing glances at her before were instantly dissolved in laughter as she good-naturedly covered her very naked derriere and mimicked a mock stage bow toward their tables.

It was then that the man first caught Dieter's attention. He was wearing an ordinary beige suit jacket with an open-collared shirt and he had a rolled newspaper under one arm, but unlike the others surrounding Sofie when the breezelet "attacked" her, he had turned away quickly and stepped back into the shade. If he had been a priest in a cassock, it might have been an appropriate movement of modesty so near a suddenly bared behind. But he was a very ordinary-looking pedestrian who apparently did not want to be seen. Dieter kept the man at the edge of his vision as Sofie completed the delivery of her greetings and her reward to the sand artist, and then turned again toward her destination. When she had moved forward about twenty meters, the man folded his newspaper and moved in the same direction, never focusing obviously on Sofie but duplicating her pace. *Is someone shadowing Sofie? Who? Why?* Dieter thought to himself. As he rose to greet her with an affectionate hug, he saw that the man had taken a seat on a nearby bench and was reading his newspaper, never looking in their direction.

Octavio Oliveira had been trained in the United States by the US Secret Service so that he could provide protection for Brazilian President Getúlio Vargas, and he had served on that team for ten years until Vargas's Liberal Alliance Party began to come under popular criticism. Octavio's wife had encouraged him to find some other position, sensing that the pressures of government work were growing and there could be better pay in a suitable private capacity. When the position of Chief of Hotel Security opened at the Copacabana Palace in 1943, Octavio had presented himself to the manager, and his impressive credentials landed him the job almost at once.

With 222 guest rooms and 146 suites plus some of the largest dining and meeting rooms in the nation, "The Copa" required a dozen permanent security professionals, augmented on special occasions by members of the Rio de Janeiro police department and even some private detectives. Octavio thoroughly enjoyed his new responsibilities, which afforded him the opportunity to move among the many world celebrities who stayed, played, and dined at the hotel. He had immediately liked the "Piano Man," who was hired at about the same time as he, and Octavio frequently enjoyed a complimentary luncheon in the popular Bar do Copa, where good food and some of his favorite music took much of the stress from his work. He had been working that busy room on the day when Sophia had first materialized there and captured the sophisticated audience. Dieter and Sofie were now his friends.

On Monday morning, while Dieter was tuning and refreshing the Bechstein in his "domain," Octavio and a pair of uniformed police entered at the rear of the room and commenced checking doors, windows, and smaller side alcoves. Octavio waved at Dieter and said, "Olà, Piano Man—we'll be checking a few things for twenty minutes. How 'bout some Fats Waller music to keep us company?" Immediately Dieter began playing the upbeat "Honeysuckle Rose," which he knew was a favorite of the security chief, and he watched the usually sedentary man shuffle and jive like a New Orleans waiter chasing a big tip.

"Music hath charms to soothe the savage breast," he mused to himself, pleased that he could do that for a friend. "What's happening? Some politician coming to the room for lunch?" Dieter asked.

"Can't tell you. It's a big secret, but King Farouk from Egypt moved into the Presidential Suite last night and he's throwing a party at his embassy tomorrow. Could be he'll be lunching here sometime soon. Got to be sure it's secure just in case. We can cover the room with five people—and he always has his own torpedo, too."

"Torpedo?"

"Armed bodyguard."

"Oh. You have such interesting work, Octavio. May I ask you something about that?" Dieter didn't wait for a response but took a short breath and continued, "I believe that someone has been following Sofie when she moves about outside the hotel, and it concerns me. I want to know who and why. Do you have connections who could help me with something like that?"

"Man?"

"Yes, yes—a man who stays at a comfortable distance with a newspaper under his arm and seems to want to go undetected. He is very good at that, too."

"Is he? You seem to have noticed him—that's not so good for a shadow, Dieter."

"Ah, I understand your point—but you must remember that

in Europe we existed with the Gestapo and their informants, and sometimes I think that created a whole new field of awareness. It forced us to be cognizant of people who were somehow—how do I say it?—somehow out of place, that's it. I know that Sofie's appearance often begs attention, and I have seen men and women fixate on her movements. You have seen how she can 'wear' a blue spotlight as if it were a cellophane bathrobe, and that carries over when she is just strolling on Atlântica. But this person doesn't watch her so much as he watches where she goes and what she is doing."

"How tall?"

"Average—maybe 170 centimeters—he's average everything! Height, weight, coloring, clothing, movements. Nothing says 'Look at me!' I haven't even seen facial expressions."

"Right or left-handed?"

"Now how would I know that, Octavio?"

"Under which arm is the newspaper? His dominant side will be opposite that. See, I'm helping you to be a detective, *meu amigo*!"

"*Obrigado.*"

"Might he be armed? Coat a little too big and front button open? I'm playing with you—sorry. So how can I help you? I'd like to, but what do you want to learn? You said 'who and why' earlier, but I almost have to begin with 'whether'—I mean, is my friend Dieter especially perceptive or totally paranoid? You may not like my conclusion at all. Do you want to chance that? If he turned out to be someone she fancies and he is waiting for her to be away from you, are you going to kill him, or me, for suggesting it? You see, Dieter, these things can be complicated, eh?"

"I know, I know. But I have learned to trust my instincts when they speak to me. I've seen this fellow a couple of times and there is a pattern. I don't want to ignore what I'm sensing, and I want someone other than me to see this. She will be leaving by the south side entrance—onto R. Fernando Mendes—about three o'clock and will probably stroll southward on Atlântica for an hour, stopping often to look at things and chat with locals. Can you have someone observe her very quietly and see if there is a shadow? Don't engage him in any way, but see if there's an identity you can establish."

"I won't do it myself—I'm too recognizable. But I do have a fellow on the house staff who was a military police officer and has done this sort of research before. It will cost you a little money, but it will be worth it if it puts your mind at rest, eh? See you here tomorrow at about this time. Bring fifty American dollars. Let's hope there's a good explanation. Hey—have you shared your concern with Sofie?"

"Oh, no, Octavio. She'd be upset. It's probably nothing and she's already edgy about going on tour. No—right now this is just between you and me."

12

A Little Girl from Gdańsk

Elsa had rendered nearly all of her wartime service in Bohemia, that section of Czechoslovakia dominated by the city of Prague. The Nazis had literally talked Britain and France into permitting them to occupy and oversee the area in exchange for a hollow promise that, by doing so, a second Great War in Europe would be avoided. When German businessmen and military personnel began descending into Bohemia late in 1938, Elsa and other trained Polish intelligence agents were already there to interact with them and extract information that could be useful in defending against Nazi conquest of the entire European continent. Elsa's initial weapons in this subtle warfare were a winning smile, extensive knowledge, language capability, and a durable body.

She had appeared younger than her chronological age of twenty-six when she first arrived in Prague in 1937 to work as part of an escort service available in the city's luxury hotels. She had been raised and educated in Danzig—Gdańsk—where it was not unusual for residents to be fluent in German, Polish, and Russian. The Polish intelligence agency known by the initials SWW actively recruited young women who, like Elsa, were patriotic, smart, and attractive. The lure of travel and good pay was highlighted by SWW recruiters, but by 1945, Elsa understood fully that her career description should also have included bedding down a procession of pigs.

Elsa now kept a tidy apartment on Růžová, near Prague's principal railroad terminal, Hlavní Nádraži. She no longer was an employee of SWW, but she frequently met with incoming visitors at the agency's request, and her encyclopedic knowledge of the city found many applications.

Tonight she was to have dinner with a functionary of the American OSS, who had been directed to her by her wartime SWW boss, Lilka Rudovska. The man's name was Carney, and he would be arriving on the afternoon train from Vienna and met by a US Embassy driver. Elsa decided to observe the gentleman in advance of their dinner, and, since she had not recently retrieved mail from the box she rented at the station, the short walk could serve dual purposes.

A black 1940 Buick with diplomatic plates and a military driver was instantly identifiable near the station's main entrance; the driver was apparently sharing a cigarette break on the sidewalk nearby with a young Czech woman Elsa recognized immediately as one of the city's priciest English-speaking professional escorts. Surely Mr. Carney wouldn't be so imprudent as to be joined in a public place in broad daylight by a known prostitute, would he? She concluded that possibly he was being set up for some purpose, and if Lilka had directed Mr. Carney to Elsa, there was an implied duty for Elsa to warn him. She pulled the single white envelope from her mailbox, looked at it briefly, and wrote *CARNEY* on its reverse side with her lipstick, then walked briskly to the track where the Vienna train was easing to a stop. She knew almost as soon as he stepped from the train which passenger would be Mr. Carney, and when she held the envelope in his path, his reaction confirmed her choice.

"I'm Elsa Danzig; our mutual friend Lilka in London has arranged for us to meet."

"But not until dinnertime tonight, right?"

"Right, but I just observed something I wanted to share with you before you leave the platform. Indulge me for just a minute, and possibly I will owe you an apology when you have heard my reason."

The well-dressed man lowered his small suitcase to the platform and looked in all directions to see if the unexpected woman was alone, then, apparently satisfied, he pointed to an open archway marked *ČEKÁRNA* and said, "I'll find a place to sit in there. Wait a minute and come sit by me." Before Elsa could respond, he had moved through the waiting room entrance and been lost to her view among scurrying passengers. She walked a full circuit of the room before she recognized him reading a timetable, seated on a corner bench. When she sat beside him, there was no glance in her direction, just the words, "So, what is it, Elsa?"

When she had finished her explanation, he folded his timetable and said only "Thank you" as he departed under the arrow indicating the direction to *STANOVIŠTĚ TAXI*. Elsa concluded that he had sufficiently valued the scrap of information she provided to pass up the embassy car, and that he possessed at least a rudimentary grasp of the complicated Czech language, which was quickly replacing the offending German in public signage. She hadn't met many American professionals, but she had heard that they were all "cowboys." Mr. Carney didn't fit that description.

Back in her apartment, Elsa remembered that there had been one piece of mail, and she had converted it into a sign to greet him. What had she done with it after that? Ruffling through her handbag contents and searching the pockets of her light coat yielded nothing but frustration. "Come on, Elsa," she urged, "You're trained to be observant, so what the..." She tried to visualize the envelope. It had colorful stamps and a big, round postmark from another country. The envelope was embossed with a business logo—maybe a hotel? And it wasn't typed; it was written by hand. Legibly. Addressed to her box number without her name. One of those stamps was an airplane, so it was sent by airmail—maybe from overseas? The airplane was over a pointed mountain, and it said *Correio aéreo* under it. And, yes—it was sort of tangled in a green and yellow flag. Who did she know in Brazil?

13

⸎

Unmasking the Shadow

Octavio's choice to trace Sofie's observer was a young man recently discharged after military service. He looked like many other young Cariocas who relaxed along Avenida Atlântica on sunny days, smiling at passing *gatas* and nursing cool drinks in the warm air. Octavio had nicknamed him Samson because of his muscular chest and shoulders, but wrapped in a soft cotton sweater of indistinct color, Samson's appearance was unexceptional. He had been standing near the corner of Av. Atlântica and R. Fernando Mendes talking to a friend for half an hour before the recognizable blonde woman emerged from a service entrance, checking the contents of her oversized purse as she passed by. They both assessed her, then resumed their conversation, while covertly observing her movement around the corner and across to the beach. Samson waited for a decent interval, then left his friend and sprinted across the street, avoiding traffic. He could see Sofie about fifty meters ahead and decided that would be a suitable margin to maintain.

After walking at a leisurely pace for ten minutes, Sofie paused and sat down on the beach, looking out toward the ocean—

apparently deep in thought, because she failed to see a man stepping quickly from the shadows toward her. In a single motion, he swept up her bag and began running along the beach through a maze of sun worshipers—directly toward Samson. The young detective had to decide quickly whether to intervene, and he couldn't resist the opportunity to deploy his military training. The unsuspecting runner was dropped immediately when Samson's elbow noisily intersected his moving jawbone, but then, as quickly as he could regain his feet, he ran across the street through traffic and disappeared in the general direction of the favelas, leaving her unopened purse on the sand.

Samson brushed the sand from the bag and walked toward Sofie, who was already hurrying in his direction. She thanked him gratefully and held out a 100-*cruzeiro* note, which he declined. On the sidewalk nearby, an observer tucked a newspaper under his left arm and walked northward toward a waiting car.

Octavio listened with growing impatience to Samson's description of the encounter. Obviously this child of the favelas was not the shadow Dieter had observed; he was an ordinary *trombadinha*—a pickpocket—preying on easy marks in the popular tourist area. "But," he pointed with his raised forefinger, "if there were someone stalking Sophia, he would have seen this skirmish and would remember the young man who recovered the purse in such dramatic style—and turned down a reward—so, Samson's usefulness is blown! *Jesu Cristo!* Do I have to do everything myself?"

Dieter was embarrassed, thinking that he was now causing his friend to go out of his way. Yet he raised no objection, and so on the following afternoon Sofie departed through the hotel's main doorway, and a slightly overweight man soon slid out of his rocking chair in the lobby and traced her path. "Jesu Cristo, how far is it to her flat?" he grumbled to no one in particular, after walking only a few hundred meters. It had been a long time since Octavio had walked that far.

As Sofie crossed the intersection of Rua República dio Peru, a block south of the hotel, Octavio saw someone lighting a cigarette in the doorway of a *tienda*. The man took a long pull on the cigarette he had just lighted, then flicked it toward an overfilled trash can, missing his target by a wide margin. Soon he was moving in Sofia's wake, with his head lowered and the newspaper tucked away under his left arm. When she paused to give directions to a tourist couple, the man was quickly leaning against a storefront with his head buried in the newspaper—just another reader along the Atlântica.

Octavio had observed two more similar instances before he blurted, "Jesu Cristo, look at that! This bastard has a tiny Minox camera folded into his newspaper. He takes a picture of anyone she interacts with!" He tailed the shadow for another twenty minutes before Sofie took a key from her bag and opened the door to her apartment building. The man stood across the street "reading" for ten minutes before he folded his paper and walked away.

Octavio was feeling hunger pangs and lame legs by now, but he had an investment in this inquiry, so once again he walked inconspicuously at a distance until the man stopped at a taxi stand and took one of the three cabs waiting there for fares. Puffing furiously, Octavio got to the next cab in line within a minute, and he asked the driver if he had heard the earlier rider's destination. When the polite response, "No, senhor," was directed casually over the driver's shoulder, Octavio shoved his police badge into the driver's view and said, "See if you can catch up to that cab—quickly!" That seemed to motivate the driver, who soon pointed ahead and offered, "That one," indicating a vehicle less than thirty meters ahead. "Keep following," Octavio responded, as he leaned forward over the divider to see if he could catch a good look at his prey.

The first cab pulled to the curb across the street from an ordinary-looking granite building with metal lettering over its entrance that spelled *Embassy of the United States of America*.

"Don't stop—but keep moving slowly," Octavio blurted as he craned his neck to look out the rear window of his cab, trying to catch a glimpse of the fellow now entering the building. All he could see was a newspaper under the left arm of a very ordinary-looking guy. It was just as Dieter had said.

❧

When the two met over cafezinhos at the end of the day, Octavio told the Piano Man that his instincts had been accurate: someone was tailing Sofie, and he was photographing anyone with whom she met on her walk, as if there might be a covert relationship with a wanted person. More important, the stalker had entered the US Embassy without any apparent difficulty, so possibly, he was one of the personnel working regularly from there.

"As security director, I will try to determine whether there is a directive regarding any risk here. After all, the distinguished playboy president of Egypt is a guest in one of our suites, and we are caring for his well-being, eh? I am entitled to know their precautions against trouble in my territory."

Dieter did not want to share this with Sofie, but he knew that soon he must include her.

14

∾

Spies' Night Out

Elsa looked her best as she walked through Staré Mesto, Prague's "Old Town," where the massive stone buildings dated from as early as the eleventh century. She intentionally arrived at the Restaurace Bellevue, by the Vltava River, fifteen minutes before the agreed time, because she had learned that a gentleman arriving at a seated lady's table was perceived differently from an attractive lady being guided to a lone gentleman. They had, of course, seen one another at the railroad station, but Carney was not prepared for the understated elegance of his dinner companion.

"Is this a really good place to eat?" he smiled, "because you—"

"It's the best," she interrupted, saving him from completing an awkward observation. "They have Czech specialties and Continental favorites, but none of your American hot dogs, I'm afraid." They both laughed artificially and then Carney leaned a bit closer and lowered his voice.

"Look, I really want to thank you for your alert earlier. I did not want to be seen with that lady in public or at the Embassy, but I needed to receive some information from her, so I suggested that she be waiting in the car when I entered. By spending time outside an official car with the driver, she defeated the whole purpose. I took a cab to the Embassy, and someone else will have to debrief her."

"Then, she works for your OSS?"

"Not exactly—but she may possess some information we would like to evaluate. You and I aren't going to discuss it further, but thank you again for being so alert."

"Madame Rudovska was my handler for seven years and our relationship was rooted in mutual trust. When she referred you to me, a certain duty of care was implied. I know you understand that concept. Shall we look at the menu, like two friends dining out? And maybe you would like me to select a good Czech wine?"

Carney explained that the OSS had been assembled hastily in response to an unanticipated need for intelligence within the complex European community of nations. The United States had originally intended to maintain neutrality as war clouds gathered, and only when there was an unaddressed need had President Roosevelt launched General Donovan on his mission. And now, with victory in hand, the new US president—Mr. Truman—had set a sunset date for the wartime intelligence agency. Military and diplomatic leaders now understood that postwar Europe could become an area of intrigue, and the nation's interests would necessitate a flow of accurate intelligence. The retired Lilka had been consulted and had offered her help in identifying experienced field personnel, and that had precipitated the evening's conversation.

Elsa listened patiently, and when it was appropriate for her to respond, she said, "Mr. Carney, I'm bone-tired after eight years in the field. I have no home to which I can return and no close friends waiting to greet me. My dearest friend left the SWW and emigrated to the USA in 1943; she has a husband and child in Chicago and has asked if I would like to visit her. I have saved some money and I am thinking about making that trip. Recently I have taken on small assignments, but I have enjoyed my independence from permanent employment with one entity. I appreciate your interest and would like to think some more."

"Do you also have a friend in Rio de Janeiro?" Carney asked. "Today you wrote my name on an envelope mailed from there, and placed it on the bench where we spoke. I brought it tonight."

Elsa felt a flush of concern, then embarrassment, and finally anger. Pushing those emotions aside, in her calmest voice she gushed, "Oh—I grabbed the only paper I had available to make that sign. Never looked to see the sender. Thanks for returning it. I can read it at home tonight." He placed the envelope in her extended hand and smiled at her. She glanced quickly to see if it had been opened. Not obviously. Would she have looked inside under those same circumstances? That's what she was paid to do; of course she would read it for whatever advantage it might provide. Damn, damn, damn! What was in there?

For the next two hours they chatted over dinner about the war and some of the odd experiences and alliances wartime can produce. They agreed that the failing Roosevelt and neophyte Truman had been no mental match for canny Stalin, who had negotiated considerable advantage for the USSR in postwar Europe without giving up anything in exchange. They discussed Europe's surviving Jewish population and the need to find and establish a suitable homeland for them. Elsa mentioned that Roosevelt had secretly dispatched American aviatrix Fay Gillis Wells on a flight through Africa to look for the right place to settle Europe's homeless Jews, and that she had returned with the enthusiastic recommendation that Angola would be appropriate. But Roosevelt had gotten ill and then died without ever trying to implement the suggestion.

❧

The late American president's active search for a new Jewish homeland was obviously unfamiliar to Carney, and Elsa knew that he would be seeking to verify it as quickly as possible. For now, she had established a conversational advantage, as they moved quickly through a variety of other subjects that might confirm her suitability as an American intelligence source in postwar Czechoslovakia.

Did she know about Theresienstadt? Of course. Had she heard of a shadowy figure who had murdered several Gestapo professionals in Prague and possibly even eliminated the Butcher, Heydrich? Yes, but perhaps he was like the mythical "Kilroy," who was credited with being everywhere during the war. Had she heard about a German general who had removed vast sums from the Polish banking system? Several of them—it was there to be looted after the nineteen-day collapse of Polish resistance. Elsa was waiting to hear Carney ask specifically about General von Seigler, but she could see that her answer to the Polish bank reserves' looting was all the verification Carney needed for now.

By that time, Elsa was churning with concealed discomfort and uncertainty, not knowing the content of Dieter's letter and now convinced that Carney did. She considered excusing herself for a quick lavatory break to read the letter, but rejected that idea as an amateurish confirmation of her involvement. She needed to change the subject quickly, thrust Mr. Carney into a defensive position.

"Mr. Carney," Elsa asked, "did you drive along the river about five minutes south from where we are sitting? Where a beautiful monastery and hundreds of homes lie destroyed?"

Carney was surprised by the question. "No. Should I?"

"Perhaps you should. It was the only significant wartime damage to this beautiful city—and it was inflicted by bombers from the United States. Forty of your Flying Fortress bombers carpet-bombed historic residential areas and destroyed the homes and people there. The only explanation was that they got lost and thought maybe they were over Dresden. Mr. Carney, Dresden is over 120 kilometers north from here. Now you ask if I would consider joining the intelligence-gathering service of a nation that sloppy with deploying its power and so calloused that it cannot acknowledge and apologize for its errors? Do you understand my reluctance?"

When they parted, Carney gave Elsa his card and asked her to consider an opportunity built around her knowledge of the Czech capital city, with the assumption that it would soon come under Soviet dominance. He offered to have an embassy car take her to her home, but she declined, wishing to keep her location a secret. After walking from his sight in Staré Mesto's crooked streets, she would be able to snare a local taxi.

❧

Elsa's joy in receiving a communication from Dieter was dampened by the question of whether someone else had read it first, and so as she perused the letter, she did so under this overarching question: Could any of its contents precipitate discovery or even harm upon people dear to her? She read it slowly:

Saturday, 12 May 1945
Copacabana Palace Hotel
Avenida Atlântica
Rio de Janeiro, Brazil

My Dear Elsa,

This letter is long overdue, but until we learned of the Allied victory in Europe on Tuesday, I could not safely send it. As it is, I am not using your name on the envelope, but only the box number at Praha Hlavní Nádraži Station, which you gave to me. I hope you will acknowledge your receipt. Just use the hotel name above and indicate that it is for "The Piano Man."

Elsa, I believe that I have been born twice. First at Dr. Hoch's Konservatorium in Frankfurt, on 20 June 1911, when an elderly Jewish physician used his forceps to ease me from the body of a young music student named Eva Rosenberg. She was destined to perish in the Great Influenza Pandemic before my eighth birthday. I was born a second time on a roadside outside the Theresienstadt Detention Camp near Prague, on 6 March 1943, when you and the big Gypsy fellow pulled my moribund body from a large garbage can filled with putrid fish entrails. You both risked your lives to free me, and then you nursed me back to some semblance of health and delivered me to the next link in my escape path.

That journey took me to Lisbon, where I became a supernumerary crewman on a freighter bound for Brazil.

Once here, with an introduction and endorsement provided by my former (Portuguese) manager at the Fischerstube in Berlin, I became "The Piano Man" in the lounge bar and restaurant of Brazil's most famous luxury hotel. You can imagine the change in my life! For over three years I had wallowed in the filth and sickness of Theresienstadt—and had survived only by providing piano music for the guards and billeted military. I also cleaned their dining areas, latrines, and kitchen, and augmented my meager meals with leftover scraps salvaged from their dirty plates. Then, in only a few weeks, I was miraculously transformed into a well-paid, well-fed entertainer in an overpriced luxury hotel, observing the eccentricities and foibles of the world's "celebrities." I had truly been born again, and you were the midwife!

I will always remember how you cleaned and dressed the sores on my body and massaged my limbs each day until I could move about on my own. You bathed me as if I were a child and encouraged me to eat and read and speak and think like a free person again. Most importantly, you sheltered a fugitive at the risk of your own freedom—perhaps even your life.

Elsa, of course I know that you were a professional gatherer of intelligence working in enemy-held territory. I also realize that your work was generally performed as part of an "escort service" where your charms could loosen the tongues of occupying military and businessmen. It was depersonalizing and undoubtedly humiliating for you. In the last moments we shared, I reassured you that "... you are not a whore—you are a warrior," and more than ever I know how true that was.

With the war now ended, I want to reverse our roles and help you to be born again—and I have already put this in place—so you cannot say "no" to me.

A year ago at a place called Bretton Woods in the USA state of New Hampshire, the finance people from many Allied countries set the base for postwar business and trade. They agreed on exchange rates which are now in effect. I have most of a Swiss franc account—which was set up by a friend who you know, to help my escape—sitting untouched with Bank Julius Baer. I have instructed them to release the contents to you, using the name by which I know you, plus the date on which you freed me, expressed as dd/mm/yyyy. The account's assets, at the Bretton Woods exchange rate, will provide you with about 19,000 US dollars. I am told that dollars are the desired postwar currency and that you should be able to acquire a cozy apartment almost anywhere in Europe with that amount.

You are a talented and charming woman, but we are both approaching our 35th birthdays now, and it is time for us both to emerge from the chrysalis stage into our newborn selves. You made that possible for me and now I can partially return the favor—so do not deny me that.

With warmest affection and unbounded gratitude,
D.

Tears were proceeding slowly along the small lines from the corners of Elsa's eyes, and she paused twice to dab at them with her handkerchief. Then she blew her nose noisily and emitted an unmuffled sob when she had finished reading. She remembered vividly the pitiful escapee on that chilly March morning in 1943 and the rewarding work of helping his recovery. She pictured him now moving freely in a sun-bathed city by the ocean, and wanting to share some of his good fortune with his accessory. Were there really happy endings like that?

15

Pursuer Unmasked

Octavio smiled at his friend when Dieter inquired how much he owed for the detective work. "Ah, Piano Man—that Samson was a *pessoa estúpida*; he don' get nothing for that. Almost blew the whole thing. Me—I'm glad to help you, and I needed the exercise anyhow."

"So—what do you think? Was I right?"

"Damned right, amigo! That *cabrón* is one of the FBI fellows working out of the US Embassy. They come down here when the German submarines—the ones they call U-boats—were sinking freighters and tankers all down the coast. Don' matter what flag they fly—one torpedo, and boom! They sink. Over four thousand ships. Pretty soon we got FBI guys in every city on the coast, finding shortwave radios and checking out all the Germans, looking for Nazis sneaking in, eh? My friends at the US embassy, they tell me we now got maybe three hundred or more FBI people here. An' the war's over, but the FBI's still here, looking for Nazis.

"Would Sofie have any German friends here? If she does, that could be the reason. There may be someone they're looking for who Sofie knows. I know that the Germans who come to the hotel sometimes ask her to sing German songs—an' she always do that when they ask. I watch them—they love to hear German songs so far from home, and she always sings the ones they like best."

"I understand. Perhaps that's the reason, but I can't think who it might be. I suppose I should ask her, but I don't want to frighten her. She loves her independence in Rio, and it might deprive her to know that she has a shadow."

Everyone knew that Farouk was in the Presidential Suite, and heads craned to catch a look at him when he came and went in a limousine with miniature green-and-white Egyptian flags extended from the front fenders. The hotel security staff formed a bow wave for his movements inside the huge building, and on the few occasions when he visited the public rooms, they blanketed the entries.

He must have heard about the attractive singer who performed regularly in the Bar do Copa, and today hotel employees were busy moving tables when Dieter entered to attend to his Bechstein. A single long table with ten chairs facing the small stage had been set up about five meters from the piano. All other tables had been separated a comfortable distance from that one. When Sofie peeked in on her way to Room 626, Dieter explained that there would be a special audience, and she immediately hurried to find her most flattering performance gown. She was always motivated to be her best in front of a blue-ribbon audience.

When she returned, Dieter smiled his approval and handed her the lyric pages for three French-language songs, which were said to be among the king's favorites. She glanced at them, then said, "Dieter, do you see that fellow standing by the kitchen door?

I'm pretty sure that's the young man who saved my purse on the beach. Why would he be here?"

"Hotel security," he retorted, without thinking, "Extra attention for the king."

"But nobody said anything about hotel security when he smashed that purse snatcher. Did you know his identity? I thought he was just a nice young guy passing by. Is this a coincidence, or is there something you haven't told me, Schatzi?"

"Nothing important, but I did know that he works for Octavio. And I'll tell you all of the story after we finish entertaining the king and his party. It can wait, and it's nothing to concern you. Get warmed up."

When the manager opened the double door and motioned for some waiting people to enter, Dieter was watching in that direction to see his first real king. But instead, the tall form of Baby Pignatari, flanked by beautifully dressed women, materialized, and followed the manager's beckon to their special seating. It would be another ten minutes, during which the outer tables filled, before a large man with a substantial mustache and a handful of guests filled the other chairs. Baby and Farouk greeted one another and chatted amicably while Dieter provided some standards as background music for the clinking of glasses, plates, and silverware.

Exactly on the hour, he nudged his microphone volume a bit higher and launched into the top-ranked American tune of the day, Bandleader Les Brown's composition, "Sentimental Journey." The undramatic singer Doris Day had recorded it, and her rendition had quickly become the benchmark—sweetly delivered and upbeat. Sophia was greeted by applause as she entered the room and briefly acknowledged the presence of notables at the special table. Then she held up her hand for Dieter to stop playing and took the hand microphone.

"We had planned to open with the wonderful new melody that the Piano Man has been vamping, but suddenly as I looked around the room at all of you, I decided that it might be a good time to revert back just a little while—to when our world was at war—and to offer once again a song which meant so much to so many in 1944. It is called 'I'll Be Seeing You,' and it summed up the hopes of so many people then—which have finally been fulfilled now. Piano Man, let's do that in the key of E-flat major, like Billie Holliday does."

Dieter noted that her flair for capturing an audience had only grown stronger over the period of their musical partnership; once again she had seen an opportunity to involve her audience in the song selection, and soon even the two distinguished gentlemen at the head table were mouthing the familiar lyric, *in all the old familiar places, that this heart of mine embraces, all day through* . . . Sophia had left the stage with her trailing microphone cord and moved directly in front of them, keeping their eye contact and projecting incredible sensuality in a song about people drifting apart in wartime. She embraced the song's final phrase like a lover determined not to leave.

"I'll be looking at the moon"—her mesmerized audience held its breath through the long pause—"but I'll be seeing you."

The room was totally quiet for a collective deep breath, and then Egypt's king rose to his feet and applauded with an appreciative nod in Sophia's direction. She executed a perfect theatrical curtsy and extended her upward palms toward the large man. The room erupted in applause.

Dieter thought back to a night seven years earlier when she

had first sung publicly in Prague, and he was suddenly filled with emotion, thinking of the journey they had shared since then. Now it really was time to play "Sentimental Journey," and he clued her in. How he would miss her during her time on tour!

Back at their apartment, after a quiet dinner on the Atlântica, the two reclined together in an oversized chaise on their private terrace. The sun had just dipped below the mountaintops behind them, and a low crescent moon was reflected over the ocean to the East. Sofie took a sip of the drink resting on her side table and turned toward Dieter.

"What is it that you haven't told me about the pickpocket? You knew that the young fellow who engaged him and returned my bag to me is part of hotel security, and it probably wasn't coincidence that he was nearby. Right? Something's afoot, Dieter—and I'm entitled to know."

"You're right—and I will tell you as much as I know. I noticed recently that someone—a man—seemed to be walking behind you on your afternoon strolls by the ocean. When you stopped, he stayed nearby. When you started again, so did he. I asked Octavio to help me—first to determine if I was correct in my suspicion, and, if so, to identify the man. He assigned that young fellow to observe your movements and to see if there was what they call a 'shadow.' It was his first day, and he spotted the thief immediately. He had been in the military and knew how to deliver a blow, and he did so. If the real shadow was anywhere near, he could not have missed the commotion and would have recognized the young man if he saw him covering you again. So, Octavio himself took over the vigil and he has concluded that your 'admirer' is an FBI operative attached to the US Embassy."

"But, why? I sing—nothing more—I'm an entertainer. You know that."

"Octavio concluded that you have been watched to observe your contacts. The shadow apparently snaps photos of people you talk to and Octavio thinks they are hoping to identify someone. But there is more, Sofie. Do you recall that envelope delivered to the hotel, with the list of people freed from Theresienstadt?"

"Yes—with the name Dieter Meister highlighted."

"Right. Well, when Octavio questioned Carlos, the night deskman who received it, he said that there was a driver from that same Embassy, but he didn't want to tell us and get into trouble. If we had known that, we would have sought an explanation and probably would have unknowingly disclosed my identity. By never reacting, we confused them."

"And you think it is my father they are trying to find, don't you, Dieter?"

"I do. I'm sorry, but I can't think of another reason for the FBI to care a fig about us."

"First the Gestapo and now the FBI. Probably the NKVD will be next—or maybe MI6. I hate this, Dieter—when will it stop? A damned *king* liked my singing today, and the best-known businessman in the country joined him in applauding me—and tonight, do I feel elated? No, I'm not allowed that pleasure—I'm hunted like a fugitive by a country I've never visited." She belted down the rest of her drink and slammed the bedroom door as she left the terrace, leaving Dieter with a glowing cigarette and a full measure of confusion.

16

Elsa's Safety Net

During the war years, Bank Julius Baer had expanded its small network of offices to participate better in the movement of funds within the Continent; it had even extended itself into the US by affiliating with a commercial bank in New York. This redistribution of assets was also a defensive maneuver to protect against the possible loss of any one location. In Prague, Elsa found a listing for the company under Komercni Banka BKOM, and she walked past the listed street address three times before deciding to ring the bell at the entry door. When she did so, there was no invitation to enter from the dour matron who had responded— only a curt question about whether the visitor knew that this was a private bank. Elsa was pleased that she could assure the sour face that she had rung the bell knowingly because she had business to transact with Bank Julius Baer and wished to speak with the branch manager.

"That would be Dr. Maximilian Ullrich," Sour Face responded. "May I tell him who is requesting to speak with him?"

Years before, Elsa had paid an unreasonable price for five hundred elegantly engraved calling cards with her name and the spurious title "Assistant Director/ International Trading Corporation GMBH," below which appeared the city names "Berlin/Cairo/London/New York/Zurich." Of course, it meant nothing, but was just real enough in appearance that many people hesitated to question. Sour Face was one of those, and she pivoted away toward a closed door at the rear of the reception area, leaving Elsa alone for a few moments. The door reopened and a smallish man with wire-rimmed spectacles perched above his brow looked out at her. "I am Dr. Ullrich—how may I assist you, Miss Danzig?"

Elsa nearly choked. It was "Two Minutes Max," a regular patron of the escort service where she had once worked. He was a favorite of all her compatriots there, because a typical evening with Max consisted of a wonderful restaurant meal on his expense account, followed by the modest time demands of this little fellow, who always wore Chinese silk underpants reaching below his knees. Elsa recalled asking a friend how her encounter had gone, to which the laughing reply had been "Two minutes, max." From that point onward, the man's nickname became iconic.

She gathered herself quickly, hoping that Max would not remember her, and said, "Dr. Ullrich, one of your depositors has authorized the release of certain funds to me, and the code name and number are written on this paper. I would like to effect that withdrawal now because I have a trip coming soon which may require the funds." She handed an envelope to the small man, trying to avoid him looking at her face. The glasses were now resting squarely upon the bridge of his nose and Elsa thought that he was trying to place her.

He turned away quickly and pointed to a small, comfortable meeting room with deep leather chairs. "Please wait in there, miss. Would you like some coffee—or perhaps something stronger?

This should take no more than ten minutes, and there will be a signature required, plus your official identification. Nothing more."

"Thank you. Coffee with a little cream would be nice." He *had* remembered her and wanted her gone as quickly as possible. Good. If he had said "two minutes," she was afraid she might have dissolved in laughter. Before she could finish the coffee, Sour Face had returned and was counting out 19,341 US dollars, then presenting a standard receipt form for signature. Elsa's name had been typed below the signature line and only her passport number was entered on the address line. Done!

17

———

OSS Makes Its Case

Carney and Joe hadn't sat together in three weeks, and each had uncovered some interesting material in the interim. Joe had been cultivating his friendships within the FBI and had convinced at least a few that OSS leads and investigations in progress should not be dropped just because the agency was being phased out at the end of September 1945. He had recounted the Wiesenthal catalogue of Nazis now falling outside the grasp of the Nuremberg investigations and had stressed that important money which had once belonged to Poland's Jewish citizens might be traced and recovered if certain key Germans could be found.

Carney said that FBI/Rio had delivered a "bait envelope" to the singer known as Sophia at the Copacabana, but gotten no response. They had gathered scores of photos of the woman chatting with men in that city, but none bore any resemblance to the escaped General von Seigler, believed to be her father. Nevertheless, everyone agreed that Sophia the singer was Zofia Lena von Seigler, the daughter to whom the general had once assigned his military benefits. They also agreed that surveillance should be continued—unless, of course, she detected it.

Carney withheld his biggest piece of news until the end of his report. "As you know, I have been interviewing several established intelligence specialists in Europe to see if any could be useful to us. Entirely by chance, when I was in Prague I came into possession of a letter sent from Rio to my interviewee there. I was able to read it and am convinced that it is from that mysterious fellow who was protecting the general's daughter at one time. He really did escape from Theresienstadt with help from the lady I talked to. And he was sending her some money in appreciation of her service to him. How do you like *that*!"

"Okay, here's my question," Joe shot back. "Suppose for a minute that one of these photos *does* show Zofia Whatshername talking to a guy who really looks like General von Seigler, and we can find out where he lives and see that he's living the lush life. What do we do then? We are in somebody else's country where we operate out of our diplomatic mission. We have no right to do anything to apprehend anybody. The best we may have is an extradition treaty, which allows our government to ask the other government to return a convicted or indicted person to our jurisdiction. But there's no case against this guy—only Wiesenthal's personal list of bad guys. That doesn't have standing. We don't even know if it's accurate."

"Yeah. I had a terrier who always ran out and chased the milk truck when it went by. He never caught it, but I wondered what he would do if he did."

"Come on—be serious. We have picked up some facts that seem to fit together. If we can add a little more, we take it upstairs. Maybe they arrest the guy. Maybe Wiesenthal's people grab him. Maybe nothing happens right away, but later there's a case with plaintiffs and defendants and a judge. At least we have shown an ability to gather intelligence, and someday there will be an agency that specializes in that. We can be part of it, right?"

18

New Life

"No, there's nothing abnormal about your breasts, senhora. You are a tall, athletic woman and they are large, healthy, and well-formed. Very appropriate for a thirty-year-old late in her first trimester of pregnancy."

"But, Doctor, I'm not pregnant, and I'm experiencing this feeling of fullness and even a small sensitivity—"

"Senhora, you are indeed pregnant—perhaps as much as eleven or twelve weeks. Would that correspond to your sexual activity at that time?"

"No, no—yes, but no—really. We have sex regularly—for over two years. Most nights after work, but I didn't think . . . Oh, damn. This just isn't the right time for me. Damn! Doctor, may I ask you something that may seem silly?"

"Nothing is silly when you are surprised by your condition. What's your question?"

"Well, how can I put this? If I don't tell anyone, how soon will it become apparent? And, if I am moving about a good bit, could that endanger my health or the baby's?"

"Moving about? You mean like dancing or swimming? What

moving are we talking about, senhora?"

"Doctor, I am a singer. About three weeks from now, I am committed to leave on a tour which may last as long as ten weeks, where I will be appearing in front of audiences, wearing—er—ah—form-fitting gowns, perhaps five evenings of each week; four hours each evening. On my feet. Walking around with a microphone. Trying to project energy and vitality as well as my voice. And traveling by air among half a dozen locations. Can I reasonably do this, Doctor?"

"This is your first pregnancy?"

"So far as I know. But, I didn't know this time, did I—so—no, I don't recall this sensitivity before. This must be the first."

"Have you been ill at all during the past two months?"

"No—I'm *never* ill, doctor. I've never missed performances. I sleep soundly. I get lots of exercise. About my only excess has been a fondness for cognac, which relaxes me in front of audiences and soothes my vocal cords. A few times during the war I overdid the cognac and passed out—in my own bed, of course. Usually alone."

"Senhora—pregnancy is a natural condition in women and, sensibly managed, it is only a bit inconvenient. You are marginally late for a first pregnancy, but certainly in fine physical condition. The singing will not suffer—but the gowns may seem to shrink a bit, especially the top parts. Try not to wear anything too small, eh? I am not suggesting that you stop the cognac, but please limit the amount and try to have a little food at the same time. If you begin to feel nausea, then stop altogether. Please see me again as soon as you are back in the city. Good luck—and congratulations!"

Sofie dressed and groomed slowly, with an unanticipated whirl of thoughts competing for her attention. Was there anything else she should be asking the doctor? Were there any prescriptions she should carry with her? Was she going on a fool's errand to be enhancing her career just as her life was about to take a different direction? Should she tell Dieter now?

"Doctor—one thing. I am probably going to make the tour, because it is the capstone of a long professional effort. And I'm probably not going to tell the child's father until I return, because that could burden both of us unnecessarily. But, would you be willing to write a brief note on your letterhead stationery saying that you examined me today and confirming your professional opinion that I am several weeks pregnant?"

"You don't want there to be any question regarding whether the pregnancy was initiated while you were on tour, am I correct?"

"Precisely."

"Of course I will."

19

⎯⎯⎯⎯⎯⎯

❧

Prague

My dear Piano Man,

Your recent letter and its generous contents left me trembling. I still have not stopped. You owed me nothing.

As you disappeared down that isolated country road, I had the great satisfaction of contributing to the rebirth of a courageous human. After years of war, treachery, and deception, that was payment in full for the help I was able to lend you.

Lest you think that I am preparing to return your gift, I hasten to tell you that USD 19,341 was transferred to me efficiently and gives me the opportunity to pursue many things which have been beyond my reach. Trembling again!

One caveat to you: On the day when I received the letter, I also was meeting an American intelligence man at Hlavní Nádraží. I was sloppy, and as a result the letter ended up among the things he carried *away. He returned it "unopened" at the end of the day, but I have been in this profession too long to believe he did not examine the contents. Without much imagination, he will conclude that on 6 March 1943, I helped a Piano Man to slip away from Theresienstadt, and that the escapee is now in Rio de Janeiro. He will also know that the escapee has provided me with an important amount of money from an account with a private Swiss bank.*

This may not be of any interest to the man, but you know how investigators never stop turning over stones. The trail of money from a numbered account to a former SWW operative may be too appetizing for Mr. William Carney to ignore. When he returns to Prague, I will try to evaluate further. So sorry for my error.

Your faithful nurse, ED.

Dieter reread the letter several times. He was glad that he had initiated the correspondence, but wondered whether too much information had passed between them. If one could identify the correspondents, then a wider circle could be drawn to include Sofie and General von Seigler. If money reposed in a private bank for this purpose, how did it get there? How much was there? Who could control it? Where did it come from? Any one of those questions could set off relentless pursuit. He hoped that Elsa's feeling that the Carney fellow had read his letter was not logical, but she had lived in the grey world of intrigue for many years and her instincts had served her well. Dieter had the feeling that the war's end was only a termination of military activity, leaving many matters still to be sorted out.

20

The Tour

Sooner than he could prepare himself for it, the date of the tour's beginning was upon Dieter. Sofie's bag was remarkably small, containing only five performance gowns, as many pairs of shoes, and two "traveling outfits." She would be wearing a third. "After all," she had reasoned, "I'm going to some of the most fashionable cities on this side of the Atlantic. I can find anything I need—and perhaps some of it will be provided." He could visualize her strolling through Buenos Aires' Recoleto neighborhood and trying on beautiful creations that shop owners would like to have displayed on stage. Perhaps she was right.

Sofie's excitement bubbled over. After all, the tour was to begin with her very first airplane ride, and she would soon be greeting audiences in countries different from any she had previously encountered. Most of all, she would be working with a full orchestra enhancing her vocals. This would take some of the work off the shoulders of the vocalist, as instrumentalists provided lush background harmonics for the best tonal quality she could deliver. On the other hand, she knew that an orchestra could never abandon its arrangement in mid-performance and follow her through unplanned improvisations, the way Dieter frequently did.

A Brazilian, Alberto Santos-Dumont, was credited by most of the world with having invented the airplane. Citizens of the United States never heard his name, because, of course, the Wright Brothers were accorded that honor in their own nation. But in Rio de Janeiro, the principal airport was named for Santos-Dumont, and the pioneering Flight #201 of Pan American World Airways touched down there six days of each week on its journeys between New York City and Buenos Aires. Sofie and Dieter first saw the glistening Pan Am Douglas DC-4 in the late afternoon light. It had four large propellers driven by Pratt & Whitney engines, which could carry the aircraft and more than sixty passengers at speeds approaching 250 mph and reaching altitudes of three miles and more above the earth.

Those amazing facts were all set forth in the materials that the popular American airline distributed to its passengers, and Sofie devoured them while wondering how her beautiful city and endless beaches would look from above. She also wondered secretly how she would react to being lifted suddenly from earth's security and propelled through the cold air at such ridiculous speeds. Most of all, she wondered whether a tiny being within her would feel different inside a metal tube high above earth. There wasn't anything about that in the descriptive materials; apparently it wasn't considered a high risk like exploding beverage bottles or wearing heels in a life raft.

Her ruminations were interrupted by a familiar American voice—Buca's.

"Sophia, you must hear this. We just got a big break at the beginning of our tour, and your friend Baby was our benefactor."

"Come on, Buca—you're going to get me in trouble with the Piano Man. Baby and I have never exchanged a single word. Just a bunch of white roses and some applause, that's all. But tell me what he has done for the tour; it must be something very special to excite you like this."

"Well, do you remember that a little while ago there was a huge earthquake in Argentina? More than ten thousand people killed outright and God knows how many injured or left homeless. It was a real national tragedy. It was in all the papers and newsreels here."

"I do, but . . . ?"

"Okay, there's now a big effort by the Argentine government to provide relief. There's one flamboyant fellow—he's the Argentine Secretary of War and Secretary of Labor and Vice President all kind of mixed together—and he is heading up the whole relief effort. His name is Juan Domingo Perón. He and some popular actress have booked the Teatro Colón—it's a gorgeous, big opera house, kind of like La Scala—for a relief concert. Baby is making a generous contribution—he thinks Perón may be Argentina's president someday, good for his business—and Baby has suggested that the Pittman Orchestra and its outstanding vocalist be featured at that concert!"

"When does all this happen? Sounds as if we may have to add some special numbers. Will we have enough rehearsal time in our schedule?"

"We'll have to make time. If we can kick off the tour with a great performance for a blue-ribbon audience in a famous opera house, everything else can fall into place for the whole tour! Oh, and there's more—they are putting us up at the Alvear Palace Hotel. It's the grandest hotel in all of Argentina, much like the Copa in Rio. And—and—you will have your own room!"

"I thought I was going to be sharing with our wardrobe mistress on the tour."

"Well, Baby and I agreed that you might be subject to constant interruptions—because she is—and that could be a distraction. I want you to be able to rest properly and get dressed and ready before your appearances without any unnecessary diversion. You are our featured vocalist on this tour, and eyes will be on you just about every hour we are performing."

"And did Baby suggest that?"

"Come on, Sophia—Baby just got this one gig for us, but it's my tour and I'm calling the shots. I don't even know if we'll see him in BA."

"Right." She also thought to herself, but didn't say, "Well, that didn't go very well, Sofie."

The name of handsome Brazilian businessman "Baby" Pignatari was synonymous with extravagant generosity and beautiful women. (Photo by Ralph Crane/The LIFE Picture Collection/Getty Images) Used by permission.

21

Working Clothes

Elsa spent several days strolling randomly along the walkways that flank Prague's beautiful Vltava River, a broad, swift-moving stream that flows from the Bohemian Forest northward to where it joins the Elbe. The Vltava divides the majestic city into two distinct parts, which are connected by several bridges, most notably by the fourteenth-century Charles Bridge, a lovely stone pedestrian crossing from which she could ponder the flowing river and the ancient buildings at the same time. She loved the sights, sounds, and aromas of Prague, which had been her home for nearly eight years. But it was a bittersweet collection of memories that she sorted through on her walks. Her dedication to Poland had dominated those years, as much so as if she had been a soldier serving on the front lines, and with that perspective she had lived a lie and now had a portfolio of regrets.

She could remain and live comfortably, working for whatever intelligence service she might choose, or she could close the chapter and venture into a new life, much as her friend Magda had done. Maggie the housewife, Maggie the mother—no longer Magda the spy or Magda the whore. Elsa was happy for Magda and envied her new status, but she was unsure whether she could make such a transition herself, even if it were available to her. It would mean lying about her past on every day of her future, a frightening prospect.

Elsa treated herself to a delicious *trdelnik* pastry and a cup of *turecka kava* at one of her favorite cafes in the old city, and then walked at a fast pace through the winding streets with unpronounceable names leading to an ancient stone building in which she kept her very private apartment. It was her refuge; she could slip in and out unnoticed—always alone—and even after several years she did not know any of her neighbors.

A small envelope, with only its corner protruding, had been fitted carefully under the heavy wooden door. She opened two sturdy locks with her keys and then moved the door carefully to dislodge the note without tearing it. By the time she had done so, her curiosity was fully aroused, but the envelope provided no ready answers—it contained only the Czech addressing title "Gospodica Danzig" in firm handwriting. Rather than skewer the envelope with a blade to get at the contents, Elsa elected to steam it open, using the teakettle in her small kitchen. It seemed silly, yet her training had made her especially cautious whenever she encountered the unexpected.

Inside, a note in the same handwriting delivered a simple message:

My dear Elsa,

A work assignment has brought me back to Prague for a few days, and it would be a delightful change of pace if you will join me at dinner this evening. I am sending a car and driver for you at 6:30 p.m. He will wait outside your door for five minutes. If you cannot make it, perhaps we can find a more convenient time. Hoping to have your company and a good appetite tonight.

The note was signed simply *Bill C*—nothing more—but of course she knew that it was from the suave OSS agent Carney, with whom she had dined and spoken recently. Her first reaction to the communication was that he had somehow traced her to her flat after that evening, even though she had taken normal precautions against being followed. So, he wanted her to know that he was very resourceful. Okay, so was she.

Second, his "invitation" offered no information about where or with whom this evening would be spent. Seemingly it was intended to measure whether she would trust his motives and her own ingenuity sufficiently to be there on the curb at 6:30. "So. It's a challenge or a test," she mused. "He must know that those have been my bread and butter for a decade. There's no way I can duck this."

Finally, the note's content suggested to Elsa that Mr. Carney had indeed taken advantage of her slip-up and had read the letter from Dieter Meister in Brazil before returning it to her. From that source, the OSS operative might easily assume a connection to Sofie von Seigler and probably to her vanished father as well. That was the ultimate prize—that and the possibility of recovering some substantial amount of stolen money or bullion. "When you make a mistake, Gospodica Danzig, you make a really big one," she chided herself. "Now, how might I turn this into a positive opportunity? I must get the resourceful Mr. Carney to share his knowledge with me—just as I have done hundreds of times since I came to Prague, with hundreds of other men who were tightly wrapped around their precious secrets."

She chose a simple black cocktail dress—one that could be worn comfortably without undergarments—and she laid out a single strand of pearls that could lead a gentleman's gaze unerringly toward her attractive cleavage from across the dinner table. Her bare arms were still firm from the intense training that had always been a part of the SWW regimen, and currently they were a uniform tan color from those daily riverside walks in the Prague sunshine. The final product was intended to look like a current favorite movie pin-up, the Canadian star Yvonne De Carlo. Elsa had done her work well.

Under the apartment's only bed, Elsa still kept some of the standard tools of her trade, which could be fitted easily into a lady's dainty evening bag. First there was a metal lipstick tube, which also contained two capsules of chloral hydrate, the potent knockout potion made famous by turn-of-the-century Boston bartender Mickey Finn. A Chanel perfume dispenser had a second port that could dispense two ccs of sodium thiopental, which Elsa thought was overrated as a truth serum, but nevertheless carried for the right occasion. And, finally, the handle of the purse itself converted into a sharp four-inch blade with which she had shredded a score of stuffed training dummies and one Wehrmacht Colonel with malevolent intentions.

At 6:25 p.m., an attractive, lone woman entered the rear door of a waiting black Buick sedan.

22

⸻

❦

Blues in the Night

Santos Dumont Airport was exactly ten kilometers straight north from the Copacabana Palace, with the sea on its east side and the signature lumpy Brazilian coastal mountains to the west. Dieter followed the blinking wingtip lights of Pan American's sleek aircraft as it paralleled the shoreline then climbed higher into the fading twilight. There was one final flash of reflected sunlight off the silver plane's surface, and then it disappeared from his view into some wispy cloud cover. He knew that Sofie was seated on the plane's starboard side and so she could look down on the city's early-evening lights, and then at the pink glow behind the mountains where the sun had disappeared. Oh, what an adventure for her, he thought—and what a lonely evening for me.

Rather than return to their apartment, Dieter had a taxi return him to the hotel, where he could immerse himself in familiar surroundings for a while. The Bar do Copa was very lightly populated, and the sound level was that of intimate conversations, bartenders mixing a few cocktails, and some vile recorded music playing at a mercifully low volume. Dieter opened the Bechstein and began playing some of the blues melodies that had gained popularity in the United States. Without intending to do so, he slipped into a beautiful composition titled, "When Your Lover Has Gone," and found himself mentally tracing the lyrics, which seemed to have been written intentionally for that evening:

When you're alone, who cares for starlit skies
When you're alone, the magic moonlight dies
At break of dawn, there is no sunrise
When your lover has gone.

He must have been working over variations of the beautiful melody for several minutes when he realized that the lyrics were not only in his head, but also being delivered in a soft, accented voice a few feet away. Alone at a table, the singer gave an apologetic wave in his direction but continued twining the lyrics skillfully around his accompaniment. They completed the thirty-two bars with the sad conclusion:

Like faded flowers,
Life can't mean anything
When your lover has gone.

"That was beautiful, Miss . . . " Dieter smiled, as a ripple of applause floated across the room. "You caught me totally off guard; I was just exploring a favorite song and suddenly you gave it a lovely treatment. Do you sing? I mean, do you sing as a profession?"

"Aha, you don't recognize me, Senhor Piano Man. My name is Lola, and you heard me sing with the Buca Pittman Orchestra a short time ago. Do you remember?"

Lost for words, Dieter nodded and slapped his head lightly in embarrassment. "Of course, of course—Buca's featured vocalist! *Estupido*—asking if you sing professionally. Please forgive me; I should have recognized you and your lovely voice."

"Would you care to do another?" she asked. "We both seem to be in the mood for soft ballads tonight. How about the blues ballad by the Englishers—Maschwitz and Strachey—called 'These Foolish Things'? Do you know Billie Holiday's recording of that one?"

Once again the lyrics bit deep into Dieter's thoughts as if they had been especially chosen:

> *A cigarette that bears a lipstick's traces*
> *An airline ticket to romantic places*
> *Still my heart has wings*
> *These foolish things remind me of you.*

The two continued their accidental collaboration for nearly an hour, and very gradually, people walked into the Bar do Copa to listen until more than half the tables were taken and the bartenders were busy shaking and pouring a good many cocktails. The next surprise was the manager, who had walked in to see what was going on.

"Do you two realize that we were planning to close early? And do you know that you're not being paid to perform tonight? How'd you even find each other? Am I missing something?"

Dieter felt the need to respond. "Buca and Sofie and the orchestra flew off to BA tonight, and I was feeling lonely—so I walked in and started noodling around in the empty room."

"And I did the same thing," Lola interjected. "He didn't even recognize me. I was just sitting there with a *limonada*, feeling sorry for myself, and Piano Man started playing some nice lonesome songs—so I sang them and sucked on the lemons. I guess we should stop now, huh?"

"Well—I think the bar guys were planning to take off. But I'm gonna offer to pay them until eleven if you two will stay another hour. How's that?"

Both nodded affirmatively, and Lola said, "I gotta idea, Piano Man—let's call this 'Blues Night.' We can kick it off with that Harold Arlen/Johnny Mercer song, 'Blues In The Night,' yes?"

Dieter was on it quickly, vamping a few chords, then Lola raised her hand and offered:

Mah momma done tol' me
When ah wuz in pigtails . . .

Whatever sadness had been gripping them earlier had been flushed out by the enjoyment of creating unrehearsed, harmonious sounds together. They waved a smiling good evening to their appreciative audience, who had been provided with a final round on the house when the room closed officially at eleven. The manager also handed each musician a US one-hundred-dollar bill and said, "Let's give this some thought and get together tomorrow. Maybe we can build a regular weekly night or two around your blues music format." Lola pressed an unexpected light kiss on Dieter's cheek and said, "Thanks, Piano Man. That was good for me." She was out the main door and into a cab before Dieter could gather his thoughts, so he waved at the departing vehicle and took the elevator to the sixth floor where the solitude of Room 626 was awaiting him.

23

Last Libation in Prague

The driver said, in unaccented English, "Good evening, Miss Danzig—it will take us only about fifteen minutes in this light traffic."

"To go where?" Elsa queried. "I just guessed that it would be a quiet, more formal restaurant when I decided what to wear."

"Aha—then you won't be disappointed, ma'am. They say that U Malīrů 1543 is the oldest restaurant in Europe. The ceilings are painted—like the Sistine Chapel, you know—and the food is served by candlelight. It is in the area called Malá Strana, the Lesser Town, on the west side of the river."

"Sounds romantic," she observed, with just a hint of irony in her tone.

"I guess that's the idea," he responded with a sardonic smile. "I've never eaten there myself."

The next ten minutes were entirely silent in the Buick, as Elsa gazed out the window at the lighted buildings along the Vltava. Once again she realized how incredibly beautiful this city was. She wondered if Maggie, in Chicago, had anything so nice in her daily view. As promised, they pulled to the curb in front of a beautifully preserved building after the fifteen-minute drive, and a doorman helped Elsa to exit the car and proceed through the arched stone entryway. Inside she was seated at a corner table while her eyes adjusted to the candlelight.

"Mr. Carney will be here momentarily, Miss. May I get you an apéritif—perhaps a nice Dubonnet—while you are waiting?"

"Why, of course," she responded. "Mr. Carney will just have to catch up if he is too delayed."

When Carney hadn't yet appeared twenty minutes later, Elsa began to wonder whether she was supposed to be tipsy even before he arrived, or if there were OSS people ransacking her apartment at that very moment while she stared at the ceiling murals. She was never content when she felt someone might be taking advantage of her, and now a bit of that discontent was creeping into her evening.

"Garçon," she signaled to the nearby waiter, "Do you think that you might get us two glasses of sparkling water with ice?"

He nodded his understanding and returned with the sparkling water quickly. "And perhaps you could fetch a second glass of Dubonnet for me," she added, even though her first was far from empty.

Chloral hydrate sometimes imparted a slightly bitter taste to plain water, but in sparkling water it was undetectable. A droplet of the Mickey Finn ingredient dissolved immediately into the water glass across from her before the second Dubonnet had arrived, and that second glass was transferred to the empty position at the table, awaiting Mr. Carney—if indeed he came at all.

A warm hand unexpectedly touched the bare nape of her neck, and a soft voice intoned, "I hope you can forgive my tardiness, but something came up just as I was preparing to leave, and I thought I could deal with it more rapidly than I did. I hope they offered you an apéritif and that you were able to check out the surroundings. This place is four hundred years old, and a lot of the furnishings and decor are genuine. I'm sure you noticed."

"Of course! I had time to earn an associate degree in antiquities and consume a liter of Dubonnet," she scolded, but softened it with a winning smile. "There's your apéritif for you, if you're thirsty. It's very good. I haven't looked at a menu, because I'm sure you have favorites to recommend."

Carney took a few swallows of the inviting ice water to clear his throat, and then recited from memory four of the highly recommended offerings of U Malířů 1543. Each description was elaborated with personal asides on the preparation and presentation, allaying any thought that he might be new to the place. When he had completed his recitation, he also finished his ice water and queried, "So, what appeals to you, Miss Danzig?"

"I like the sound of the boeuf bourguignon—and perhaps you could select a nice Burgundy wine to go with that, Mr. Carney?"

"Good choice. I think I'll have that, too—and we can split a bottle of 1940 Romanée-Conti. That's an excellent Burgundy year and a leading Domaine Romanée. After waiting so patiently, you deserve the best."

It was, indeed, a delightful dinner, and their conversation was limited to food, wine, and the pleasures of consuming both. Nothing about becoming an OSS stringer in Prague or about Elsa's plans for the future. She noticed her host stealing an occasional glance at her strategically draped string of pearls and knew that the candlelight on her exposed skin gave it a smooth, silky appearance.

Finally, Elsa leaned confidentially toward Carney and said, "You read the letter from Brazil, didn't you?"

"Why would you think that?"

"Because we are both spies, and I would have read your letter under similar circumstances—isn't it obvious? That's what we do. That's who we are."

"And if I read your letter, what would I have learned?"

"That I was a part of the plan by which a young German Jew escaped from imprisonment in Theresienstadt and fled the country successfully. And that, in appreciation, he gave me some money which I now have available to restart my life."

"But, would I wonder how a young Jewish piano player in Germany could accumulate that much money while imprisoned?"

"You would have read that a friend of his provided it so that he could resume life after his imprisonment—he mentioned that in *my* letter."

"Yes, I'm curious about that friend. Might you know the friend's identity? The escaped prisoner seems to indicate that you would know that person. Do you?"

"Perhaps. But if so, I wouldn't reveal it without adequate reason. That would be an important breach of trust. Can you think of any reason why I would cross that line? Before even considering it, I would want to know the use to which the information might be put."

"Well, for discussion's sake, let's suppose it could help lots of people recover a part of something stolen from them while they were being mistreated. Hey, maybe a public restaurant isn't the place for such a discussion. We're a short walk from my flat, where we won't be overheard."

"Oh, surprise! Let's take a walk."

They strolled southward for five minutes in Malá Strana to an area where upscale apartment buildings overlooked the Kampa Park area, and beyond it, the river. Carney stumbled twice on the cobblestone streets, but each time righted himself quickly and continued his flowing conversation. Now he was describing the FBI's "Special Intelligence Service" and how it operated as an overseas agency in South America during the war years to keep tabs on the estimated five hundred thousand Germans spread across that continent. "There are more than ten thousand operatives down there—lots of them in Argentina and Brazil and Uruguay where the governments had some sympathy for the Nazi causes and allowed them to immigrate and settle in.

"When they tol' me that OSS din't have any operations in South America, I wasn' sure we could help that Wiesenthal guy, who had the goods on so many escaped Nazis. But the FBI SIS has a crew in Rio and we were able ta put a tail on that singer, Sophia—the general's daughter, y'know. We think her father's somewhere there—in Br'zil—and he may have a whole bunch o' money filched from the Jews."

"Mr. Carney, what happens if you do ID the general—what then? How do you recover anything he has stolen?"

"Dunno. The SIS guys are only surveillance. They can' arres . . . arres . . . arrest people or shoot 'em or anything. But, I think the Jews can snatch 'em an' pound bamboo shoots unner their finnernails until they say *Onkel*—thas' German, y'know—who the hell cares."

"So you watch the general's daughter and hope she'll lead you to him, right? Why are you interested in the escapee who wrote to me from Brazil?"

"Aha! We think he was her bodyguard—an' maybe her lover, too. Real mystery man, but he could maybe help find th' general, too! Anyhow, your letter pins his location down an' we can put the screws on him. Hey, thsh is where I live. Gotta sit an' relax onna balcony with me. Helluva view."

"Nice tits, too—huh?"

"You're hilarious, Elsie . . . Elsa—yeh. Real nice—the part I can see. Ha!"

Five minutes later Carney was sprawled in a lounge chair, passed out completely. Elsa had fixed him a short whisky and water spiked with the additional chloral hydrate and she had left without the need to unbutton a single button. She had gotten the answers she set out to obtain, but instead of buoying her spirits, they precipitated a sense of true sadness as she contemplated that this might be the last evening she would ever spend in the elegant old city she had come to love.

Timeless Prague, late at night. Photo: Robert A. Neff.

24

Buenos Aires

The Spanish explorer Pedro de Mendoza had founded a settlement in 1536 and called it Nuestra Señora Santa Maria del Buen Aire. It was on a broad river leading into the Atlantic Ocean, which seemed to bode well for its future as an agricultural source. But the indigenous people of the region shut the community down, and its surviving settlers moved farther south and east along the river. Eventually they ventured back to the original site and attained some success, but their region at the southern end of a huge continent was officially a part of Peru, which was governed from the city of Lima, far to the north. This delayed the growth of Buenos Aires for generations, but eventually the grains and cattle that thrived there found a market in many places reachable by sea, and the settlement became a prosperous "frontier town."

When Sofie looked down on the city shortly after the conclusion of World War II, its metropolitan population was approaching three million, and beyond the city limits a proliferation of other inhabited areas nearly doubled that. Buenos Aires was big and bold and quite beautiful to the new arrival.

From the air she had no way of seeing the domestic struggles within the area as the working class and entrenched "upper" class squared off in a battle for control of the naturally rich region.

Sofie's first impression was that BA was much more in the mold of Paris or Berlin than Rio had been. It boasted wide boulevards and classically inspired architecture, and the residents dressed and conducted themselves more formally than the Cariocas she had left behind so recently. She had completed her first airplane trip without major discomfort—despite the long distance over which she had been tightly confined in a cylinder—and now she longed to stretch her arms and legs and perhaps walk barefooted along a sandy beach where the air felt fresh as she inhaled. Despite the miracle of flight, the aroma of cigarette smoke and recycled air was really a miserable traveling companion. It was two thousand kilometers from Rio to BA, and even in a modern aircraft, that had been a hardship for Sofie.

For the next two hours, she seemed to be buffeted between receiving lavish attention and being totally ignored. She was not permitted to carry any of her luggage or open a door or move a chair. That was all done by smiling faces, but between those episodes were stretches of dead time, when she felt detached from the rapid conversations in Spanish and the constant shuffling of paperwork by little men in important-looking uniforms. Finally, all twenty-five of the people in their traveling party were in a bus, honking its way into the heart of this humming city, where in twenty-four hours she was supposed to sing for an important audience. For just a moment Sofie felt a sensation suggesting she might vomit.

When they finally unloaded at the Alvear Palace Hotel, she took a few moments to look at all of the beautiful Louis XV furnishings and art in the public area, and there she saw a large signboard announcing the gala performance being offered at El Teatro Colón for the benefit of families suffering hardship as a result of the recent *terremoto*. The evening would be hosted by actress Eva Duarte, whose smiling face was depicted next to the names of those who would be donating their talents to the evening's success. And, there it was, near the bottom of the poster: *Music provided by the Booker Pittman Orchestra, featuring international vocalist Sophia.* She almost wished that she could pick up the large board and send it to Dieter in Rio; he would be so proud of the billing she had been given! Now, if only she could relax and rest for long enough to recharge her energy.

Once her passport had been examined and she had signed in at the main reception desk, Sofie went up to her room. It exceeded her expectations, with an ornate bed and matching chairs and desk. Velvet draperies had been drawn away from the broad single window looking out onto the beautiful Recoleto neighborhood, and her clothing had been transferred to hangers in the mirrored closet and to drawers left partly opened to display their contents. She felt like a celebrity in these tasteful surroundings.

Then a table in the farthest corner of the room caught her attention. It was a simple piece, not in the same style of the other furnishings, causing her to conclude that it had been added especially for her visit. Atop the table was an ornate vase containing more than two dozen beautiful white roses, emitting a wonderful aroma that seemed to cleanse the residual tobacco odors still clinging from her air travel. "Oh, Dieter!" she blurted as she walked to the bouquet.

The small card tucked beneath the vase said simply, *Enjoy your time here—you will soon be the toast of Buenos Aires. Baby Pignatari.*

Sofie remembered her father's frequent references to

Virgil's *Aeneid*, when he would wink at her and remind her, "Beware Greeks bearing gifts: every nice gesture comes with a price tag." At some point she would learn the fare for this beautiful room and the stunning bouquet, but for now she needed to stretch out on the bed, catch up on lost sleep, and let her churning stomach settle.

25

―――――

✎

New Sounds at the Club de Copa

Two days after their impromptu duet, Dieter again saw Lola walking through the lobby of the Copacabana Palace, and he called out to her. She looked his way and then crossed the lobby toward him, offering a warm smile and her extended hand. They captured a small, out-of-the-way table and by some unspoken understanding began to chat. Dieter ordered a Ramos Fizz and asked if Lola would join him in that choice, whereupon she smoothed her dress over a slightly protruding belly and said, "No, I've sworn off alcohol until this little one is safely delivered. I'm thirty-seven years old, Piano Man, and this may be my only opportunity to have a child. I want it to be a good, healthy one."

"Ah—I hadn't noticed that you are ... well, I didn't really look. Congratulations! You and your husband must be very excited; I know I would be."

"Well, I am excited and feeling blessed—but I have no husband or life partner, Piano Man. I'm not even certain who the father is. Probably one of the woodwinds—they are usually the roués on the road. Ah—I've shocked you. I'm so sorry, please forgive me. It is very lonely for a woman traveling with an orchestra, and it is very easy to get familiar with people you are constantly seeing. The band became my family, and sometimes, when we are tired, it's just natural to . . . you know . . . let go! I'll bet you know Irving Berlin's song, don't you? It says,

> *You've got yourself tied up in a knot*
> *The night is cold but the music's hot*
> *So come—cuddle closer; don't you dare to say 'no sir'*
> *Let yourself go!*

"It was good enough for Ginger Rogers, and seemed to work for me, too—until one day I noticed some subtle changes. And here I am out of work and expecting a little saxophone player. I get mad at myself, but then I imagine ten years from now when I'll have a great little pal sharing life with me."

Dieter was amazed at the total honesty and independence Lola projected. He liked her and wondered if she was as open with everyone. Lola seemed to read his mind as he studied her.

"I know, Piano Man—you're thinking that this is a very personal conversation to be having the second time we see one another, but I'm like that. If it's in my head, chances are it will be out on the table pretty quick. But I heard you were in a German concentration camp for a long time, so I know you understand. Loneliness—it can create a—convenient intimacy—from time to time, yes? We're mostly all social beings and we are fueled by breaking rules if our lives have become dull and boring. So I banged a few drunk musicians in colorless cities and you buggered a few guys when you were in cold, concrete rooms. Does that make us bad or does it just keep us from wasting away of boredom and neglect? Tell me what you truly believe, Piano Man."

Dieter was trapped. Even admitting that he had ever been in

that situation went well beyond his previous disclosures to friends, although he understood that until he could discuss those events comfortably, they would continue to draw him back to the horrors of his captivity.

But didn't they say that confessing one's sins to a total stranger on a train or to a curtained wall in a church confessional could, indeed, provide a fresh start? So would washing his moral laundry with a lascivious singer he hardly knew be a good idea? Perhaps the fact that he was even considering it was an acknowledgment that the prospect was strangely appealing.

Dieter patted his tunic pockets until he found a folded pack containing two crooked cigarettes, then he ceremoniously removed one and attempted to restore it to its original cylindrical shape. When this ritual had produced a reasonable result, he stepped away to a nearby table, where a small candle still burned between the emptied cocktail glasses of the table's last occupants. He lighted his cigarette and returned to Lola. Perhaps it was finally time to open his version of Pandora's box.

"Have you ever been in love, Lola? Not just childish infatuation, but an attachment that dominates your thoughts around the clock? Have you ever wondered if you might murder someone who came between you and that object of your affection? Have you wondered whether life would even be bearable without that person? And, if you have been there and have lost that attachment, have you just said 'the hell with it—I'm going to grab what tastes good and do what feels good and go where my whimsy takes me until I tumble over some cliff' . . . have you?"

"Seems like we both have, Piano Man. You couldn't express those feelings unless you had experienced them—and I certainly understand the questions, because I've considered them before. So here we are, a couple of lonely musicians exploring the blues and maybe giving a little audience a chance to shed their private tears in a public room. We're like musical priests, Dieter! That's your name—Dieter. I checked it with the front desk. Do you think we can build a little program around that theme, Dieter? It would have to be a late-night theme. Maybe we could use that Harold Arlen lament, 'One For My Baby and One More For The Road.' Did you see Fred Astaire sing that in the movie? It was about three years ago."

Lola swung her legs around and stood unsteadily. "Fred was supposed to be getting really drunk because of lost love, and he goes into this stumbling dance where he breaks lots of glasses on the bar." She laughed as she deliberately tipped Dieter's glass over. "Then he jumps to the top of the bar counter and does moves that would kill most dancers." She spun gracefully and ended up facing her astonished companion with both hands extended, as the American dancer might have finished.

"I'm afraid I was in a concentration camp—in a room with two dying friends—about that time."

"Sorry, Dieter. That was thoughtless of me. But let's grab a piano and I'll teach you the song. It would be a great intro to a program of American blues."

"You play piano, too, Lola?"

"And the marimba and saxophone and eight-string guitar. Whatever it takes to get a paycheck. Music, she's a jealous mistress—always challenging you to get better, always presenting someone more skilled or better looking than you are. But I still love it—for those times when everything comes together perfectly and you hope someone else noticed. Know what I'm saying, Dieter?"

"Well, I'm not sure which is worse—nobody noticing when you've just delivered your best, or somebody waxing poetic about your playing when you know you were mediocre. We struggle to approach perfection and then realize that it is wasted in a room of tin ears. In the long run, I am the critic I want most to impress and please." Dieter took one last pull on his revived cigarette, then ground the glowing tip into one of the small Copa ashtrays that visitors to Rio stole in unbelievably large numbers.

"*Bastardo!* You are absolutely right. But . . . but every once in awhile there's that rare *compañiero* who really knows you and cares you do your best. Hey, we might could do that for each other, Piano Man, eh? I already asked the manager if I can do a little blues review in the Lounge tonight, and he gave me ninety minutes to try it out—with waiters an' tables an' everything. You wanna try with me at ten o'clock, Piano Man? I think maybe it's a good chance for both of us."

"Well, you've done a lot of work, Lola. Sure—I'll try it out with you. Maybe you can write down about twenty titles and the keys you want, and I'll see if I can handle at least half of them."

"Already have done that. Take this with you and I'll meet you at nine-thirty in the Lounge. Let's make this fun!"

Dieter watched the lady walk away, feeling that he had been assaulted by a mountain lion. Obviously the "chance encounter" had been a setup if she had already spoken with the manager and written a list of song titles. But, he reflected, what could possibly go wrong trying out some songs with a pregnant lady in a public room? Certainly there was no implicit scandal in that scenario in postwar Rio.

❧

Dieter was surprised when he arrived at the Lounge doorway; there was a tripod holding a nicely lettered sign reading:

AMERICAN BLUES IMPROVISATION 10:00 PM TONIGHT

PIANO AND VOCAL / COCKTAILS AND BAR FOOD

NO COVER OR MINIMUM CHARGE

Beneath the wording were the hotel's individual stock photos of Lola and the Piano Man.

"Don't you think we look like movie stars?" asked a soft voice over his shoulder, and Dieter turned to see Lola snugly packed into a floor-length silver gown with a feather boa draped around her bare shoulders and covering her waist discreetly. She did look like a movie star! He wished for a moment that he had matched her level of elegance, but then reminded himself that the vocalist, not the accompanist, should be the focal point in this kind of recital. They entered the empty room and sat together for the next half hour on the wide piano bench, picking the melodies they would be spinning out for their impromptu audience. From time to time, Lola addressed the keyboard long enough to demonstrate the turnbacks and rhythm shifts she envisioned. Dieter was delighted with her input and frankly surprised at her knowledge of his instrument.

Promptly at ten, the doors were opened and a few waiting hotel guests were seated in the room, then some more materialized and they could hear the familiar sounds of drinks being mixed and hors d'oeuvres being sampled. It was time to begin. Dieter tapped his microphone and spoke.

"Thank you for joining Lola and me this evening. This is a bit of an experiment for us, and we hope that it will be enjoyable for you. Music has been around in one form or another for ten thousand years, but only about five hundred years ago it began to take on a more disciplined form where composers actually wrote down—in their own hieroglyphics—the exact notes and tempo they envisioned. That trend has continued, and surely the large orchestras of our twentieth-century world would be chaotic without the reams of paper notations that knit them together.

"However, around the turn of the century, it became popular in some parts of music's world for smaller groups to begin playing a song precisely as written, and then to invite individual improvised solos by members, while the rest continued the pace and structure of the song. This format was embraced by the jazz bands and blues bands that began performing in New Orleans, and it moved up the Mississippi River through the heartland of the United States. Then it jumped the Atlantic Ocean to the bistros of Europe where it thrived, even as war engulfed that continent.

"Tonight Lola and I are going to improvise our way through some melodies we have selected. Most are the so-called "blues" songs—they are slower-paced and sometimes in a minor key, which can be used to create that tired and lonely feeling we have come to know as 'the blues.' This performance is spontaneous and unrehearsed, so we will be watching one another to build our rendition as we deliver it to you. Please join me in welcoming the popular vocalist Lola Morais."

Lola walked confidently to Dieter's side and placed one hand lightly on his shoulder. She raised her head slightly as she faced the audience, then closed her eyes and began:

I hate to see . . . the evenin' sun go down
'Cause ma baby, he done lef' dis town

W. C. Handy's "St. Louis Blues" was a solid beginning to their evening because nearly everyone in the Lounge already knew the song, and it set feet to tapping and lips moving as the audience became a part of the evening. When Lola had finished with her vocal offering, she pointed toward the keyboard and said, "Mr. Dieter Havlik, the Piano Man," and Dieter explored some variations of the melody as Bach and then Mozart might have imagined them. Then Lola nudged him to the end of the piano bench and added her two-handed improvisations while Dieter provided the rhythmic structure, Both were obviously having a good time, and it seemed infectious, as the seated patrons began reinforcing the beat, clapping in rhythm with it.

As they ended the song there was an appreciative "Wahoo!" from the rear of the Lounge area, and Dieter could see that it came from Octavio, the head of hotel security. It was indeed a good beginning, and the two performers were able to sustain the audience appreciation for over an hour, at which time the manager commandeered the microphone, thanked attendees for joining the experiment, and said that, regrettably, the bar must close in the next ten minutes. "But not before one final song from our wonderful artists and one round on the house for our patrons."

Lola cupped her hand by Dieter's ear and, in a hushed voice, said, "I think he liked it, Piano Man."

26

El Teatro Colón

Sofie had left her mother in Poland and joined her father in Berlin when she was sixteen years old. It was an exciting time in that city, which was then generally credited with being the third largest metropolis in the world. There had been crime and debauchery aplenty, but her proud father had shielded his only child from Berlin's tawdry attractions and instead escorted her to the city's equally heralded cultural scene. She recalled vividly their visits to Staatsoper Unter den Linden, a lavish opera house where the great Caruso and other icons of classical music had been enjoyed. Those old memories were turning over in her mind as she dressed to go to their rehearsal in El Teatro Colón.

Even reading a tour pamphlet's description of the famous Argentine opera house did not prepare her adequately for the reality of entering one of the world's finest performance venues. There were twenty-five hundred plush velvet seats for viewers, plus open galleries that could accommodate a thousand standees. But the real magic seemed to be in the lighting and acoustics, which maximized the sights and sounds of El Teatro Colón. That very evening, a truly sophisticated audience in the legendary building would focus its attention upon one voice—that of Sophia. She folded her arms as if suddenly chilled and imagined the mixture of power and fright that might grip her as she heard her voice resound among the columns, the chandeliers, the walls, and the ornate ceiling.

Perhaps this should be that exception her doctor had allowed when urging her to minimize her brandy consumption during the pregnancy. She would have just enough to create that reckless creativity that had always helped her to achieve her very best vocal delivery. Sofie assured herself that she would be calming the source of nervousness in her brain and warming her vocal cords and air passages to create good sounds, not poisoning a little being known only to her. For that passenger, she would have a portion of rare Argentine beef and a medley of fresh vegetables, washed down with just a swallow of red wine.

Buca interrupted her daydreaming. "What do you think? Not more than a half dozen places so grand as this in the whole world, and our audience tonight will be strictly top drawer. If they and the papers are kind to us tomorrow, we'll have new opportunities everywhere. You know, Colonel Perón's girlfriend—or wife or whatever—is a movie and radio actress here, and I'm told that news agencies from all over South America will be filming tonight. That's all about pushing her career, but we get a free ride because all the celebrities will be filmed right in front of our orchestra. Get yourself a glass of water and come on over to the stage; I want to rehearse three vocals with you—two listed in the program and an encore, if it's needed. Your first will be more or less addressed to Vice President Perón, who has an ego of major proportions. We're going to put a soft spot on him while you sing to an otherwise dark audience."

"What song, Booker?"

"Gershwin's 'The Man I Love'—that should send the message he's trying to put out there to the voters. This guy intends to be the most powerful leader on the continent a year from now, and we all have to genuflect now. He should love the fact that a beautiful woman—and a good singer—directs that at him. What do you say, Sophia?"

"I like the song if the room isn't noisy. If Colonel Perón thinks I'm sending it personally to him . . . well, we'll see if he flashes a big smile. Don't want to embarrass him. Not going to sit on his lap or get close to him at all. You know, I sang that song to Hermann Göring at a political function when I was in my early twenties and he got all sweaty. Politicians don't like to look sweaty or unnerved in public."

℞

Sofie was introduced to Eva Duarte de Perón about an hour before the Gala to Aid the Victims of the Great San Juan Earthquake was scheduled to begin. She understood that the Argentine Vice-President, Colonel Perón, had made this relief effort a key part of his current campaign for the presidency, and he was relying heavily upon his popular young actress/wife to orchestrate such public appearances. Eva was four years younger than Sofie, and at 1.6 meters was half a head shorter. She was perfectly dressed in a tailored white suit, and her off-blonde hair was rolled upward from each side into a height-increasing chignon mound atop her pretty face. The popular "Evita" could flash a broad, engaging smile instantaneously, but could transform it to a commanding glare just as rapidly. It seemed to work effectively, as several people scurried about the stage area carrying out her clear instructions.

In due course, the shorter, younger woman turned her

attention to Sofie, who could sense that Evita was not pleased to share the spotlight with other females. "You are the band vocalist?" she began, knowing the answer but wishing to establish their relative importance before they shared a stage that evening. "And you know that you will be singing a song to express the country's and my affection for our future president, Colonel Perón? Of course you do—I can see you aren't stupid. Do you speak Spanish, dear?"

"I can understand spoken Spanish, but I'm afraid that I mostly communicate my responses in some butchered Portuguese; I've lived in Brazil since 1943, but this is my first trip outside."

"I see. Where were you before Brazil, dear?"

"The Continent—Europe, that is. I'm a Swiss subject, but have lived in Germany and in France, too. But I never learned Spanish—except the words to songs, of course. It is a lovely, melodic language and I really should become better at it."

"I hope you will. Do you know Gershwin, dear?"

"Oh, Gershwin songs have been very popular in Europe— except with the Nazi leadership, of course. He lived in France for a while and composed some of his best music there. But you know he died when he was only thirty-seven or thirty-eight years old— much like Mozart did. Don't you wonder what people like that might have done with longer lives, Señorita Duarte?"

She smiled—finally. "I do, Sophia. Both Mozart and Gershwin should have had long lives to give full range to their genius. Let's hope that we will be more fortunate. And, please call me Evita, dear—I am really Señora Perón now, but the working class of Argentina—*los descamisado*—like to call me Evita. I'm twenty-five years younger than Colonel Perón, and they think it is funny to use a diminutive name for me, but they chant it at our political rallies, and I am happy to wave back when I hear it. You understand?"

Two hours later the immense Teatro Colón was jammed with formally dressed Argentines who hoped to be recognized while giving their support to the Peróns' relief effort. Many of the men in attendance wore military uniforms replete with sashes, medals, and braid, while the ladies at their sides showed creamy necks and shoulders accented by dazzling jewelry and expensive fabrics. Sofie reflected that it could as easily have been a Berlin audience ten years earlier as people struggled to befriend that country's emerging political leadership. Buca had his orchestra playing background music softly for the milling crowd; he had chosen the music of the popular Argentine guitarist Hector Ayala, who had composed something called the *Suite Americana*. It had a tango rhythm, which Sofie appreciated with several sips of brandy and a light swaying of her body. That evening, she had chosen an Argentine-blue gown with a white sash and large gold clasp, and when she was dressed she had saluted herself in her hotel room's high dressing mirror with a sip from her snifter. "You look like an Argentine flag with big tits, dear!" she mocked Evita's verbal style. "Please don't bow deeply toward the man I love."

She wished that Dieter were there; he would grasp the humor and laugh with her, then talk her down into a really good performance. *Inspired but controlled* would be his message. "I can do this alone!" she had proclaimed to the mirror—and now she was on stage, ready to test that resolve.

27

———

❧

On the Run

In 1939 an eccentric millionaire named Howard Hughes had achieved control over a US air carrier which had started in business as Transcontinental & Western Air. After WWII, Hughes pushed the company, as TWA, into the forefront of international carriers offering transatlantic carriage to the public. From major cities in Western Europe, one could fly to New York for about $350, and the trip would take between eighteen and twenty hours and include a refueling stop in Newfoundland.

Elsa departed from Prague before her dinner companion awoke the following morning, and she went by train to Paris, from which there were multiple transatlantic flights each week. Nothing of interest remained in her small apartment, and she entered France using a German passport, which was discarded once she reached Paris. After a few quiet days for shopping and a new hairstyle, Elsa presented herself at the Paris office of TWA and negotiated the cash purchase of a ticket to New York. Her instincts warned that the OSS agent, Mr. Carney, would be furious at having been humbled by a female, and that he would go out of his way to squeeze Elsa's friend in Brazil in an attempt to flush out General von Seigler. He had said that OSS had no organization in South America, and further that President Truman was closing the doors of that wartime intelligence service. So she concluded that Mr. William Carney would be pursuing his prey using the US diplomatic services in Brazil and the FBI SIS agents there as his point men. That would take time—enough time for Elsa to alert her friends in Brazil, she hoped.

William Carney never slept past sunrise. There was something decadent about people who did that; it would be totally out of character for one serving in the OSS and charged with being the early bird. Carney never drank as much as those who dined or partied with him. Being a bit more alert gave one the advantage in all such situations, and the whole purpose of the OSS was to create an advantage by acquiring better intelligence. William Carney was profoundly disappointed and looking at the morning sun high in the sky through eyes that literally ached. He rubbed them angrily and looked about his disheveled apartment, hoping to see another sleeping body—that of Elsa Danzig in her damned low-cut dress with the look-here pearls accenting her promising cleavage. There was no sign of her beyond a lipstick-rimmed glass with the water from melted ice at the bottom.

A second glass was inverted by the bar sink. No doubt it had been washed, rinsed, and dried so that no trace of its soporific content remained. Bill had been outwitted, and he felt humiliated. She had used the oldest lure of all to capture her advantage, and he had no idea how much information he may have provided through his unfiltered ramblings. About the last thing he remembered was her unexpected "nice tits" interjection and the overwhelming carelessness it turned on. He rubbed his eyes again with closed fists and then admonished himself with a light knock on his forehead. "Idiot!" was all he could say, and he repeated it several times as he tried to reconstruct the evening, but there was nothing after that last glimpse of the pearls—and he judged that to have been about twelve hours ago. "Idiot!"

Carney knew he must get back to Elsa's covert apartment just to verify his conclusions, but if she was clever enough to incapacitate him in his lair, he doubted that she would be waiting for his visit. So, should he skip that step for now and go immediately to Hlavní Nádraži station and check the destinations for departing trains this morning? Where would a career spy who spoke Czech, German, Russian, Polish, and adequate English run for cover? Certainly not to any of the cities with new Soviet presence—that would eliminate Vienna, Berlin, Danzig, and Warsaw for starters. Zurich and Paris might be attractive because they were transportation centers, but did she even speak French? Her former SWW handler, Lilka Whatsername, was probably still in London where Carney had interviewed her, and Lilka had directed him to Elsa when he first mentioned an anticipated need for a good stringer in Prague. That might be a more logical place to start a search for her rather than some wild goose chase at the railroad station.

And what would be the purpose in finding Elsa anyhow? Originally Carney was looking for a talented information source in Prague, and by accident he had found a possible link to the missing German general who Wiesenthal believed to be involved in stolen bullion or money. By her actions the previous night, she had shown that her loyalty lay with the escaped fellow in Brazil and perhaps with the general's daughter—hey, maybe with the general himself! So, Carney reasoned, it was he who had won the confrontation, because he had forced her to reveal all of that. It was distorted thinking but it made him feel a little better. But what would she do if his conclusions were accurate? She would try to warn those people in Brazil! So he should be tipping the FBI people in Rio that the suspects might be aware of their surveillance. Damn that Elsa—she really was an intriguing woman. Carney suddenly realized that he would like to see her again.

28

⸎

The Melody Lingers On

During the week following their impromptu "Blues In The Night" show in the Copa Lounge, the hotel manager had arranged for three additional appearances by Lola and Dieter. It was an efficient moneymaker for the hotel, because most patrons ordered two or three rounds of drinks during the ninety-minute program, and the small morsels of overpriced bar food seemed to be a requirement for people, even though only about half were consumed. The two featured musicians were happy with a hundred dollars each for their nightly work, and their flow of tips for special requests grew with each repetition of the show.

Lola lived in a small apartment over a gift shop on R. Julio de Castilhos, about six *quadros* inland from Ipanema Beach. It was a busy little area during the daylight hours, but less inviting at night because several streetlights had been stolen, and the storefront businesses were closed and shuttered after dark. Since it was in the general direction of Dieter's beachfront apartment, he waited for her to gather her personal things and then hailed a taxi to drive him home, first dropping her at her doorway on Castilhos. That seemed to please her, and so it was their routine at about eleven o'clock, four times that week.

"My little saxophone player is driving me cuckoo tonight," she said unexpectedly on their fifth such drive together. "I need to get some food into my belly, or I'm not going to be able to sleep. Would you mind stopping at one of those little *mercearias* near the beach so I can quickly pick up a few things?"

"Sure," Dieter replied, and the driver, listening to their conversation, assured them he knew exactly the shop to visit at that hour. The purchase took only minutes and they resumed their drive. When they arrived at her door, Dieter held it open and wished Lola, "*Desfrute de bom apetite*, my partner; you have earned it tonight." She smiled at his improving Portuguese, but when she turned he could see small tears sparkling on her cheeks. "Are you okay, Lola? "he asked.

"I'm just miserable, that's all," was her laughing response. "Don't pay any attention—I get this way when I climb the stairs to an empty flat and fall asleep talking to walls. Maybe it's good training for a blues singer, Dieter. What do you think?"

"Well, maybe we should take those *chouricos* and cheese to my terrace and savor them under the stars with a few sips of good Miolo—would you like that? It's only another five minutes from here, and it's easy to get a taxi there at all hours. The breeze from the ocean should be cool and salty tonight—it can help anyone to sleep better."

"Sold," she laughed, and popped back into the cab with surprising agility. Almost too quickly, they were on his terrace, seated in the open air, listening to endless waves rolling toward Ipanema's empty beaches. Dieter opened a rich-smelling red wine and poured two glasses, which they touched together in an unspoken celebration of their successful new partnership. "Look!" she whispered. "No more childish tears."

Two hours and a liter of excellent wine were consumed over personal recollections, with each describing circumstances that had tested their resolve. Dieter found himself discussing the seemingly endless days in Theresienstadt—actually 1282 days— each represented by a line scraped into the wall of his cell. It was a mosaic of frustration, and he had risked his life to escape it.

Lola described a stepfather who had visualized her as a wanton streetwalker at age twelve, demanding her exclusive attentions until she slipped away at sixteen to dance with a touring samba band. She had performed for two years in small bars and clubs around the state of Mato Grosso. "While you were marking your days with scratches on the wall, my nights were counted with bruises on my arms and scratches on my back from cowboys who thought that the price of a beer earned them the right to feel up the dancer," she admitted with regret.

"So, here's to our survival of all those miserable days and nights," Dieter said.

"And to our freedom to grasp all the happiness we can find now!" Lola added.

A second bottle of Miolo softened the evening's breezes even more, and soon both slept soundly on the terrace overlooking darkened Ipanema.

❧

The sun rises over the Atlantic Ocean and sends sharp blades of light through windows on the east perimeter of Rio. Along Ipanema Beach, early body surfers gather and catch white-crested swells before they curl forward. Sea birds hang majestically above the water, awaiting the appearance of schools of small fish near the surface; then they swoop effortlessly and pick their silvery breakfast cleanly from deep blue surroundings.

On a flower-decked terrace on Rua Francisco Otaviano, the Copacabana's Piano Man opened his eyes with a puzzled expression and took in his surroundings—two chaises flanking a small table containing horizontal, empty wine bottles. A fluffy white bathrobe draped over one chaise and a pair of sandals dropped randomly on the wooden deck. A feathery boa trailing across the open space toward an open bedroom door. And, finally, a clear contralto voice singing musical scales to the accompaniment of a running shower. "Oh, oh, oh—she never went home. She's here and it's . . . let's see, it's nearly ten o'clock. Oh, Dieter. Think! What happened? We had wine and little things to eat, and we fell asleep still talking. Did we touch? Oh. Dieter."

"You're awake, Piano Man! You were so cute curled up there that I didn't want to waken you, and I thought I might be able to tiptoe out and catch a cab. Any chance I can borrow a shirt from you? That gown would look too weird in the street at this hour, but a man's shirt tied at the waist over my tights will look fine. I'll help you to pick things up and then be on my way—you were so sweet to just sit and talk me down last night. I needed that. Hope I didn't shock you, Dieter. Did I?"

He hadn't been shocked by the previous night's conversation, but now here he was—seated on his terrace in broad daylight, speaking with an attractive, moderately pregnant woman wearing only a bath towel draped over her moist shoulders. No matter how innocently it had occurred last night and how uneventfully it might end this morning, Dieter sensed that the thin edge of the wedge had been set.

29

It's in All the Papers So It Must Be True

Argentina had many good newspapers in the immediate postwar period. In a country and at a time marked by intense political rivalries, each had its favorite themes, but one on which there was unanimous agreement was the need to help the thousands of families which had experienced losses during the tragic 1944 San Juan earthquake. It had been that country's greatest natural disaster ever. And in the province of San Juan, thousands were dead and one-third of all families remained homeless.

Vice president and presidential hopeful Colonel Juan Domingo Perón, together with his popular new wife, Evita, had made this cause the centerpiece of his campaign for the presidency. And the benefit performance held at the venerable Teatro Colón had been attended by the country's elite and covered by every publication of importance.

Sofie—well, Sophia—was awakened in her room in the Alvear Palace hotel by the sounds of a full breakfast tray being wheeled to her bedside and heavy curtains being drawn aside to admit the bright sunshine of a ripe Sunday morning. Outside she could hear bells from the nearby Torre de los Ingleses together with the busy noises of a wakening metropolis. Her first reaction was that the light hurt her eyes and the bells fractured her ears—and she was a mess. She cupped her hand over her nose and mouth and inhaled the breath she had exhaled. It was awful. And who was that standing by the bedside? The chambermaid with her breakfast cart, of course. Was there a pot of coffee? Good Brazilian coffee?

"Good morning, Señora Sophia," floated out via an all-too-cheery voice. "Here you have the full Alvear breakfast—and the morning newspapers, too. Look at *Clarin*; it is the top one and you are on the front page! Everyone in Buenos Aires knows you today!"

Clarin was a tabloid, fashioned after the popular new journalistic publications in Europe's capital cities, and of course the gaudy New York tabloids. Candid photos and headlines in rubric print shouted at readers and promised revelations in their related stories.

The center photo on this morning's *Clarin's* front page was of four smiling people knotted closely together under the banner, *PERÓNS AND CELEBRITIES UNITE AT BENEFIT GALA*."

There was the presidential candidate, resplendent in a tailored military uniform, and his popular wife, fashionably dressed in her signature flawless white suit. There also was the tall, handsome Francisco "Baby" Pignatari with his arm draped familiarly over the shoulders of a disheveled Sophia, threatening to pour out of her clinging gown.

The story was even worse than the photograph: "International chanteuse 'Sophia,' appearing with the famous Buca Pittman Orchestra at a Teatro Colón benefit performance for victims of the San Juan disaster, publicly challenged her escort, Brazilian magnate Francisco Pignatari, to match her donation of CHF 10,000 to the worthy cause. Then, to the obvious delight of Evita and Vice President Perón, Senhor Pignatari doubled that donation and Sophia raised her contribution to match his. Although the ultimate beneficiaries of this flamboyant generosity will be the homeless earthquake survivors, certainly Colonel Perón's campaign for the presidency has received immediate impetus from these colorful and generous visitors to our country."

As Sofie stared at the tabloid, she suddenly realized that she was sitting quite naked in the large bed, and the server was still standing at her side holding a pot of coffee and a pitcher of cream, awaiting instructions. "Si, por favor—café," she blurted, as she gathered the sheets around herself. "¿Que hora es?"

"10:00 de la mañana, mi señora," was the quick reply, followed by, "El señor salió hace dos horas y dejó ésta para usted" as she held out a folded paper for Sofie.

To no one in particular Sofie mumbled, "What gentleman left two hours ago leaving a note for me?" although unfortunately she had no trouble imagining the answer to her question.

She unfolded the notepaper.

I would easily have gone to CHF 50,000 for an evening as glorious as that! Cariños, Baby

She rolled it into a tight ball and hurled it toward a vase of white roses staring down at her from a nearby table. Sofie fought to recover her last clear memory of events the previous evening and realized that whatever occurred after her delivery of "The Man I Love" was now shrouded in a hazy amalgam of lights, applause, *abrazos*, and cognac. How did she get into the company of those three people in the photograph, and what had motivated her donation of CHF 20,000 in a public setting? She knew that each franc was worth about twenty-five USA cents, so she had given away 5,000 US dollars, and Baby had matched that! Stupid girl! If an FBI SIS shadow had been watching her before, he would certainly be convinced now that Sofie was concealing something.

And what about Dieter? If the newspaper found its way back to Rio, he would have no explanation for the outrageous photo and bad judgment it conveyed. He would have to conclude that Baby had escorted Sofie to the grand affair at Teatro Colón, and that she had unwittingly bragged to a whole nation about her cache of Swiss money. Worst of all was the possibility that Sofie had spent the night in the company of an infamous philanderer who seemed to encourage that reputation and, in the process, could damage hers.

The notion of such gross stupidity—or possibly the chemistry of reproduction tiptoeing through her body—suddenly dropped a wave of nausea over Sofie, and she began sobbing uncontrollably, wishing she could return to Rio and Dieter. Eight more weeks away might be more than she could bear.

30

The Fazenda

Brazil's Santa Catarina is a pie-shaped state in the country's southern "stem," with the pie's wide eastern "crust" curving along the Atlantic Ocean and its narrow western "point" forming a short border with Argentina. As Brazilian states go, it is quite small, but its area of 37,000 square miles is nevertheless about the same size as the European country of Hungary. Nearly all of Brazil lies north of Santa Catarina. There is a range of small mountains running north/south through the state; the abundant rainfall in that high country divides and flows either eastward toward the coastal plain or west toward the mighty Rio Paraná in Paraguay and Argentina.

Rich soil and temperate climate suggested to Brazil's political leadership in the mid-nineteenth century that Santa Catarina should be populated aggressively by ambitious, intelligent, and hard-working settlers, and so they actively recruited people from northern Europe to immigrate. In the mid-1800s, Europe was struggling with unrest, and many from Austria and Germany answered that call, hoping to retain the best parts of their culture in a virgin setting. The result one hundred years later was a

Brazilian state with the flavor of Bavaria. The German language was the first language of more than half of Santa Catarina's inhabitants, and various other European cultures were also prominent in the small state. By 1945, Santa Catarina enjoyed Brazil's best standard of living and its highest literacy rate.

On August 22, 1942, Brazil joined the Allied nations, opposing the Axis powers. The Brazilian government understood that Santa Catarina state was truly a German and Austrian enclave, where the annual Oktoberfest celebration was second in size only to that in Munich. They passed a law requiring that all European descendants living in Santa Catarina master the Portuguese language, and hundreds of thousands of adults complied.

At the end of a sunny day in early October, a young language teacher named Lucia DeSimone from the university in Joinville waved goodbye to a middle-aged couple standing on the broad porch of their *fazenda's* main building. They had been her students for nearly a year, and they had made excellent progress in their efforts to master speaking and writing in Brazilian Portuguese. She judged them to be in their mid-fifties, although each seemed very fit and trim and, from a short distance, might be mistaken for being much younger. They paid her well for the weekly sessions and sometimes invited her to stay after the formal lessons to dine with them and chat socially in their new language.

From the outset, the teacher was aware that the senhora already had a good working knowledge of conversational Portuguese but pronounced many common words and used expressions which were suggestive of the language as it was spoken in Portugal rather than here in Brazil. She had also noted that when the couple wished to exchange thoughts privately, their aside remarks were not expressed in German but in a language she could not understand—perhaps Polish? However, when she intentionally explained something in German, they were both quick to understand the point, and they responded easily in that language.

The man had the short beard favored by local cattle farmers, while the woman had henna-colored hair that had been professionally cut and shaped. She called him Kurt and he addressed her as Gerda. Their teacher had learned, from a clerk in a nearby mercearia, where most locals shopped for grocery items, that their surname was probably Hahn, and her search of a telephone directory did contain a number for *Hahn, K&G,* without a corresponding address.

When Lucia dined with them, their dinner table was set with elegant Rosenthal chinaware, crystal goblets, and engraved silverware, all suggesting that their origins were not humble and that they might have immigrated more recently than the older families in the area. The meals were served by two attentive Italian girls and prepared by a loud "chef" who seemed to be the girls' father. The teacher was the granddaughter of Italian immigrants who had come to Brazil during the time of Italy's civil strife, and from childhood she had been fascinated by the stories of many of the region's adopted citizens. This couple and their household were hard to figure out, so she constantly looked for small clues.

Oddly, there were no family photos on the walls or tables in the living or dining areas, but Lucia had asked to use the lavatory once or twice and used those opportunities to peek into two large bedrooms. In one of them she saw a framed photograph of a young blonde girl, perhaps in her late teens. She guessed that it might be their daughter, but decided not to ask the question until a more appropriate time. There was also a framed poster from a Czech hotel featuring a blonde singer, and she concluded that it could be the same girl a few years later.

The name on the poster was "Sophia."

A special dinner menu will be featured after each performance.

The fazenda's entrance was more than a kilometer from the house, its few outbuildings, and stables; all were tucked into a concealing grove of Araucaria pine trees. At the entrance there was simply a sign announcing *Propriedade Privada—Nao Entre.* Not the usual finca designation or ownership name, but a warning not to venture up this private driveway without an invitation. At about the midpoint of the entry road, there was a gate that had to be opened by a burly farmer who apparently lived there with a young woman and two small children. The teacher had noted that a telephone line extended to the tidy little house and that the farmer always had a handgun strapped to his waist. The well-kept garden beside the house was only large enough to feed a few people, and a chicken coop to the rear had just two or three dozen healthy birds feeding inside their fence. It seemed obvious that the primary occupation of this *companheiro* was security rather than agriculture.

31

⸼

Selisia

Carney and Joe held their bi-weekly progress review in London, and each brought a full portfolio of findings. Carney led off the review.

"Well, I fucked up big-time in Prague—but also got important confirmation on several points."

"Okay, let's hear the bad stuff first."

"That Elsa, who we were looking at as a possible contract agent, skipped town on me after our last meeting and I haven't turned up a clue on where she is now beyond her mention of a friend named Magda or Maggie in Chicago—and how she now has funds to travel. So—maybe. Dunno. We checked out her Prague apartment and it had been picked clean, as a pro would do. No calendar; no lists; no pictures or notes. Only some tired furniture, a few dresses on hangers, and basic groceries."

"Well, she *is* a pro, so that's to be expected. What's the good stuff, Carney?"

"Okay, once she convinced herself that I had read her letter from the guy in Brazil, there was no more nice-nice from her. That Dieter *is* the mystery man who was with the general's daughter and who somehow got out of Theresienstadt a couple of years ago. So, we can be pretty sure that the Sophia in Brazil is the daughter—and I'm guessing that sooner or later she'll slip up and lead us to the general if we are patient."

"Well, did you at least get to poke her before she split? You said she's a looker."

"Hey, you know me, amigo. I never fail in that department. But she slipped away after we fell asleep at my place."

"Ah, you rascal! Must have slept pretty soundly if she had time to sanitize her apartment and get out of Prague without you knowing it, huh?"

"Shut up! She's missing and possibly headed to Chicago. We're going to have to find her if we can, and we can be pretty sure she'll be tipping off Dieter and the general's daughter about our interest. Whatta you have?"

"Okay, here's the scoop on Sophia—the singer. She's on tour with the Buca Pittman Band and made a big splash in BA. She hobnobbed with Perón and got her picture in the papers there. But, here's the clincher! She personally donated USD 5,000 to the earthquake relief fund. Five thousand bucks, Carney! Where does a singer get that kind of throw-away money? I'll tell ya—from her Nazi father who stole it!

"Here's another link. Remember Wiesenthal talking about Nazi trains moving gold shipments when he was working on the railroads? Okay, now our guys in Silesia have discovered that old Hitler was building a whole network of underground tunnels and rooms in the mountains there. It was going to be a safe headquarters for the Nazi leadership—farther east than Allied bombers could fly. This complex has train tracks running right into the mountains, Carney! They could run the damn trains there with all the stuff they stole and hide it!"

"Where's Silesia?"

"Geeze—it's that little tit of Poland that juts into Czechoslovakia east from Prague, and it's mainly populated with Germans—that was Hitler's big argument at Munich when he got the Brits and French to let him take over that area without any fight. He said they were ethnic Germans and should be united with their 'fatherland.' Remember? If they gave him that, no war! He lied. It's all old castles and spooky mountains and forests—great place to hide things and people."

"So—what happened to Hitler's big underground project?"

"Well, after his army zipped through Poland in nineteen days, he made the mistake of spreading his armies too thin. He took over northern Europe pretty easily too, and had England on the ropes. But then he broke his non-aggression pact with Stalin and started a war in the East, and that didn't go so well. In fact, those Soviets eventually started to push back, and while Silesia was safe from our bombers, there appeared to be a possibility that the region might fall to them. So, the underground headquarters was put on hold and covered up pretty well. They could go back later—or that's what they thought, at least."

"Okay, what's the connection to our assignment?"

"Remember, *our* general—von Seigler—was the Germans' authority on Poland and Polish banking. He was exonerated from any complicity in the Oster Conspiracy and restored to full command by Göring following his successful participation in the victory over Poland. So then—he disappears! So does his daughter. And now she's down in Argentina with extra money to flaunt. Sound fishy?"

"Well, I certainly can understand the connection, and I can see that if we tie Wiesenthal's story to these Germans and then pinpoint their location, it would be a feather in the cap of US intelligence operations. Have you shared this with our FBI contacts in Rio and BA?"

"Sure have. And I've also got the feds in Chicago checking for that Magda and perhaps Elsa, if she shows up there. I'm pretty sure Elsa would like to protect Dieter rather than helping us, and she's one smart cookie. But remember—she has been operating in a limited area for several years, and there's a learning curve when you move away from familiar territory. Right now I'm having the Chicago feds look for a Magda emigrating from Europe four or five years ago. She was probably okayed by State because of her SWW service, and she supposedly married in Chicago not long after going there. She's about thirty-five, because that's Elsa's approximate age and they trained together. She's had a kid, who'd be two or three now. The feds will probably start with the "Polish Corridor" in the city and check with each of about twenty Polish churches there for marriages and baptisms. They could get lucky and find a match in just a day or two—or there could be so much obfuscation that we never locate the right Magda."

"They can also check the manifests of incoming flights at Chicago Municipal Airport for anyone named Elsa traveling alone and using some European passport for ID. Look at the two weeks after Elsa skipped Prague—probably only two or three hundred names to check, don't ya think?"

"Ah—I'd say that's a long shot. She's a pro, as you say, and a pro may have a whole box full of identities. But, what the hell—give it a shot. Could get lucky. But what do we do if they do ID this Elsa?"

"Nothin'. Put a tail on her and see if she leaves again. We might want to have her questioned later on, but for now I want her to feel that she's outta the jungle. The first thing I'd do if we're sure it's our Elsa is get a warrant to read her mail."

32

───────

The Closing Number

Dieter arrived early for their evening performance and found Lola already in the empty room. She looked up at him with a pleasant smile, but he detected that she had come early for a reason and that she might be about to launch one of her unexpected and uninhibited reflections on matters of concern to her. It was an accurate guess, and after a brief greeting she was wading into a condemnation of inflexible norms.

"Do you know what the manager said to me today? Well, of course you don't—you weren't there. I was there and I can hardly believe it myself. We two have transformed an empty sitting room off the lobby into a popular late-evening gathering place—at almost no expense to this big roadhouse. Sixty or seventy people—maybe even more—come every night and consume two hundred fifty to three hundred overpriced drinks and eat fifty pounds of expensive, non-nourishing doo-dads and leave nice tips. Right?

"It doesn't cost Mother Copacabana nada! They don't even put tablecloths on the puny little tables, so what? They burn fifty candles or so and keep the dishwasher an extra ninety minutes. It's a helluva efficient moneymaker, Dieter—and they drop a hundred US dollars on each of us like it was gold bars. They should kiss our asses. So what does Mr. Manager say to me? Huh? He wrinkles his nose like he's smelling something and says, "Lola—you have to get some modest maternity gowns because a few of the ladies don't think it's 'appropriate' to have a pregnant lady singing blues and ballads in a cocktail outfit.

"Dieter—you know I'm tasteful in my dresses. I'm not wiggling my ass at the gentlemen or singin' party songs like Florence Desmond or somebody. Who does he think he is? You gotta tell him to back off—we're making him look good on the bottom line by presenting some music that's not available around town. There are even a couple of places trying to copy us, but they're empty. I'm mad!"

"Come on, Lola—you're getting all upset and gonna have a sour evening. Get a smile on your face, little girl. Tell you what—I'll fix you a plate of *coxinhas* on my terrace after work to celebrate twenty successful performances, if we pull it off tonight. There's going to be a full moon and we can celebrate with piña coladas afterward."

"Hell, Dieter. You're too nice. You won't even allow me to have a little tantrum when I need one. I'm gonna change into something really tasteful and sing like Jenny Lind tonight."

❧

By eleven o'clock at least a hundred patrons had signed chits in the lounge, and frequent bursts of enthusiastic applause had drifted through the reception area, giving endorsement to the two veteran entertainers. For her encore that evening, Lola had chosen Cole Porter's "You'd Be So Easy To Love," which three sensuous ladies of color—Billie Holiday, Josephine Baker, and Maxine Sullivan—had taken turns infusing with sultry undertones. Lola seemed to capture some of the passion from each in her rendition, which was directed playfully at Dieter. As the last lyric floated over the patrons, Dieter realized that he was dripping with perspiration even though the room was comfortably cool. He wished he had not promised Lola hors d' oeuvres and drinks on his terrace. But he had, and Dieter kept promises.

"Did you like my encore choice, Piano Man? You were sweating like a whore in church when we finished. I think several people saw that and laughed because you were being such a good actor as well as a fine musician."

"Wasn't acting," Dieter chuckled. "Cole Porter reminds me of myself in some ways, and I really get into his music when it's delivered well. You did a great job with that song tonight, and I felt as if you were singing it to me in a room where we were alone together. Good stuff, Lola."

"How does Porter remind you of yourself? Because he writes both the melodies and lyrics of his songs and fits them together so well? Or, because he's a homosexual guy married to an older lady and able to move freely through both worlds?"

"Ah, come on, Lola. That's 'way too heavy to get into at one o'clock in the morning. Can't we just pour a nightcap and look at the stars and be happy our performance went so well tonight? I was afraid the manager was thinking of shutting us down—but there's no way now."

"Shutting us down because I'm showing and in good circles pregnant ladies don't sing in bars, Dieter? Is that what you were worried about? Well, damn it—that's not fair. There are billions of people on earth and every damned one of them came from a pregnant lady. So it's not some weird or uncommon malady that has to be hidden from view. We have the same feelings, needs, faults—you know—same as we had before. Did you ever make love to a pregnant lady, Piano Man? Was she any less involved?"

"Oh—I didn't even know—you know—I thought maybe they kind of—well, stopped for a while."

"Well, they don't—we don't—I don't. As you get fatter and more awkward it gets even more important to have somebody treat you as beautiful. Or at least desirable. It's not like you're squashing my child, Dieter. I'll bet you didn't even know that I get to be the one on top. And the good part is we both get to watch!"

Dieter never could remember how the next two or three minutes unfolded, only that he was on the chaise and their foreheads were touching as both watched in fascination what they were doing. He knew that the sound of waves breaking and rolling onto the empty beach below the terrace somehow was mimicked in the slow undulation of Lola's hips and abdomen. Cole Porter's melody taunted him, too; it was oh, so easy to love. He understood it but knew he could never explain it, and he hoped there wouldn't be occasion for that. Perhaps just another boyhood nocturnal emission to be filed away and not revisited? No—a real occurrence, Dieter!

33

Wiener Schnitzel

Blumenau seemed unusually busy as Lucia DeSimone drove to her favorite *padaria* to get fresh rolls and cakes; she thought she might take a few to Kurt and Gerda to enjoy with dinner after their weekly lesson. Those conversational dinners were really more useful to them than grammar and vocabulary books now that they had all of the basics in place. And the final "test," for certain, would be their ability to speak confidently on a telephone where there are no assists from hand gestures, charades, or pointing at objects while pronouncing their names. They were almost a finished project, and Lucia knew she would miss them because of their innate kindness and unfailing good humor. She reflected that success can have its downside if it results in separation.

The window of the padaria announced that it was *Backerei Blumenau*, assuring shoppers that they would find authentic German baked goods inside, and when the doors opened and closed, the escaping aroma of fresh bread endorsed that guarantee. Lucia picked the top number from a box just inside the entry, and she could see that she was fifth in line behind the person being served currently. With a few minutes to wait, she turned to the large bulletin board of upcoming community events, nearly all of which seemed to be associated with Oktoberfest.

Of course there would be Hammerschlagen contests, where young men competed to see who could pound a big nail into a stump quickest and cleanest. The more beers, the more errors, but intense grunting and shouting—and some side betting. And local restaurants lauded their special Oktoberfest offerings like figs wrapped in German ham, vanilla bean custard with sour cherry sauce, and caramelized onion pretzel rolls with caraway salt. Thousands of Brazilians of German heritage would flood the parks and streets to sample this microcosm of their culture.

A multicolored professional poster advertised three appearances by the Booker Pittman Band, flown in especially from Rio de Janeiro to offer the latest in jazz standards from America and Europe, mixed with the most popular traditional German songs. Clarinetist Pittman had been featured with the famous bands of Louis Armstrong and Count Basie before bringing his own aggregation of all-stars to Brazil. And—near the bottom of the poster—the public was invited to hear the vocal renditions of European favorite Sophia, who had recently enchanted Buenos Aires at a special fundraiser hosted by Argentina's Vice President Perón in the grand Teatro Colón.

Lucia thought that she had seen the singer's name and photograph before, but she couldn't connect it to any activity or source. It would come to her eventually, she reflected, as her number was called by the baker.

❧

Kurt and Gerda greeted their teacher in Portuguese. "Boa tarde, professora. Nos esperamos que voce fique para o jantara noite." It was a perfect greeting as well as the hoped-for dinner invitation for that evening. The young woman smiled broadly and offered a bakery box filled with fresh rolls and sweet cakes. She told them of her visit to the nearby town and described the Oktoberfest preparations she had seen. A large contingent of the state's German population would be on hand, especially for the three-day weekend, when music would be popping up everywhere. She mentioned that there would even be a famous American band appearing in the grand *pavilhão de música* in Blumenau's large park. The baker had told her they were expecting more than ten thousand attendees for those concerts, and that all the food purveyors and local brewers would have booths around the perimeter to keep the party going. Such excitement!

"Você vai participar?" Lucia asked.

"Possivelmente," they shrugged. It was a possibility, but certainly not a strong commitment. The young woman concluded that well-to-do middle-aged people might prefer the comfort and quiet of a remote fazenda to the jolting and beer-spilling of a partying crowd. Well, there would just be more space for her, because she wouldn't want to miss Oktoberfest in Blumenau for any reason—even though she was Italian.

Their dinner was a rich wiener schnitzel, which Gerda pointed out could only be called that in Germany and Austria if it was made exclusively of veal—which, of course, hers was. It was actually the law back there that a restaurant which used pork or turkey in making the schnitzel had to give the dish a different name on the menu and had to differentiate clearly the meat ingredient. The teacher was fascinated by this gastronomic discrimination but actually was more curious about Gerda's most recent experience in a restaurant in Germany or Austria.

Lucia couldn't resist the temptation to ask. "Senhora Hahn, when did you last eat in Germany? Perhaps the war and the postwar recovery will change that tradition. I'll bet that veal has become scarce and prohibitively expensive over there. Maybe the restaurants have gotten more imaginative in grinding their schnitzel meats."

Kurt was quick to fill the awkward conversational gap. "We like to think that good things never change—that the Germany of the early 1930s is still there as we remember it. At least, under this roof, you will always know that wiener schnitzel is made of veal, and in September we serve it to you with Hefeweizen, the best Oktoberfest wheat beer! Here, let me fill your glass again! You can't fly on one wing, professora."

Three full steins of Hefeweizen later, she desperately needed a bathroom break. Lucia excused herself from the table and bumbled down the hallway to the door, except it proved to be the wrong doorway, and she was again in that private bedroom, looking directly at the framed poster from Prague's Majestic Plaza Hotel announcing the featured singer Sophia. That was it—the same name and face she had seen in Blumenau on the posters trumpeting that American band in the park. She tried to clear her mind—should she tell the Hahns, or would they be offended that she had entered their private quarters? Or might there even be a reason that they never spoke of a daughter who sang in Europe during the war years and is now in Brazil? After finding the correct door, she sat for several minutes trying to sort through the considerations, and finally she reminded herself that it is never a mistake to keep your mouth closed and know something others do not. Their daughter was going to be singing in Blumenau and they did not want to share that knowledge.

As she drove away that evening, Lucia DeSimone had an uneasy feeling that she had stumbled upon knowledge which she should not have and which could have serious consequences for her if shared with others. Nevertheless, she was intensely curious and knew that she would have to dig a little deeper.

34

❧

Montevideo

Sofie was glad to get out of Buenos Aires. The thought that she might see Baby again actually frightened her because she still had no recollection of events in El Teatro Colón that could account for the photograph with Perón and Evita. And there was an even larger blank obscuring the hours between midnight and ten o'clock the next morning. At one point, she tried to get help from the chambermaid who had wakened her, but the middle-aged woman had been well trained by the hotel and replied simply, "I never see nothing, señora—the peoples in Alvear all dee same for me. Eat, sleep, drink, make love, take pictures, go home. I not watch and I not remember what I see. You very pretty lady and no dirty up room— thas all I know."

A week later the orchestra had travelled by boat from Buenos Aires to Montevideo, Uruguay's elegant capital city. The trip was advertised as a five-hour journey on the broad Río de la Plata, and she had used the time to rest in a deck chair and mentally reorganize her wardrobe. She was certain that she had gained weight during the early part of the tour, so she had cut back on food intake and was taking short walks whenever there was time. On a stroll around the boat's deck, she encountered Buca, smoking a cigar and studying the horizon.

"Hi, boss. Everything okay?" she asked.

"I suppose. We exceeded our projected numbers in Argentina, and Colonel Perón said that if he's elected we will be invited back to perform at his inaugural. He liked the band and was quite taken with you, Sofie. I'm not entirely sure Evita shared that fascination, but ladies who are accustomed to the spotlight sometimes don't like to share it."

"Sorry, Buca. That evening sort of got away from me. I think I was still tired from the trip—and then I had a snifter of cognac to settle my nerves. Hope I didn't mess up any of my numbers."

"Your singing was excellent—never better. My problem is when a vocalist gets too sensuous, the boys in the band notice right away and their attention strays. That happened with Lola—good singer and hard worker, but sending signals to the boys and pretty soon they're all trying to get a piece of the action. They get mad at each other and even try to sabotage one another's solos sometimes. You know how the big band leaders back home handle that?"

"No—I haven't any idea. I never even understood the problem until you explained it. What do they do?"

"The vocalist becomes notoriously the bandleader's girlfriend— and nobody else from the band goes near her for fear of losing his job. A little like the kings' favorite mistresses in the old days."

"Whoa, Buca—that's either the worst solution to the problem I could imagine or the worst line I ever heard. I'd like to just forget we had this conversation if it's alright with you. I'm serious about my singing and you've given me a great opportunity to test it against some good critical audiences. I really appreciate that, but there's no offstage quid pro quo—just my best work as your vocalist wherever we perform. Can we agree on that?" Sofie waited for a response, but instead, Buca directed a small cloud of fragrant cigar smoke in her direction, then turned back toward the railing. She thought that she detected an enigmatic smile as he looked away, and hoped that she had not sacrificed their professional relationship.

Sofie had read about Nazi Germany's famous battle cruiser *Admiral Graf Spee*, which, early in World War II, had terrorized the sea lanes along these Atlantic coasts of South America, sinking many merchant ships belonging to the Allied countries. The mighty ship had been engaged in these very waters off Montevideo by warships from Great Britain and New Zealand, and the ship's captain had determined that he must scuttle the damaged *Graf Spee* to save the lives of her crewmen. Then he had committed suicide when his ship was gone.

It caused her to think about her father and to wonder how much of this history he knew. Wouldn't it be glorious to make this visit with him and to walk through the Barrio de los Artes, which fanned out from the Esplendor Hotel Montevideo where she would be staying for a week? It was futile—she had no precise location to contact him and shouldn't wish for things she couldn't have.

After looking out her window for a while, Sofie picked up the room telephone and asked the receptionist to connect her with Mr. Pittman. When he answered, she said, "Boss—I'm sorry I was rude to you on the boat. Yes—I was. How'd you like to walk through the Barrio together and see if we can find a little café where we can get some tasty local specialty and maybe look at the waterfront? Dutch treat—I'm feeling guilty and need to apologize. About fifteen minutes from now in the lobby? Good!"

Buca had been to Montevideo previously and knew a little of its history; he had chosen the Esplendor because it retained the style of the twenties,, when it was built. It lies near Montevideo's Teatro Solís—a beautiful classic-design theater where the Pittman Orchestra would be performing each night during their stay. Already there were placards in the restaurants and galleries nearby telling strollers about these prime performers of the most popular musical numbers from the Broadway stages to the jazz bistros of Europe. And near the bottom of each was Sofie's professional photo. She leaned close to Buca and planted a playful kiss on his cheek. "If I ever do have a boyfriend on the road, boss—it will be you," she smiled.

Two casually dressed men seemingly immersed in deep conversation at an outdoor table duly noted the gesture. One asked, "Are you sure that's our target? Very attractive lady and apparently on intimate terms with the gentleman. They have been chatting constantly since they came in. But he doesn't look at all like a military man. What do you think?"

"Well, I think that's Sophia the singer, alright; she looks just like the billboard pictures. See if you can get clear Minox shots of both their faces. Take my photo, but move me around so you can catch them in the frame. Exchange some swishy comments with me so people will think we're two of the queers who are all over this barrio. Then I'll get a shot of you, and between us we'll get what we need."

After posing for one another, the two returned to their conversation. "What does the FBI care about a girl singer from Europe? I'm missing something."

"Me, too—but apparently she's the only child of some big Nazi general who fled Europe and came to South America a couple years ago. And the Jews say he grabbed a lot of money or gold and they asked OSS to help them find him."

"OSS isn't even here—and they're shutting down in Europe. I don't get it."

"Washington wants us to follow her and see if she meets a guy who might be the general. She's on tour with a big band and they're performing in several cities where Germans, Italians, Jews, everybody has run to. There's half a million of them in South America and she might be a link to an important one. That's all I know."

"Oh, wow. That's far-fetched. But having to watch her isn't the worst assignment I've had. Do we get to see her perform?"

"Well, the hotel tells us every time she goes out. So, when she goes to sing one of us gets to attend."

"What if the general goes to the hotel? How do we know that? Maybe he just sees her in her room."

"Hotel gives us the word and we plant somebody in the lobby to watch for him."

"Seems like a lot of attention for one girl singer, don't you think?"

"What the hell—there are still three or four hundred SIS guys around South America and the war is over. I think J. Edgar likes to keep us busy and wants a bigger role. Roosevelt's gone and he has to show our efficiency and value, so catching an important Nazi down here would sell back home. John Q. Public loves a story of intrigue and beautiful women. That's my take on it."

"Oops—she's getting up to leave. Let's get crackin'."

35

Chicago

Chicago Women's Club
11th Street
Chicago, Illinois USA

Dieter,

A lot has changed since I last wrote, and some of it concerns you. As you can see from the Air Mail stamp, I am no longer in Prague. The Soviets are moving into Czechoslovakia quickly. When the US General Patton crossed into our country in May of '45, Czechs went to the streets to fight the occupying Nazis. But just as quickly, the Americans stopped—the explanation we heard was that General Eisenhower ordered that unwise action to save casualties, but it just gave Prague to the Soviets and they marched in and raised the red flag of the Czech Communist Party.

I was considering staying in Prague with my Czech identity to work with the remaining US intelligence team in Europe, but the more I saw of it the less it appealed to me. That is where you come in. The agent who was evaluating me learned that I had been involved in your escape and that you are linked to Sofie. They believe that she may lead them to her father and that he could be custodian of much stolen Polish wealth.

You and she must be very careful and aware. These are not nice people.

I am temporarily in this Club, which is in the busiest part of town. Michigan Avenue is a few steps from our door, and just beyond it is the big Illinois Central Railroad yard. A little farther in that direction there is a nice green expanse called Grant Park, with a pretty fountain and playing fields. My friend Maggie works in a building named Sears, Roebuck, which is only six blocks away from my hotel. I have a temporary job there in the mailroom and am using this time to improve my American English and to decide my next steps. For now you can write to me at this hotel.

I send you what the Americans call "a big, juicy kiss."
Elsa Danzig

36

Checking In

ALVEAR PALACE HOTEL
Avenida Alvear 1891 Buenos Aires, Argentina
My dearest Dieter,

I haven't had time to write previously and now we are about to depart from this busy city and go onward to Uruguay, just a short cruise to the east from here. BA reminds me in many ways of Berlin when we first met there in 1938. All the talk is about politics, and military people seem to be everywhere in handsome, tailored uniforms. There are frequent rallies and speeches, and the biggest "attraction" seems to be Evita Perón, who has become patron saint of the working classes. I'm sending a page from Sunday's newspaper showing the Peróns and me—plus Francisco Pignatari, whom you may remember from Rio. He believes that Colonel Perón will be the next Argentine president, so he is advancing his business interests here. The Pittman Band and I were featured at a big benefit for victims of the earthquake—but really it was a Perón rally.

When Brazil joined the Allies in the war, Argentina decided to remain neutral. They were mad at England for continuing to assert their ownership of the Falkland Islands right off the Argentine coast. (Argentina calls them the Malvinas Islands and contends that Britain stole them.) There were lots of Germans and Italians in Argentina who preferred the Axis powers to the Allies. But, when the war was almost won, Argentina decided to join the winning side, which was probably a smart move. As you can tell, things are embroiled here—again, like Berlin in 1938.

I'm looking forward to Uruguay, which I'm told is less conflicted. Buca has us booked in a nice old hotel near the theatre, where we perform for a week. I miss you and look forward to our happy audiences in the Bar du Copa, where people just seem to be interested in fun and good music.

Always in my thoughts,
Sofie

37

Reflections

"You know, Dieter, I believe that there are two places to which people can run when the problems in their lives don't offer easy resolution and they need adequate time to think about them."

"Really? Where do you think they can go?"

"To their favorite music or to satisfying sex."

"And what is your reasoning?"

"Both fill time completely, leaving very little space for worry or planning while they are in progress, and both can be enjoyed finitely, leaving you free to return to whatever issue you have put aside temporarily. It is a bit like a coffee break in the workplace, where you make a little stack of unfinished tasks and walk a few feet away to the wonderful taste and aroma of your favorite cafezinho. After the break, you return refreshed and sometimes more creative than before."

The two musicians had now been appearing together for a month, during which their musical improvisations had become more facile and their audiences more enthusiastic. After their awkward initial forays into personal familiarity, they had drifted into a casual routine of eating a nightly snack along the Oceanside and then exploring carnal pleasures where only the stars could look down on them. They laughed frequently at one another's discussions of hidden insecurities, and they had become shamefully immodest together.

Dieter found it easy to reflect, in Lola's company, upon the loneliness of his childhood, his fears of being Jewish in Nazi Europe, and the seemingly eternal damnation of Theresienstadt. He confessed to the guilt of his current wellbeing, which he contrasted with the waning lives of the living skeletons he had left behind in Europe. There was still the lingering notion that he had deserted them.

Lola lamented that she had too early learned how to gain attention through flirtation and aggressiveness, which had progressed from a young girl's technique into full addiction before she reached her twenties. "I was really quite pretty, you know," she complained, "but look at me now with this big belly and over-ripe breasts reaching downward to touch it. This is not the pinup girl on those American magazine covers, Dieter—this is nobody's dream!"

He wrapped his arms around her bare shoulders to offer a reassuring hug and immediately knew that he was giving himself permission to again be the willing partner in Lola's ritual escape.

An hour later they resumed their conversation. "You know this has been a totally unfamiliar adventure for me," he smiled, "but you haven't made me feel ashamed or embarrassed for my sexual illiteracy. There's a basic warmth in you, Lola, which I can't explain—but it is nearly impossible for me to resist. Now I find myself looking forward to our evenings alone together, even though I have nothing more to offer you than temporary escape.

"Now, let me ask you something. You said there are two easy refuges from problems, but isn't there another popular one—drinking?"

"I said there are two which can be visited temporarily while the problem is set aside. Either of them allows us to revert easily to our task when we're ready to do so. But a *borracho* loses track of his mission, gets blinded in the process, and becomes captive to his diversion. He may try to resume with his instincts dulled and, if so, he risks the possibility of adding to his worries with unwise decisions. Booze is no competitor for soothing music or drowning sex, Dieter."

"Drowning? Drowning? That's a funny adjective, Lola. How did you come up with drowning?"

"Well, think of it. If you are in deep water, you can try to stay afloat and flail your arms and legs—at least for awhile. Or, you can sink willingly into the sea and let it toss you this way and that until you succumb completely. Drowning is the total experience, not just superficial, uncontrolled splashing around on the surface."

"Well, tell me—has all the music and all of the drowning you've sampled during the past month helped you to imagine a plan for your future? What do you see yourself doing two or three years from now, Lola? You know, the whole world is restarting right now, and the best choices will be rewarded. What do you imagine for yourself?"

"I really *do* have a near-term goal, Dieter. Now, don't laugh, *querido*, but I would like to own and operate a little music bar on Praia Leblon. Both Copacabana and Ipanema beaches have gotten way too expensive, and in just a few years the shift in interest will be a bit farther south along the shoreline. Leblon has broad beaches and the Dois Irmaos behind it, sheltering from west winds. Property there costs only a fraction of what the same thing sells for on Ipanema, so there will be young people moving to the area, and they'll want entertainment nearby. I could have a sort of 'greenhouse' for new talent—most would probably appear for free just to try building a following. What do you think?"

"I can see that being a timely move—yes. And I suppose you could begin by living right in the same building so you'd be near your little saxophone player much of the time. And, you could be a star attraction yourself—sing only when you feel like it and choose the songs you like best. Good. Good. Have you calculated a start-up budget? And do you know where you can get some investors or lenders to help you?"

"Well, Dieter—I'd probably start with you."

38

Porto Alegre

Copacabana Palace Hotel
Avenida Atlântica,
Rio de Janiero,
Brazil

Dearest Sofie,

*Y*ou are at about the midpoint of your tour and finally back in Brazil after experiencing two of the most sophisticated Spanish-language cities in the world. Porto Alegre should accentuate the differences, because it is still considered a "frontier town" by the Brazilians I know here. They tell me that the gaucho mentality still prevails, even as a modern city springs up along Lagoa dos Patos. Bordering on a big lake must give it a different feeling than we get in Rio, on the ocean.

I know that the Pittman Orchestra is giving several musical performances at Theatro Sao Pedro, in the old historic center of the city, and that probably means Spanish *and European favorites. Your language skills will no doubt be featured—and appreciated!*

My rescuer, Elsa Danzig, has written to tell me that she has departed Prague rather than remain there under the new Communist rule. Before leaving, she was being evaluated for some position in the U. S. intelligence service; she passed along a caveat that you and I should be alert to the possibility of being followed by agents searching for people we knew during the war in Europe. After that annoying "shadow" Octavio identified back here, I believe that you'll know what to watch for.

As for me, I have been exploring improvised blues music and Brazilian sambas with Lola (from Buca's band) in appearances in an evening lounge off the main lobby of the Copa. The manager offered the opportunity shortly after you buzzed off to BA, and it has achieved modest popularity with hotel guests and others. I suspect it has been valuable to Lola, both in terms of her current salary and tips as well as her plans to start a little beach bistro after her child is born.

I miss your warm smiles and countless attentions— and send my love across the miles.

Your Dieter

Sofie folded the letter and slipped it into her travel case. She, Buca, and five other band members had flown from Carrasco Airport near Montevideo to Porto Alegre's Salgado Filho Airport using the Brazilian carrier, Varig. The rest of the contingent would be covering the same 800 kilometers by land in clumsy busses bouncing along the coastal road. It would take them two days to accomplish what the twin-engined deHaviland DH 89 "Dragon Rapide" had overflown in less than three hours. But, unlike the big Pan Am aircraft that had provided Sofie's first flying experience, the Rapide could carry no more than eight passengers. She was flattered that Buca had included her on the flight, and she concluded that it might be his way to emphasize the special relationship between the bandleader and his vocalist. Or perhaps it was just chivalry.

In any event, they were now in their hotel with an hour to burn before dinner. Dieter's letter had awaited her arrival, and since it was her first communication from him in a month, she tried to analyze the message within the message, as she had learned to do early in their partnership.

First, since she hadn't provided the venues of their performances, and Dieter knew where she would be singing in Porto Alegre, he had gone out of his way to follow the course of the tour. However, he hadn't commented at all about the theater or events in Buenos Aires, even though she had provided him with many details, and the news picture had certainly been provocative.

That meant that he wasn't happy that Baby had been pawing at her in public or that she appeared to have forgotten decorum even in the company of the country's most famous political figures. Dieter sometimes drew attention to things by choosing to ignore them when it would be natural to comment.

Then there was the mention of Elsa Danzig and identifying her as his "rescuer." Elsa had indeed been his nurse after his escape and had hidden him until he regained his strength. Sofie had always thought that the petite Elsa had strong yearnings for Dieter, which was why she referred to her in their conversations as a fat Polish girl. So he mentioned her departure from Prague, but gave no idea of where she was going. Either he was afraid others might be trying to follow her, or he didn't want Sofie to know.

Then, tucked away in that mention of Elsa was a very important message that Dieter and she might be followed wherever they went by US operatives looking for her father. The clumsy fellow in Rio had been unmasked easily, but there was no Octavio in any of her tour cities to spot them and she had to have her antennae up constantly.

Then finally there was Lola. She remembered the night at the Copa ballroom when she had first sung with the Pittman Orchestra, and Dieter noted that Lola was sulking alongside the stage as Sofie took over her featured role with not so much as a thank-you. If Dieter's new exploration of blues improvisation began shortly after her departure on the tour, she was reasonably certain that Lola had conceived the idea earlier and was waiting to spring it on Dieter before her airplane was over the horizon. Sofie laughed to herself as she pondered how her favorite Greek tragedian, Euripides, might put together the story of two pregnant women and a fat spy vying for the attentions of a shy musician who is too innocent to understand the plot. "I guess that makes me Medea," she said, as she observed her body in the full-length mirror of her hotel room. "It won't be very long until someone other than I notices that there are changes in progress."

39

Sightseeing

She was forty-eight hours ahead of the main group of musicians, which meant that she had almost two days in Porto Alegre during which to relax and also to be alone. Sofie did not want to provide any opportunity for misunderstandings with Buca, so she left her hotel early in the morning to find a local *café da manhã* for breakfast, after which she intended to visit the Museo de Arte do Rio Grande do Sul and then stroll through the city's *Parquinho da Redencão*, a wooded park with its own little lake. She carried a folio of songs to study those she would be singing. The weather was perfect and she looked forward to the solitude.

Two hours passed quickly, and she found the little lake plus a sun-drenched wooden bench near the water. It was a wonderful vantage point for people-watching as young mothers pushed strollers along the walkways and older children launched model sailboats in the shallow water. Everything was perfect except perhaps a lone man who seemed dressed more appropriately for the office than a park. He was about thirty meters behind her right shoulder on a similar bench, and he had dwelled upon the same newspaper page for too long to be reading.

Sofie took a small makeup mirror from her purse and pretended to examine an imperfection on her chin, but actually she continued to watch the man behind her shoulder, who clearly was observing her. She decided to assemble her reading matter with no appearance of urgency and then to move quickly to the bus stop on Av. Joao Pessoa and take the first conveyance that arrived there. She could exit it as soon as it was out of sight from the park without losing her sense of direction in this unfamiliar city. She surprised herself with the swiftness of her movement to a bus, which departed before she could sit down. But she was able to glance back at the park as the bus pulled into traffic. There was no one on the bench any longer.

At the first stop, she stepped quickly from the bus and started walking in the general direction of her hotel, without knowing precisely where it was. There was just a slight feeling of vulnerability beginning to grip Sofie, and as she turned corners and walked swiftly through the narrow streets she became aware that she no longer had any clear sense of direction. A car slowed beside her and someone asked, "Are you looking for an address?" As she turned to respond, she felt strong hands on her arms as she was virtually lifted into the car and pressed against the back seat. She was flanked by two large men, and a third was driving the car. It would be futile to try to escape at this point, and furthermore she had no idea who her captors were or what they wanted from her.

"My name is Sophia Havlik and I am a Swiss subject currently on a musical tour with the Booker Pittman Orchestra from Rio de Janeiro," she blurted. "You have no right to confront me this way and take me anywhere in your car. Please stop at once and let me out. *Here!*"

"Well said, Sofie!" the man on her left chuckled, and in that instant she understood that her captor was the most amazing man she had ever known—her father, General Otto von Seigler.

Sofie could not stop crying, and for fully five minutes there were no sounds other than the tires hitting road seams and the young woman sobbing with her head buried in the shoulder of the man holding her. When she finally regained her composure, Sofie said, "Poppy—how did you find me? What are you doing here in Porto Alegre? I'm totally confused and ecstatically happy all at once. This is like the old days in Berlin, when you surprised me regularly. Oh, God—I have missed you, and I think of you every day. Turn this way so I can look at you!"

"Well, first," he began, "the Oktoberfest celebrations in Santa Catarina have been announcing the orchestra's appearances for a month, and our Portuguese teacher brought to our attention that the featured vocalist with that orchestra will be the same person as is pictured on a poster from the Majestic Plaza Hotel in Prague, which is framed in our bedroom. Branka and I did not react to her suggestion beyond acknowledging the similarities, and we changed the subject quickly.

"You should know that in our little village we are known as Kurt and Gerda Hahn, and, as many of our neighbors do, we have German roots. We have become as proficient in Brazilian Portuguese as possible, which is often evaluated by people who are curious about more-recent arrivals. There is quite a lot of snooping in this southern part of Brazil and in Argentina, because there is awareness that the wartime refugees from Europe include both victims and perpetrators of wartime excesses. As you know, we departed from Europe in 1943 because the war had been taken on a sadistic course that I couldn't serve any longer—but that is a distinction which is incredibly difficult for a military professional to be making. So, Kurt and Gerda Hahn live quietly but well in a secluded fazenda somewhere in southern Brazil. We have a small staff of people who remain personally loyal to me, and I have only one person beyond the fazenda who is truly important to me. That is my beautiful daughter."

"Poppy, you now have another such person. That is your first grandchild, who is currently seated next to you and rubbing against your elbow. Other than my physician, you are the only person who knows this."

"This is Dieter's child?"

"Well—either that or the first virgin pregnancy in nineteen centuries," she laughed. The unexpected encounter had suddenly taken on even more importance for both of them and they looked at one another through moist eyes and a happy mixture of little laughs and stifled sobs.

Finally the newly minted Kurt Hahn interrupted the shared emotion. "I must tell you a few things before I forget. Because of our caution, I will be in the crowd at Blumenau, but will not be greeting you there. Gerda and I will be just two locals attending Oktoberfest. We checked the bookings at your hotel in Porto Alegre and could see that you were preceding the main group of musicians to this city, and decided to abduct you 'softly' for a dinner with us. Gerda is waiting in a quiet little restaurant in Canoas, a few kilometers north from here. We can speak freely there; it belongs to another loyal friend from Berlin. After dinner, my driver will return you to a corner near your hotel and monitor your short walk back to the front door."

"Poppy—that seems so elaborate to me. Why?"

"My dear, resentments from the war years will live into the next century, and there will always be a price upon my head. It is well known that I have a daughter and some may try to find me through watching you. It would be natural for us to meet at something like Oktoberfest in Santa Catarina, and that event will be monitored. Two or three of my friends will also be observing the concerts, so you can relax and enjoy the festivities. This is the only time you'll be abducted in Southern Brazil." He laughed as he delivered that assurance, but the reality that she would continue to be followed had finally settled in, and it was an uncomfortable feeling for Sofie.

"I hate the fact that I am some political pawn, when all I have ever wanted to be is a singer with an uncomplicated life. I hate that, Poppy; it is so unfair."

"I know that, my love. Wars are always wrapped in injustice, and the collateral damages ripple outward like waves from a stone thrown into a quiet pond. I have done my best to protect you, but my shield is imperfect, and, in the final analysis, you are your own protector.

"We are coming into Canoas now, and I hope we can celebrate all of our good news and not dwell upon problems. Be strong, sweet Sofie—you are a general's daughter!"

She thought of adding "whose mother is a spy," but swallowed the words before they could complicate the happy reunion. For now she wanted only to relax with Kurt and Gerda Hahn somewhere in the state of Rio Grande do Sul and share good tidings.

40

———

Reviewing the Bidding

Joe and Carney sat together once again at #70 Grosvenor Street and picked through a stack of reports from the FBI's South American SIS personnel regarding their elusive target.

"Well, Sophia's not hard to find," Joe laughed. "She was all over the front pages in Buenos Aires—even upstaging Evita Perón with that cascading blonde hair and those luscious knockers. Did you see the front page of *Clarin*, Carney?"

"Yeah, yeah. Remember, I told you to read more?"

"You did—Madame DeFarge, right? *Tale of Two Cities*. Dickens. Wiesenthal's list of uncaptured Nazi criminals. That's how we started all of Hoover's SIS guys standing on street corners in South America. Is it getting us anyplace, Carney?"

"Well, we have gotten lots of little pieces, and somewhere under that pile of horseshit there has to be a pony, Joe. Sophia Havlik is certainly the same person as Sofie von Seigler, the general's daughter born in Poland. She was his hostess while she lived in Berlin, and then she slipped away to Prague. When she went there it was with some kind of bodyguard, apparently provided by Göring himself. His name was Dieter Meister and somehow he ended up as a prisoner in

Theresienstadt. But after a long time he pulled off an escape with the help of that Elsa Danzig I interviewed in Prague.

"Now—suddenly—Elsa disappears, but we know she has a friend named Dieter in Rio, who has funded her retirement, and she has a fellow SWW friend in Chicago who worked with her in Prague all through the war, squeezing info from Germans."

"Okay, Carney. Here's something about Sophia I got out of all those reports. First of all, she's easy to follow in Rio and in BA and in Montevideo. During that time our sources link her up with Pignatari and then with the bandleader, Booker Whatsisname. So, she's a healthy singer having a good time on the road—and not sneaking off with any Nazis. Then she gets to Porto Alegre and slips away for a whole day and absolutely nobody knows where she is."

"So—you think Porto Alegre may be the linkup between Sophia and the general and they pulled that off right under SIS's noses. Didn't they have someone in the hotel set up to track her?"

"Apparently he was on her from the time she walked to breakfast. Never let her out of his sight. Couple o' hours sightseeing and then she sits wide open on a park bench and looks at a pile of papers. Casual. Relaxed. He could toss a ball into her lap if he wanted to. No sweat."

"And?"

"And the broad bolts off the bench while he's lighting a smoke, and she runs . . . runs to a bus stop and jumps on one that's already moving. He can't catch it and it goes outa sight around a corner. By the time he gets to where he can spot it, the bus is leaving another bus stop and he thinks he sees her walking away around another corner. So, he jogs to that corner expecting to see her, but the street is empty. Gone!"

"Well, I guess we can assume she made him, so it's no longer a secret that she's being followed. Now she'll get more cautious, right?"

"I guess so. Here's a funny thing, Carney. There's another SIS guy at the hotel—so they can switch off and she doesn't see the same suit too often. When our guy gets to the hotel—it's not far from where he lost sight of her—the SIS guy sitting in the lobby says she never came in. The desk confirms it. And for the next ten hours she doesn't pick up her key. Then she just materializes and goes to her room around midnight. No escort; no packages; no indication of where she's been. Our guys checked all the nearby restaurants during the time she's gone, and they're pretty sure she wasn't in any of them. They even followed Booker Whatsisname, and he eats alone in the hotel. So whatta you make o' that?"

"Once she knew she was being tailed, she shook him and met the general. That area around Porto Alegre is loaded with Germans and German restaurants—I'm betting they were in one of 'em together. Too late to trace 'em now, but a good indication that he's somewhere between Porto Alegre and Blumenau, where all the other Krauts are hunkered down."

"Y'know what bothers me, Carney? The war hasn't been over very long, but the lines between bad guys and good guys are getting fuzzed over already. Take this Dieter—he's a German who the Germans put into a detention camp. The Polish SWW helps him escape from the Germans and he goes to Brazil. The general's daughter joins him in Brazil after she has been singing in Europe and we think the general has gone to Brazil, too. Everybody's starting over!"

"I'll tell 'ya what's weirder than that, Joe. Remember the Gestapo guy they called 'the Butcher of Lyon'? The one who tortured so many French? Actually, our stats connect him to fourteen thousand deaths there."

"You're talkin' about Barbie—Klaus Barbie, right? Awful guy! What's weird about an awful Gestapo guy, Carney?"

"Well, you remember a minute ago saying how the lines are getting fuzzy after the war? Guess who *our* Army counterintelligence has recruited to help them develop effective methods for interrogating Communist spies? That would be good ole' Hauptsturmführer Nikolaus 'Klaus' Barbie. Now he's on our side and the Soviets, who were our allies, are the bad guys!"

"So, we're chasing a general who skipped in '43 and went to Brazil, and our counterintelligence is employing the services of a villain who electrocuted people and did some of the cruelest torture of the war for the other side?"

"I'm afraid that's about it."

41

Button, button . . .

It had become an unrehearsed duet for the two musicians—first, a seaside snack on Avenida Atlântica, followed by an intimate encore under the late-evening skies. The final act was nearly always a free discussion of personal hopes, fears, and histories.

"Did you once think you were inalterably homosexual?" the pregnant woman teased as she wrapped a robe around her swollen body. "Because, if you did, you were grossly mistaken, Dieter. You obviously take great satisfaction from our times together, and I'm nobody's idea of beautiful right now."

"Of course you are beautiful, Lola. Not in the pinup sense of the word, but in your openness and unabashed participation; in your no-nonsense honesty about what pleases you and me. Beauty comes in a variety of packages, and you are superb in yours. We don't ever lie to one another, but we care deeply about the human concerns that brought us to this point. It's going to be awkward to return to our respective lives from this, but we'll take much value with us, too."

"I like that thought, but I wonder whether it's just a convenient excuse for our weakness."

"See—there you've done it again. Perhaps we have just been

stealing from life's cookie jar when no one was looking, and are telling ourselves that we were really looking for nourishment. It isn't totally different from my early homosexual life, you know."

"No, I don't know. Care to discuss it with me?"

It was an imaginary wall Dieter had never attempted, even with his closest friends. The roots of his intimate behavior were complex and painful, and whenever others prodded there, he adroitly slipped away into some lighter conversation. Later there would predictably be doubt as to whether he had missed an opportunity that might have set him free, but that wall had always loomed too high.

Now once again he was at that threshold—this time with an admittedly flawed woman, but one who also seemed to be rich in understanding, compassion, and forgiveness. Dieter poured a glass of his favorite Miolo and stared into it as if it might offer some answer to his reluctance. Then he drank it quickly, like an elixir that could activate his repressed memories, and he began his story.

"I was an orphan living in a music school when I was only seven. My father had been a music teacher there; he was killed early in the Great War. My Jewish mother had been his young student, and lover, who got pregnant. They married before he went off to war, but in 1918 she was one of the fifty million who died in the Great Influenza Epidemic. I had no living relatives, so the head of the school generously allowed me to live there and to study music with the other students; they were all much older. In a dormitory of salacious boys ten years older than I, it was easy for me to gain acceptance by becoming a sleeping partner. That became my nature—or at least my habit.

"By the age of seventeen, I had learned much about music but nothing of the world outside our school. Then, the National Socialists forced Jews to leave such schools, and both the head of the school and I were Jews. It happened quickly. I packed my one suitcase and went to Berlin, where I was told a good piano player could find employment in various pubs. I found one that was managed by a handsome Portuguese homosexual, and we quickly gravitated to one another. We became apartment mates and I became the resident piano player in the popular place he managed."

"So, you were set. You could have stayed and done that. Why didn't you?"

"The pub was a popular gathering place for music students from a nearby university as well as for Wehrmacht military personnel in the area. Somewhere in that mix were a general and his daughter, who was a talented singer. She thought I was attractive, and even though I doubted my own instincts, over time we became dependent upon one another. I concluded that I had been a 'homosexual by convenience' but not necessarily by any quirk of nature. Later, when I was deprived of any female contact—in a Nazi prison—I easily slipped back into affection for my cellmates. Few people have understood this, because they consider it in the abstract. I've lived it and still cannot fully explain the dichotomy."

Now it was Lola who needed to re-gather her thoughts before speaking, and she broke her pregnancy abstinence and poured a modest portion of the Miolo into Dieter's empty glass. She mimicked Dieter's earlier examination of the red liquid and similarly allowed it to slide down her dry throat, then, with a reassuring smile in his direction, she responded.

"I'm flattered that you share that with me, Dieter. I was aggressive with you, because that's always been my nature. 'Get what you need by whatever device you have available' has been my pattern, because I never had anyone who cared a fig for my happiness—or even my survival. So here we are, creating music and getting paid well for it, making love like rabbits, and exchanging some buried secrets in unfettered conversations. It has made me very happy. And, Dieter, I want you to know that you don't owe me anything beyond these few weeks we've shared. I have a clear picture of what I am going to do after Mr. Saxophone joins my world, and if I come to you for guidance I know you'll help me."

"I know that," he lied.

As the last light in the apartment was extinguished, a car pulled to the curb on Rua Francisco Otaviano, and the driver stepped out and walked toward a second car already parked along the street. "I'm your relief," he said through the open window. You've been on for four hours—anything happen?"

"He and the singer—Lola—walked back here a little before midnight, and they haven't gone out again. I think I saw cigarettes being lighted up on that front terrace, but other than that it has been quiet. No other visitors and they seem to be bedded down for the night. All the lights are out."

"Thanks. You're free to go home after you file your report. I'll be here until about sunrise, and then that new guy from Washington will relieve me. This guy has a Secret Service detail watching his ass around the clock and he doesn't even know it! Isn't that odd?"

42

───────

✿

Dinner in Canoas

Once they had exited the dark interior of their automobile and entered a Bavarian-style restaurant, Sofie and her father could embrace and examine one another in a true reunion. She could see that at age fifty-six he was resplendent with thick, graying hair and a well-kept beard in the style of Ernest Hemingway. His skin was colored by the sun to a tone much darker than she had ever seen it, and he had maintained the lean, strong lines of his military training.

"Oh, Poppy—you could be a movie star! Really, you are so handsome after—what is it?—two or three years away from that grueling work in Berlin. I'm not really sure I would recognize you if we passed in the street. And I love the back-country clothing, too. I hope that your life is as relaxed and healthy as your appearance suggests—is it?"

"Sofie, dear Sofie. You have always worried about me, as a good daughter would. But really, nothing brings me more well-being and happiness than the knowledge that you are far away from the treachery of Europe and able to give life to your talent. And now you are literally creating new life! How could Dieter let you out of his sight at such a wonderful time?"

"Poppy—he doesn't know yet. I visited a physician in Rio only weeks before this tour, because I felt sort of—well, sort of different—and I was afraid to launch something so ambitious if I were getting sick, you know. Perhaps I should have guessed without having to be told, but I'm never sick and that was my first reaction to some subtle changes I noticed in my appetite and—well, you don't have to know all the lady things that change. But I wanted to see a doctor and not bother Dieter. Then when I understood the cause, I especially wanted him not to worry about my health on the tour, so I am saving it for my return to Rio in another couple of weeks."

"Let's go to the table and talk to Branka. But let's wait to tell her about your baby and see if she notices anything. Branka is one of the most observant humans on earth—but, of course, that's what she was trained to do, wasn't it? Before you ask, she has been wonderful since we came here, and we celebrate our decision to walk away every morning when the sun peeks into our window."

As Otto von Seigler led his daughter through the busy restaurant, Sofie could easily believe that she had been transported back to Zur letzten Instanz, her father's favorite old wood-paneled pub on Waisenstrasse in Berlin. There were the same solid oak tables stacked with die Vorspeisen—German hors d'oeuvres—and a crush of fast-moving waitresses daringly lifting multiple steins of beer over the heads of their seated patrons. Predictably, there were a few smaller private rooms snuggled beyond that noisy public area, reserved for dinner guests seeking a more relaxed dining experience.

Sofie failed to notice the plainly dressed woman standing at the entrance to the private room to which she was being guided, until she saw the woman's arms extend to initiate an *umarmung*, one of those full European embraces reserved for special friends and family members. It was Branka—but not the glamorous SWW stringer Branka from Lisbon who had won her father's affections during his wartime vacation trips to that neutral city. Like all capable intelligence professionals, Branka had apparently learned how to make herself invisible when conditions suggested a lower profile, and she had concluded that tonight in a popular restaurant in Canoas she might better assume a modest and unremarkable persona. This seemed to assure Sofie that Otto and Branka had transformed themselves successfully into Kurt and Gerda Hahn, respectable residents of Brazil's Germanic interior.

Gerda brushed an affectionate kiss on each of Sofie's cheeks, then held her at arm's length and assessed the lovely young woman who meant so very much to her father. "Your time in Brazil has served you well, Sofie," the older woman observed with a warm smile. "Your father and I speak of you daily, and seeing you tonight reassures us that starting anew was a good decision for all of us."

Their attentive room waiter placed a copy of the *Menu Do Dia* in front of each of his three diners and asked if before dining they would like first to sharpen their appetites with a light aperitif wine. Gerda and Kurt each requested a Caipirinha while Sofie smilingly asked for a glass of sparkling water until she could make a selection from the dinner menu.

When the waiter had departed, Sofie suddenly became overcome with the moment, and before she could consider her emotion, she was seated across her father's lap and crying happily on his shoulder. "I'm sorry, Poppy—but it has been too long since I last saw you, and I have missed you so much." The returning waiter was totally confused by the three closely grouped, sobbing occupants he encountered, and he placed the tray of drinks quietly on a serving rack and left the room as quickly as possible.

It took only a few moments for the three to collect themselves, and then their mood shifted to one of excessive laughter over the reaction of the departed waiter and the unexpected situation he had encountered. It had been a collective release of internalized questioning—a sigh of surrender to the daily tensions each had suppressed for a long time in their adopted country, combined with the realization that all their yesterdays might yet overtake them, half a world away from Germany.

Over dinner, a calmer Sofie recounted her experiences and the sights of her tour, and reviewed again the surprising events of this day. "I didn't know how to react when I was attempting to get back to my hotel and stay out of sight from that strange man. Suddenly I was literally lifted into a car in a dramatic sweep and pinned between two strong men. All I could do was recite my identity like some prisoner of war and demand to be released; it was totally frightening. And then, Poppy, there was the improbability of your familiar voice urging me to be calm. It was nothing I could have anticipated, but just what I needed."

Branka—or Gerda—sipped her dinner wine thoughtfully and then began in a measured voice. "You may know that anticipation lies at the heart of our intelligence-gathering profession. When our instincts tell us that something should be true, we employ all of our senses to find verification for that conclusion. But if we can't substantiate it empirically, then we must return to and re-examine original premise to see what was wrong."

Sofie's face brightened. "Gerda—I understand the process you're describing, but I'm not sure I understand its relevance to our getting together here tonight after two years of separation. Can you help me with that?"

"Let me give you a specific example: Tonight I encountered a healthy and very attractive thirty-year-old-woman who has, against all odds, been reunited with her consort after a long absence. They have worked and lived together happily for many months, doing something they both enjoy. My instinct and life experiences tell me that they should be starting a family of their own while conditions are ripe for that, and so I seek confirmation of my premise through observations. Sofie, I believe that you are going to make my handsome Kurt a happy 'opa' in the near future, am I correct?"

Sofie reached for her father's wine glass and emptied its remaining contents in an almost reckless fashion, then blurted, "Oh, Branka—I apologize for being so wobbly, but you just shocked the starch out of my back. Until this evening only my physician and I knew of this baby, and now it seems as if I have a big sign painted across my forehead. Of course, your conclusion is accurate—I am into my second trimester, but I thought I could keep it secret until the tour is over and I'm back in Rio with Dieter. May I ask . . . ?"

The older woman was now the one smiling. "First, you instinctively protect your little one, finding various ways to cover her with crossed arms or a purse positioned over the telltale fullness. Your hips and chest appear larger, and you regularly perform little involuntary stretches of your back muscles. And finally, there was your negative response to the request for your drink order—on a celebratory occasion such as this reunion with your father? No— there must be something else in your everyday thoughts. And that validated my hypothesis, you see?"

Uncertain whether to be assured or annoyed, Sofie was sure of one thing: this woman did not know her well enough to speak to her this frankly. And she was going to pay for that "larger hips" remark. Sofie leaned decisively back in her chair, arms folded over her chest. "I see. Now—may I do the same kind of analysis?" She took a sip of her traitorous sparkling water. "In Lisbon, when we boarded to come here, you were beautifully turned out. Each night of our voyage, you dressed stylishly and had just the right touch of rouge and mascara to highlight your lovely, high cheekbones. I must confess that I didn't recognize you immediately tonight, because you went out of your way to be plain." Sofie leaned forward, her eyes riveted on Branka. "My conclusion is that you and Poppy are fearful that I may lead someone to you—inadvertently, of course. Is that correct?"

Kurt held his hand up as a signal to preempt further discussion. "We know that individual tragedies from the war years will survive any formal armistice, and although Branka and I were originally on opposite sides of the armed conflict, over time we discovered we shared many values which were not being well served through continuation of our wartime service. So we made our decision to exit the field and begin again together. We don't expect aggrieved people to agree that we are entitled to do that—and perhaps we are not—so we are dedicated to becoming two unremarkable migrant European country folk who have resettled abroad, rather than a soldier and a spy fleeing from righteous indignation.

"Those who might want to track us down could easily conclude that at some point we will be in contact with our closest former associates or our dearest family members, and that nexus could betray us. Meetings like this one are precious and we must continue to have them, but always as safely as possible. That's as succinctly as I can state our situation, and I apologize for the difficulties it may visit upon your new life here."

Conversation stopped while their waiter removed dinner dishes and wine glasses and placed a dessert menu on the table. He promised to return shortly for their dessert, coffee, and after-dinner drink preferences. When the door closed softly behind him, Sofie took her father's hand and said, "Thank you, Poppy. Dieter and I can stay within those parameters."

Branka—or Gerda—smiled and added, "Please let an old espionage specialist suggest an avenue for our periodic communications. You use Rio's *O Globo* and we will use the Florianópolis newspaper *Floha do Norte* to post short notices in the personals section on the first business day of each month. We will be "Tristan" and you "Isolde." If either of us wishes the other to call, state the day of the month, the time of day, and the telephone number. But make each number one higher than you want us to use. So, if you write 'call on January 8 at 9:00 p.m.', we will call on January 7 at 8:00 p.m. Do the same thing with the telephone number—reduce each digit by one.

Sofie looked incredulous. "Branka, that sounds like something out of a bad movie. Can't we just send a letter to a post office address and be done with it? I don't even like Wagner's operas and don't care to be Isolde. Dieter and I both receive lots of letters at the Copacabana Palace—we have regular hold boxes at the Reception Desk. It works just fine. You can probably rent a postal box in Blumenau or wherever you live and we'll send baby pictures and updates. I promise."

Branka tapped her fingers impatiently, then concluded. "No. There is a serious need to be cautious. You have said that you and your father used code words and little signals to one another back in Berlin. Every wartime communiqué was encoded. There's a reason we go to all that trouble to maintain secrecy and anonymity. Please humor me and take these precautions."

Sofie could see that there was no point in debating on such a rare occasion as this, and she decided that it was time to change the subject of their conversation or risk estrangement from Branka and perhaps from her father as well. "I'll try it. Branka," she smiled. "But I hope we can have more warm evenings like this one—and little need for encoded messages."

All too soon they hugged and kissed goodbye, and Sofie slipped into the empty car with a silent driver who delivered her quietly to a corner near her hotel and then monitored her short walk to the entrance. As she retrieved her key from the front desk, she noticed that the lone occupant of the lounge area glanced furtively at his wristwatch before returning his attention to the magazine he had been reading. It had been an eventful day, and now she had to concentrate on being a vocalist.

43

"Bist du das, Otto?"

Florianópolis became important to the FBI during World War II because of its Atlantic coastal location midway between Rio de Janeiro and Buenos Aires. It was also the capital city of the Brazilian state of Santa Catarina, a region heavily populated by German immigrants. With the Atlantic shipping lanes plagued by German undersea raiders and a large number of Axis agents infiltrating South America, the United States had dispatched and recruited over three hundred "Special Intelligence Service" operatives to the South American continent. Now, after the nation's war with Germany had been officially ended, this elite contingent of FBI specialists remained in place awaiting future assignments from FBI Headquarters in Washington.

On a warm September morning, their section chief had assembled two dozen SIS veterans in Florianópolis to discuss an assignment the chief described as "challenging."

"The Bureau has added two former OSS fellows from London and taken an interest in their last case over there. It was walked in to them by that concentration camp survivor, Simon Wiesenthal, who has compiled files on several Nazis who are not scheduled to be tried at Nuremburg but who are accused of reprehensible behavior during the war. We know that many of them have managed to slip away from Europe, and that Argentina, Chile, Uruguay, and Brazil were among their prime destinations because of the large German subpopulations and some sympathetic political leaders here.

"Wiesenthal asserts that a particular Wehrmacht general was in a position which allowed him to divert significant amounts of Polish bullion and currency reserves, and that he may have fled from Lisbon to Brazil in '43. We know that he disappeared from Germany at that time, and if he did immigrate to Brazil, there's a strong likelihood that Rio Grande do Sul or Catarina would be his new location, because of the ease of blending into the large German communities here. The general has a daughter named Zofia, or Sofie, or Sophia, who is a popular singer. She has remained out in the open through the war and currently; she has performed in Europe and for the last couple of years in Brazil. She's billed as "Sophia," and we believe that she carries a Swiss passport with the surname "Havlik." That's not her father's name.

"This morning's meeting is convened because Sophia, the singer, is currently on tour with the popular Buca Pittman Band and they are going to perform in Blumenau during Oktoberfest. The agency's theory is that the general may try to attend one of her performances in Blumenau to hear and see his only daughter sing. The idea gains credibility because the band has previously been performing in other cities—BA, Montevideo, Porto Alegre—and suddenly she slipped our observers in Porto Alegre for a whole day and then materialized again at her hotel. We believe that she knows she is being followed and has been canny enough to disappear when she wants to. We conjecture that the 'lost day' was spent with the general, which means he's somewhere in these two states.

"The Pittman Band is giving three public concerts at the open-air pavilion in Blumenau. Each will be about ninety minutes long. Two will be during daylight hours and the third at night—with fireworks. They expect several thousand people in the area on those days, but we can narrow this down considerably by limiting our coverage to areas from which the bandstand can be observed—because that's what the general would want to do. He is in his mid-fifties, so we don't have to observe kids or oldsters. We have a file photo of him, but it is from his military years and chances are that he has changed his appearance. We do know that his official height was listed by the military as 186 centimeters, so don't waste time checking shorties. He has blue eyes, which he can't change, and the military gave him high grades for physical fitness, and he might be expected to continue that. *Don't* waste time checking overly fat men.

"Finally, his name is Otto von Seigler. You can be sure that if he has come to Brazil to hide, he is using another name here and he has official papers issued in that name. The man is no fool, gentlemen. I would suggest that you dress like enthusiastic visitors to Oktoberfest. Carry a stein of beer and some würstl or brezen. Stay in areas where you can watch and hear Sophia when she is singing. Look for men who seem particularly intent upon her performance. Our target apparently left Europe with a female companion, so include couples in your surveillance.

"Each of you is receiving a small folder with information on General von Seigler, including two official photos of him taken in 1939. Note that he also speaks Polish fluently and some English. No doubt he has added basic Portuguese to his fluency if he is indeed living here. He will certainly try not to stand out in a crowd, so look for bland clothing; perhaps a hat and also dark glasses if the day is clear.

"Finally, if you do observe someone who you think could be our man, try to get another of our team to join you quickly and run through your checklist with him. If you then agree that he is a good candidate, try to take positions nearby on his flanks, and then one of you ask in a voice sufficiently loud to get attention, "Bist du das, Otto?" Is that *you*, Otto? Don't ask it directly to him, but say it loudly enough to get an involuntary head turn from him when he hears his name."

"Then what?"

"The one who asked the question immediately waves to someone imaginary in the distance and moves away quickly, as if to reach a friend named Otto he has recognized somewhere in the crowd. Our target will probably be relieved, but may also decide to fold his tent and get out of there. When he does move we want as many eyes on him as possible—but not including the one who had originally called his name. And, gentlemen, we are all professionals, and we represent the United States. We have no authorization to apprehend General von Seigler. All of this is just a first step in pinpointing a target so that we may proceed legally to obtain extradition permission—for us or for Germany or for whatever group is entitled legally to apprehend him."

44

Carney and Joe

President Harry S. Truman signed Executive Order #9621 as soon as victory over Japan was secured. The order took effect almost before the ink from his pen had dried—actually a scant ten days later. With Executive Order #9621, President Roosevelt's wartime intelligence-gathering creation, the OSS, was officially terminated, and any remaining business of the agency was handed off either to the State Department or to the War Department. Twenty-four thousand men and women had served their country—mostly in secrecy—as OSS employees.

Many of them had undergone rigorous training in the most subversive techniques of modern warfare. They could infiltrate, spy, steal, and kill, and as they carried out their missions, they enabled the nation's conventional armed forces to function with greatly enhanced effectiveness.

Carney and Joe met one final time at 70 Grosvenor Street in London. They had both been "retained" and were now being assigned to a hastily organized Strategic Services Unit of the War Department, to be overseen by Brigadier General John Magruder, a close associate of their former boss, Wild Bill Donovan. General Magruder was supposed to effect an orderly liquidation of the OSS's clandestine projects, but to retain its major capabilities for future use, as Washington assessed the country's peacetime need for gathering intelligence.

"Whatever they decide to do, Joe, it seems to me as if J. Edgar is going to have some kind of veto power regarding the format. He doesn't want another intelligence-gathering agency eroding the FBI's position in the States and even the whole Western Hemisphere."

"So, after struggling to put OSS together and make it work, they're going to shut it down now that Germany has surrendered. Everything the Army fought for is going to be on the negotiating table, and we will be hoping that two new guys from Washington and London can keep Joe Stalin from stealing the victory—right?"

"Sort of. Roosevelt died without Truman having much knowledge of the situation, and Churchill got voted out of office during the Potsdam Conference—after leading Britain through the war. Truman plus Churchill's successor, Atlee, concluded the Potsdam Conference with Stalin and apparently the old boy stole their lunch. France wasn't even invited to be a negotiator, and the Allies came away with a jigsaw puzzle. Berlin is administered by four countries, but it is about a hundred miles inside the Soviet-controlled part of Germany. Our guys say Stalin and Communist Poland will be able to convert most of Germany to Communism in just a few years. They'll throw the old Germans out of Czechoslovakia and will be sitting on a huge part of Europe. Stalin captured about as much of Europe at a conference table in Cecilienhof Castle as Hitler got with all of his military in seven years."

"Castle?"

"That's where the Potsdam Conference was. Ya still gotta read more, Joe! One thing they did agree on at Potsdam was the continuation of the effort to capture and punish what they call 'war criminals.' " I'm thinking that our general meets that definition and our search for him will go on for at least a reasonable time. That's especially important now, because the FBI guys in Brazil say they are pretty sure he and his daughter got together recently in Porto Alegre. They're not watching for submarines anymore, and there's some pretty good assets now looking for our general. It only takes one little slipup!"

"What's the next stop on the Pittman Band's tour—Blumenau?"

"Exactly. One of the larger Oktoberfest gatherings in the world, and Sophia is going to be singing in the central pavilion in the big Parque Vila Germânica for three days. The Santa Catarina state FBI unit has a group of about two dozen agents briefed on our general, and they're going to rotate all of them into the area of her performances so that there's always a handful surveying the crowd watching her. I think if I were seeing my daughter sing to a big audience, I'd be pretty obvious. I'd be clapping longer and cheering louder, y'know. So if there's somebody like that, one of the observers is gonna say his name loud, and see if he reacts."

"But you said that the general and his daughter know they're being followed now, and she slipped away from the last pro who was watching her in Porto Alegre. I think we can assume they won't do anything too obvious at those performances. Hey, when are you movin' outa here—and where are they posting you next?"

"I asked to follow up on that Elsa back in the States, if they can pinpoint her. Looks as if she went to Chicago and we know that she and Dieter have corresponded. He may still be the one to lead us to the general if he and Sophia get back together."

"If they get back together—you mean when she finishes the tour, right?"

"Yeah, sort of. She'll be going back to Rio with the band in a couple of weeks, but our FBI guys there say he's been hot and heavy with another singer lately. Don't know how that might affect him and Sophia. There's a lot going on there, and I can't predict it yet."

45

❧

Blumenau Review

The Florianópolis-based FBI/SIS agents had obtained a closed school building not far from the pavilion to centralize their observation of the Oktoberfest celebration, and they had been able to coordinate their surveillance efforts efficiently from there. Throughout each of the three days they had personnel observing the crowd, but when the Pittman Band began setting up for their featured performances, many eyes were on them. Hundreds of celebrants came early with folding chairs to stake their claims on the broad grass apron, and others passed by to find vantage points for the anticipated music. Fifteen minutes before the scheduled starting time, the area was clogged with beer-drinking, wurst-snacking people, unaware that their faces were being scanned and evaluated by a squadron of trained observers.

As entertainment, the Pittman Band had been a rousing success. Their well-tuned instruments were a happy contrast with some of the smaller groups attempting familiar songs at the scattered food and beverage kiosks throughout the downtown area. At the conclusion of the three-day event, two dozen bleary-eyed men gathered at the school to de-brief. Twelve-hour days overloaded with beer, heavy food, and constant standing and walking had taken a toll. But more important, there was no hard evidence on which to extend their search.

"I would like each of you to submit a written summary of your activity and observations. We'll be sending a final report to HQ, and your submissions will be exhibits supporting our findings. For now, I'd like to hold a general discussion—off the record—to see what we agree upon and how similar surveillance in the future can be most effective. I'm going to lead off—but this is a general review, so everyone feel free to sound off.

"Okay, then—we had three two-hour concerts to cover and we decided to concentrate on an area extending back about two hundred fifty feet from the bandstand and with a full view of the performers up there, right? And we gave special attention to the people who came early and planted folding chairs in that area. We counted about eight hundred people who did that each day, and we got a decent view of each of them by strolling through with a beer or some food. Probably two thousand more came and stood in our covered zone— some for a short time and many for the whole concert. There were fifty-seven sightings where one or another of you got backup, and twenty-two of those got pinned for extended coverage. We really watched those closely when the girl was singing, to see if they flashed any signals or other communication. Ten guys shouted her name and got really enthusiastic, but there wasn't any feedback that we could see. Am I right so far?"

"Yeah, chief—the boisterous ones were all about twenty years old and pretty well oiled, I'd say. Certainly not general material."

"Good point. How many did you see who were 'general material' in that area? Forty or fifty, I'd say."

"Agreed. They were mostly sitting down and better dressed. Guys in their fifties and mostly with women. We kept an eye on people like that to catch a wave or some personal communication with the girl, but nobody reported any."

"Okay—let's talk about the girl for a minute. What did you observe?"

"She's a number! Tall, and good figure. Pretty, too."

"And a helluva singer! Really projected out there and sang in German and Portuguese and English. The crowd ate her up and kept her on stage a long time."

"I'll second that. She's up there with Helen Forrest or Martha Tilton in my book. And the band actually had songs built around her vocals rather than just plopping them in the middle of the number. Pittman must think a lot of her—and he should. The crowd loved her."

"Did you see her watching any particular part of the audience? Kind of looking at someone she wanted to greet?"

"Nope. Very professional. Always seemed to be focused above their heads when she sang, and kind of twirled when she waved at the applause. Acknowledged everybody on one big turn."

"Did you see anyone from the crowd approach her during or after the concert?"

"Nah. The police kept an open space in front of the bandstand and didn't let the audience move in there. Like a little corridor about seven or eight feet wide, and a cop stood at the end of it and waved anyone out who tried to set up a chair there. Good crowd control, especially when you consider the nature of the Oktoberfest. Sort of rowdy and crazy at times, but not at the concert."

"Hey—there was that one guy with the flowers the first day, remember? Little Brazilian guy with a big bunch of flowers tried to carry them to the stage for her. The cop shut him down and took the flowers away before he could reach out to her."

"Then what? Did they arrest him?"

"Nah. The cop just walked the flowers over to the stage and handed them to Sophia himself—and she was so pleased she gave him a little peck on the cheek. The crowd loved it."

"And the little guy?'

"He just walked away. He was only a delivery guy—not a general, for sure."

"Did you check the flowers after the concert to see if there was a card? Who sent them?"

"One of our guys did, and he said they were anonymous. Sophia said she thought they were from the concert committee, maybe."

"And—what about the cop?"

"Never saw him after that. Nobody else tried to get to the stage. Good crowd control!"

"No—I meant, what did the cop look like?"

"Pretty big guy. Maybe late forties. Short, close beard. Dark glasses. Authority figure."

"Like, maybe, a general?"

"Oh, shit!"

46

Viewpoints

At the fazenda, Gerda and Kurt sat by a fire burning in the hearth of their large entertaining room. From time to time, Kurt churned the components with a long poker, and each rotation seemed to bring out another wisp of flame and smoke from the disintegrating blue material.

"Sorry to see it disappear," he chuckled. "It had been more than three years since I last wore a uniform. It felt very good."

"I know—you looked quite handsome in it. I should have taken your photo, darling! Oh—I removed all the nice brass buttons and have them in a little box in my sewing basket. So, if you ever want to decorate a hunting jacket with shiny buttons announcing 'Pólicia do Santa Catarina,' I am prepared."

"Thank you, my sweet. I know that Officer Rocha will be disappointed when he returns from his vacation in Chile and can't find his new uniform. I'd return the buttons to the station house for him, but I fear it would only serve to make more people aware that Rocha's uniform was pilfered. Best to let things settle without any commentary or action on our part."

"How did you arrange the flowers, mein führer?"

"Aha! Our driver walked to the flower mart and paid the manager generously for them—delivered without a card to the stage for the singer. Officer Rocha blocked his path and said he would complete the delivery. A small gratuity completed the transaction seamlessly, and I carried them the last three meters to the stage. It earned me a kiss—and a marvelously surprised look. She was so quick to realize what was going on and didn't give it away at all. I was just a bit apprehensive that she might scream out 'Oh, Poppy, you are so clever,' and we could have been skewered.

"How did you think she looked—and sang?"

"Oh—if I hadn't seen her in street clothes at dinner, I would not know that she is with child. And, I didn't know her voice except from one or two songs in Rio, so I was truly surprised at her professionalism. She's a star, Kurt, and she's also going to have you wearing Opa uniforms soon. How special for you. *Bärchen*!"

✄

At the FBI/SIS morning meeting, the atmosphere was not so light. There was grudging admiration for the former Wehrmacht officer who had been so confident that he could stand close by his pursuers and actually nibble on the 'bait' they were trailing without so much as a shout or chase resulting.

"You know, he was clever to do it on the first night, when we had no previous experience guiding us. We didn't know whether the police were going to keep spectators back from the stage or whether to expect flowers for the diva—as at the opera. The less familiar we are, the less inclined to interrupt proceedings. He understood the art of surprise—like General Rommel."

"Ah, yes—der Wüstenfuchs—the Desert Fox! You know, they both studied at Officer Cadet School in Danzig at the same time— probably knew one another because they were about the same age.

And then they both had daughters about the same age—Rommel's is named Gertrude, and von Seigler's is this Sophia we were watching. And both generals figured big in Hitler's quick move through Poland in '39."

"Both were apparently disenchanted with Hitler sooner or later, too. Von Seigler was connected to the Oster Conspiracy back in '38, but they took the heat off him so that he could contribute to the Polish conquest. Then he disappeared and apparently is near here now. Old Rommel was implicated in an assassination attempt on Hitler in July 1944, and they gave him the choice of suicide or total disgrace in a trial. He took a cyanide pill. Kind of sad, huh?"

"Yeah. I think the really sad part is that the German professional soldiers, who had some sort of traditional honor code, got swallowed up by the Nazi movement and ended up in total disgrace."

"Well—are we gonna continue our attempt to find von Seigler, or was Oktoberfest our best shot?"

"It was meaningful in a way. We think he was in both Porto Alegre and Blumenau. Those two cities are only about 600 kilometers apart, and the area between is peppered with ex-Germans. He's somewhere in that mix. Trouble is, we could watch an acre of Oktoberfest with twenty-four agents, but we can't scour all those hills as easily, and we probably won't have many agents to devote to the pursuit. It will take some kind of break now, I think. Someone who knows he's out there and catches wind of him, y'know."

"Should we be putting up wanted signs or distributing bulletins to local courthouses?"

"Probably not until somebody cares enough to offer a sizeable reward. Remember, this area is lousy with krauts and probably most of them would prefer him to us. You gotta sweeten the pot to get them thinking of turning in one of their own."

"Guess we're 'outfoxed' right now, huh?"

The young teacher had attended Oktoberfest and taken in all of the fun, frolicking, and food. But she made it a special point to be at the musical presentations by the Booker Pittman Band and their featured vocalist. It was the same Sophia who was on that poster in the Hahns' bedroom—no question about the likeness. And, in the introduction, "Buca" had gone out of his way to mention Sophia's appearances across the Continent with Django Reinhardt, an idol to Brazil's thousands of guitarists. She watched the tall singer move and observed her mannerisms, trying to catch something reminiscent of Kurt Hahn or his wife. Perhaps it was there—or possibly she was just trying too hard to make a connection.

She was only twenty or thirty meters from the edge of the bandstand, and she scanned the seated audience looking for her students. She even passed through the random chairs to look more closely at seated couples, but there wasn't a sign of them. If this was their daughter, surely they would be there to see and hear her—and to greet her as well. But there wasn't a sign of that.

The singer was talented and beautiful and gracious. When an admirer attempted to have a big bouquet delivered to her, the police didn't permit the contact, but instead an officer carried the flowers and received a charming kiss. It delighted the audience, and he withdrew shyly to the side of the stage. And then, as quickly as he had appeared, he was gone. Did she imagine that he looked like Kurt Hahn behind those dark glasses?

If Kurt Hahn went to such lengths to see his daughter for a fleeting moment, why? Wouldn't it be normal to embrace her and leave the bandstand together after the concert and go to a quiet spot and talk endlessly? What would cause a parent to forsake those precious minutes or hours and to substitute one quick touch? The daughter advertised herself on billboards, so the answer must lie in Herr Hahn's identity.

The teacher resolved to learn more about "Sophia." The answer might lie just a few inquiries away.

Sophia stretched on her bed and ran her hands downward from her ribs to her protruding hip bones. It was no longer a flat surface interrupted by small ridges of abdominal muscle. The hands explored over a discernible rise from her sternum to a point about four inches below her navel. It was about the area of a dinner plate, and she couldn't pull it in by taking a deep breath. It didn't hurt and it wasn't particularly uncomfortable, but there was no denying that it was there and growing.

She was so very happy that she had been able to tell her father personally—and to be discovered by that witch, Branka. She wished she could turn on her side—right now—and invite Dieter to meet his child. Should she have told him at once? No use reviewing that decision now. It had been made six weeks ago, and it was made in good faith. But, why must things be so complicated? Was it always going to be something resulting from their Jewish parents and the craziness that had produced in their lives?

She thought back again to her father's two "surprises"— kidnapping her in Porto Alegre and being close enough to kiss on a stage in Blumenau. She had thought about all the money he had apparently "liberated" and with which he had decorated her life. It was done. Perhaps it should just be accepted and not revisited, especially if the discovery would threaten their happiness and even their lives.

Sofie fell asleep with a serene smile. Only two more stops on the tour and she would be back in Rio.

47

⁓

Chicago

Carney had been able to find Magda's marriage recorded in Saint Stanislaus Kostka Parish on West Evergreen Avenue in Chicago, and from that source had traced her home address, the birth of her daughter, and her current employment at Sears Roebuck & Company. The process had consumed nearly a week, but now he was standing on the sidewalk as Magda and Elsa departed from the Sears building together at the conclusion of their working day. There had been significant changes in Elsa's appearance since he last saw her in Prague; her hair was shorter and had been converted to the fashionable blonde hue now favored by American movie stars. She wore opaque dark glasses and higher heels, and she looked younger than she had at their last, lamented meeting.

The War Department had shown only mild interest in Carney's story of OSS's pursuit of a Wehrmacht general but had given him the green light to check out a source he had developed in Europe before OSS was folded away. Carney knew that his real fascination was not with the missing general but rather with the woman who had bested him so deftly in Prague. He hadn't been able to get Elsa out of his mind, and he welcomed an excuse to track her down in Chicago and to engage with her again. There really wasn't much more she could add to the pursuit of the missing general and his loot; she had already inadvertently established that her friend "Dieter" in Rio was the companion of the general's daughter, and as a result, several FBI agents in South America had invested many fruitless days and nights watching Sophia, hoping to catch sight of her father. However, their trail had gone cold as America's wartime intelligence gatherers positioned themselves for postwar inclusion in the government's evolving new intelligence-gathering alignment.

About the only justification he could construct for being on this street corner now was trying to recruit Elsa for the new intelligence agency that would soon be launched by Washington. It was to be a sort of central intelligence bureau, with skilled personnel positioned in many foreign pressure points, and after working at Sears for days and breathing the air blowing over the stockyards at night, Elsa might be willing to listen to his pitch. He understood that he was being unprofessional to include personal feelings in his working agenda, but nevertheless, he needed to be in the company of the intriguing Elsa at least one more time.

Carney had been living for nearly a week in Chicago's prime luxury hotel, at the corner of LaSalle and Madison Streets in the "Loop" area; it was a twenty-two-story building appropriately named the "LaSalle." He had fantasized sharing a Dubonnet apéritif with Elsa in the hotel's fashionable Silver Grill Lounge and then moving on for dinner together in Chicago's top restaurant, the famous Pump Room. He'd finish a perfect evening by showing her the blazing city lights from his room's twentieth-floor window. What a treat for both of them! This time there would be no falling asleep by the hunter while the ducks were on the pond.

He kept the fast-walking women in sight from a safe distance until Magda arrived at her bus stop, then resumed tracking Elsa until she entered the women's hotel that was her temporary home. There was no chance that the hotel would volunteer information on their residents, and he carried no official identity that might persuade an impressionable desk clerk to disregard that strict standard. But Carney had four years of field experience and quickly contrived a plan to get the information he needed.

Carney entered the door of the hotel within a minute of Elsa's arrival and went breathlessly to the lone desk clerk.

"Sir, I was trying to catch up to a young lady who came into your lobby from the street a few moments ago. She opened her purse when she passed me—to get something, perhaps her key—and she didn't realize that these twenty-dollar bills fell out when she did that." Carney held out four bills rolled loosely together and secured with a small rubber band. "I'm sure that eighty dollars is a significant sum for her, and it wouldn't be fair to lose it that way."

"How thoughtful of you!" the desk clerk gushed. "That doesn't happen often in Chicago."

"Do you know the woman I'm referring to?" Carney inquired, with his best innocent face open to the clerk. "Blonde hair; smallish; tan coat; about thirty."

"There's been only one guest come into the lobby in the last few minutes. That's Gretchen—and you pretty much described her. I think that's the lucky lady you want."

"Aha! Does she have a last name? I'd like to scribble a quick note to her and wrap it around the money and leave it with you—to return to her, of course."

"Of course. That would be Gretchen Hasse; I think she's German or something. Real nice lady. She'll be so pleased. Here, I'll give you an envelope and a sheet of hotel paper and you can sit over there and compose your note. Bring it to me when you're done. I'll slip it into her box."

"Ah, that's great. Thanks for your help. This is for you." Carney opened his billfold and handed a crisp ten-dollar bill to the clerk. "Perhaps both of us can help Miss Gretchen Whatsername."

"Hasse, sir. Gretchen Hasse. Thanks!"

Carney retreated to a quiet corner of the lobby and wrote a short note, then tore a page from a magazine resting on the table, to add suitable bulk to his sealed envelope—about as it might feel with four twenties inside. He addressed the envelope and handed it to the clerk with one final, friendly wave. If the little weasel opened the envelope to steal the money, he'd be disappointed, and if it got to Gretchen unopened, Carney would hear from her. Spies were predictable that way.

❧

"Oh, Miss Hasse, here's an envelope dropped off at the desk for you yesterday afternoon."

"Oh, my—I must have overlooked it. I don't know many people here, so I don't always check when I come in from work."

She walked to the small library desk in the corner of the lobby and opened the envelope with the blade concealed in her purse handle. Inside was a note on hotel stationery and a folded page from *Time* magazine, containing nothing but the names of the publication's managers and editors. Setting that aside, Elsa read the note's disciplined handwriting:

Dear Miss Hasse,

Walking behind you on 11th Street, I became aware of the striking similarity you bear to a Miss Elsa Danzig who I knew back in Prague. Alas, I lost track of Elsa after she came to America but have always hoped our paths might cross again. Now, I'd like to get to know you better.

Perhaps you would consent to be my guest at the Pump Room in the LaSalle Hotel at eight o'clock p.m. on Tuesday, and we can enjoy dinner and a quiet conversation. I even have several candid photos of my friend Elsa, and when you view them I'm sure you'll agree that there is a remarkable resemblance.

I am currently occupying Suite 2020 of the LaSalle; it is a lovely apartment that belongs to the US War Department, which employs my services. Please call the hotel and confirm that you'll be joining me. I look forward to spending the evening with you.

Sincerely,
William Carney,
Special Investigations, US Department of War

Elsa laughed for a while at the thought of Carney going to all that work to track her from Prague to Chicago—a trail she had muddied as much as possible. Persistence like that deserved some reward, didn't it?

The War Department had inherited the intelligence work of OSS under its sunset provisions, and apparently the Department had gotten the ubiquitous William Carney in that reshuffling. She was curious whether reeling in General von Seigler had retained any priority in the realignment, or whether Carney was still charged with recruiting skilled people for whatever new American intelligence agency might eventuate in the postwar world.

Her short stint in the Sears mailroom had convinced Elsa that clerical work held no fascination for her, and a lonely 15' x 20' room—well, just not the comfort level she was seeking at age 35. She had heard the Pump Room mentioned glowingly by her co-workers, as if it were a dining experience for Chicago's elite, rivaling Buckingham Palace. It had been a long time since she had gotten dressed up and gone anywhere special. But, being honest with herself, Elsa conceded that an evening of matching wits with the confident, handsome William Carney was in itself sufficient reason to leave a telephone message at the LaSalle Hotel that Miss Gretchen Hasse would be joining Mr. Carney for dinner in the Pump Room on Tuesday at 8:00 p.m.

And, so—she made the confirming call.

48

———

✍

Chefe do Pólicia

Blumenau was remarkably clean after the mayhem of Oktoberfest; it was a testimonial to the traditional orderliness of the region's Germanic residents. They could party until the wee hours, but streets were swept and trash carted away before the resumption of business. Not only that, but shopkeepers and merchants were there to open their places of business on schedule, notwithstanding some alpine-sized headaches and yodeling stomach distress. All that remained of the recent merriment were some sly smiles and whispered stories, which brought knowing laughter.

Lucia DeSimone came early to Blumenau that morning; reopening of the university in Joinville had been delayed intentionally following Oktoberfest so that local families could first attend to laundry and cleanup and out-of-towners could return to their villages. After a cup of *café forte* and a sugary *rosquinha* she checked her appearance in a store window, then walked through Avenida Central to a building prominently marked "Delegacia do Pólicia," the central police station of this well-managed community. She presented her cédula to a sleepy desk sergeant and informed him that she was composing a paper on the excellent crowd control in

Blumenau during the overflow of visitors experienced in Oktoberfest, and she would like to solicit just a few pertinent comments from the Chefe do Pólicia, who had obviously done such an outstanding job. She had learned earlier in life that a hint of flattery could send functionaries scurrying to their superiors as bearers of good news.

The sleep-deprived face of the desk sergeant seemed to come alive with her suggestion—as well as with his appreciation of the attractive lady smiling at him—and he asked her to have a seat while he made inquiry about the chefe's availability. With a nod of appreciation and one more flattering smile, she took a chair. The desk sergeant walked a few paces to a door at the rear of the receiving area, where he engaged in a mumbled conversation with a homely secretary just inside. Minutes later the sergeant returned to Lucia and in the most confidential voice he could muster—quite close to her ear—he assured her that his intervention had been effective and that if she could be patient for just a little while, Chefe Suarez would grant her a fifteen-minute interview in his office. "Delightful!" she gushed in girlish appreciation. Lucia wondered if the chefe would be equally susceptible to that approach, or if something more serious and subdued would serve her better at his level.

It took only one glance at the chefe to conclude that this was a no-nonsense public official, and with a pencil poised above an open notebook she informed the chefe that, at the university, there was considerable interest in the mechanics of controlling overflow crowds without incurring any serious crime or public disturbance.

"I attended all three performances of the Buca Pittman Band," she noted, "and it seemed to me that there might have been as many as ten thousand people splayed out from the bandstand—they were on the grass, in the streets, and even up in trees and on rooftops. But there were no fights and no theft that I saw. How do you manage such a throng so well?"

"Well, thank you. It is a challenge, but we prepare well in advance. Our own police force would not be sufficient for overseeing all those visitors, and we borrow extensively from Pomerode, Indaial, Brusque, and even Joinville. We also hire some private security forces—and in this instance, we even had a detachment of American FBI people from their headquarters in Florianópolis."

"Goodness, that's unusual! Why would the American FBI want to be present at a festival in Santa Catarina?"

"Well, I can't go into that in detail. Obviously they aren't here for crowd control. They were hoping to see a particular person in the crowd. Something left over from the war, you know—but not at all related to the study you're doing. You're absolutely right; we estimated twelve thousand in total attendance for each of those concerts, and we made only fourteen arrests, all for drunk and disorderly conduct by young men. Here is our summary, which we are going to supply to the newspapers; if you can use it in preparing your report, it is yours. My name is Chefe Emilio Suarez, if you'd care to include it."

"Oh, thank you, Chefe! I surely will do so. One other quick question: I thought I saw a man I know in uniform, but I didn't know he was a police officer. His name is Kurt Hahn—do you know him?"

"Probably with one of the private security groups—no, I don't recognize the name."

"Well, thank you for taking the time, Chefe Suarez—and congratulations on a wonderful job. I'll send you a copy of my study when it is complete, and it surely will have your name prominently included."

After her interview with Chefe Suarez, Lucia used some of her spare time to learn more about Brazil's decision to join the war on the Allied side in 1942 and how this alliance might explain the presence of a United States FBI team in Catarina. A friend who taught history at the university told Lucia that as early as 1940, US President Roosevelt had become concerned with the possibility that Germans living along the Brazilian coastline were enabling U-boats to target the ships they sank.

Lucia scribbled each additional fragment of the picture in a small notebook.

> *FBI units in South America are called SIS, for Special Intelligence Service. They are charged with interrupting info sent to help U-Boats sink shipping.*

Later, she added:

> *SIS registered here as a business company: "Importers & Exporters Service . . . something." They work from US consulates. Including Florianópolis.*

Then, later:

> *Imp & Exp Serv gerente is Jerome Doyle; his oficina principal in New York City. Comes here often.*

But, despite the fact that German U-boats had destroyed over five thousand vessels in the South Atlantic while the war raged, that was no longer the concern of those SIS people in Florianópolis after the Axis surrender. Notation:

> *SIS FBI people still in Brazil. At Oktoberfest to watch for person(s) who might attend concerts. Sophia parents?*

Gerda and Kurt H? Who are they?

World War II had not affected Lucia directly, although Italy was designated as an enemy of Brazil because of its alliance with Germany. Brazil had sent about 27,000 of its young men to join Allied troops from other nations in the Mediterranean theater, and over 1,000 of them had lost their lives. Brazil's navy had joined in the Allied effort to counter the German U-boats, which took a high toll of Brazil's shipping in the Atlantic. Italy was condemned equally with Germany as the fighting involving Brazilian troops continued up the muddy Italian Peninsula. And because her parents were Italian immigrants to Brazil, the young woman experienced seriously divided loyalties as the war ground along. Now, with the war concluded, she was not certain whether she should attempt to help America capture escaped Germans or should help her two students and fellow immigrants to avoid detection. She was certain that she had stumbled upon a "wanted" German functionary, but she needed more time to consider whether she should be their unmasker or their concealer. She needed more time—and more information.

49

A Beginning and an Ending

It normally would have been walking distance for Elsa Danzig—from the Women's Club to the LaSalle—but as Gretchen Hasse, she wore high heels and a stylish sheath dress, both of which would have made walking uncomfortable on a warm Chicago evening. And so, she summoned a cab to curbside and sped past Tuesday-evening strollers to her destination—the LaSalle. She was ten minutes early, so she seated herself near the reception desk and watched several of the Windy City's most prominent residents and guests pass by. It wasn't far in distance from the mailroom at Sears Roebuck, but light-years away in terms of self-esteem. And to think that employees of the War Department got to partake of such luxury in the course of their work! It started a thought process in the attractive young woman as she indulged in people-watching.

"Well, hi there, Miss Hasse!" came the familiar voice from behind her. "I'm so pleased that you decided to join me. Hope I can be a more engaging dinner companion than I was in Prague."

"Ah—a different place and different circumstances, Mr. Carney; I think a fresh start would be good for both of us. Let's get caught up. Obviously you know quite a bit about me, but I'd like to hear about the War Department and your new function. Can we grab a Dubonnet—for old time's sake—and enjoy getting re-acquainted before dinner?"

"That was my intention—an aperitif in the Silver Grill Lounge, and then dinner in the Pump Room. And can we begin by being Bill and Elsa again—not so formal?"

"Let's be Bill and Gretchen—that's what's on my visa. Don't I look more like a Gretchen now?"

For the next forty-five minutes the two chatted at a corner table, concentrating only upon one another. He really wasn't one of the one-dimensional OSS cowboys about whom she'd been warned; Bill Carney had wide-ranging interests and a surprisingly playful sense of humor. He observed that "Gretchen" was more than just mailroom or bedroom material—she had that typical cultural underpinning of a European education and a very sharp mind.

Over dinner, conversation reverted to the business of their earlier encounters. Bill acknowledged that he had surmised from the contents of Elsa's Brazilian letter that Dieter the Piano Man in Rio de Janeiro was the same person who had been associated with Sofie von Seigler in Europe, and this knowledge had precipitated the tracking of her recent movements in hopes of finding her father, the former Wehrmacht general. The OSS had been happy to engage the FBI units in South America in the search, but now OSS itself was dissolved and the FBI's SSI organization was also being phased out. The War Department had inherited a few portfolios and some key OSS agents, but their principal purpose now was to design a new intelligence agency to meet the challenges of the postwar period, rather than recycle old issues—like escaped functionaries.

His frankness relaxed Elsa considerably, because she still felt guilty about her unprofessional loss of Dieter's letter in Prague. But now, apparently the Americans' appetite for apprehending wartime enemies was receding and they were instead busying themselves planning a new intelligence agency—which might even be interested in her. There was one more aspect of the puzzle she felt obliged to review with Bill Carney, if she were really seeking to earn his confidence.

"Bill, you are entitled to know a few more things before we turn the page on the pursuit of General von Seigler. First of all, you know that his daughter was born to the general and his Polish/Jewish secretary during his assignment to Poland prior to World War I. But you may not have put together the fact that Zofia von Seigler's mother is Lilka Rudovska, the retired Polish SWW operative who originally brought us together and recommended my services to you. Lilka loved her daughter, but when Zofia was sixteen, she sent her to live with her successful father in Berlin and he became the guiding figure in her life.

"Second, you should know that, after I had abetted Dieter's escape from Theresienstadt, the general provided assistance in getting him safely out of Europe. He knew that Dieter and his daughter had found happiness together prior to Dieter's capture, and he was faced with the difficult choice of helping a Jew escape or crushing his daughter's feelings. He made the compassionate choice, and then left his own post and career in Europe. Some believe that he stole huge amounts from oppressed people. I don't know if that is accurate, but I know that he was no longer able to abide the direction in which Hitler's National Socialists were taking their war. I don't want to be a part of tracking him down now or of impacting the lives of Dieter and Sofie."

"Goddamnit, Elsa. You're putting me into a terrible bind by burdening me with this additional stuff. The Wiesenthal Report on General von Seigler is still an active inquiry, and now I have pertinent information which could facilitate his capture. If I fail to follow up on the matter, it is dereliction of my sworn duty. If I do cause his capture, whatever relationship I might have with you would be history."

"And, is that important to you, Bill?"

"Yes, damnit—it is important and you are important. So there—is that what you wanted to hear?"

"Well—it's what I wanted to know. Can't say whether I expected to hear it. For a thirty-five-year-old, I'm pretty inexperienced at relationships; they've all been superficial and episodal. Suddenly somebody seems to be looking at me as more than an intelligence asset—or as a piece of meat—and I don't quite know how to behave."

"Well, if you're going to become Gretchen Hasse, that might be a prerequisite, don't you think? Gretchen is going to attract some serious interest in postwar America. Slick dresser, intriguing accent, sophisticated tastes . . ."

"Nice tits?"

"Oh, God—did I say that to you in Prague?"

"Um-hum. You did a professional appraisal across the dinner table and then tried to shock the little girl from Gdańsk you were planning to seduce in your apartment. Remember?"

"I'm afraid I do."

"You're funny, Bill. Maybe we both have spent too much time playing spy and haven't matured in our social skills. Hey, thank you for letting me get to know the rest of you a bit better. I really didn't want Prague to be our last encounter."

"Wanna look out at Chicago from the twentieth floor? My windows really offer a spectacular view of the city lights."

"That would be a really nice way to end our date—but understand that I'll be leaving at a proper hour, as Gretchen Hasse would certainly do. She doesn't stay the night like those Eurotrash ladies."

The two spent another hour in close conversation while Bill pointed out the major Chicago landmarks outside his windows. They shared the common excitement of discovering someone new and special, and at eleven o'clock, Gretchen shaped a lingering kiss on Bill's lips with both hands embracing his face. She drew back just a few inches and said, "I hope to hear from you soon." And then she was gone.

❧

Shortly after midnight she lay on her bed at the Women's Club, weighing the alternatives she believed were developing for her future. There was a smile on her face as she fell asleep to the night sounds of the big city. A train whistle blew as the Illinois Central's late train departed; cars honked at one another on Eleventh Street; and in the distance, multiple fire sirens pierced the night air. Before long she was embraced by a deep sleep.

The morning papers carried the full, horrible details:

> *The LaSalle Hotel had been booked solid and most guests were asleep when fire broke out at about 12:30 a.m. on Wednesday. It originated in the Silver Grill Cocktail Lounge, where wooden counters and table tops burned, then the flames quickly accelerated upward through air passages and elevator shafts, trapping many guests in their rooms. The flames caused several deaths, but thick, poisonous smoke also contributed to the instant loss of 61 lives. Over 200 more victims were overcome and many are listed in critical condition at nearby hospitals.*

Stunned, Elsa knew instinctively that the fantasies that had lulled her to sleep had been dashed in that conflagration. Moving as if in shock, she dressed slowly and walked somberly to Sears Roebuck.

THE WEATHER
Fair and warmer tonight. Increasing cloudiness Thursday.

The Detroit News

Home Edition

THE HOME NEWSPAPER FOR MORE THAN 72 YEARS

WEDNESDAY, JUNE 5, 1946, 73rd Year, No. 266 — *A Politically Independent Publication, Not Affiliated With Any Group of Newspapers* — 40 PAGES   C   FIVE CENTS

57 DIE, 200 HURT AS FIRE SWEEPS CHICAGO HOTEL

★ ★ ★   ★ ★ ★   ★ ★ ★   ★ ★ ★

2 Pages of Wire Pictures From the Scene

Death Hits Children on Trip to Zoo

Bus Is Wrecked; Score Injured

Guests Cry for Help as Flames Spurt From Windows

LaSalle Hotel guests trapped on upper floors are shown begging for aid as tongues of flames leap from windows below them—Associated Press Wirephoto.
(Two pages of fire pictures—See Pages 12 and the Back Page.)

LaSalle Lobby Is Death Trap

Many on Upper Floors Are Killed in Leaps; Smoke Fatal to Others

CHICAGO, June 5—(AP)—Fire flashed through the lower floors of the 23-story La Salle Hotel early today, leaving a toll of 57 dead and 200 injured.

Flames Envelop Walls of Bar and Lobby

Bodies of Mother and Child Found on Roof

Bread Lines Spot Nation

Winter Wheat Crop to Bring Aid in July

Italy Votes Monarchy Out by 1,800,000

List of Identified Dead

Mrs. Patton and Son Off on Visit to Grave

Reporter Sees Fire Start

By CLAIRE COX

Crow Delays Takeoff of Plane for London

In The News Today

See EYEWITNESS—Page 4

The *Detroit News* on June 6, 1946, described the horror of the LaSalle Hotel fire.
Photo: Courtesy of the *Detroit News*.

50

The Fazenda

Gerda and Kurt Hahn sipped caipirinhas, a favorite Brazilian cocktail made from their own sugarcane hard liquor mixed with sugar, lime juice, and crushed ice. From comfortable wicker rocking chairs on the west porch of their dwelling they could look over a broad expanse of grasslands, now amber in the late-afternoon sunlight.

"Our first chance to relax together in a while, dear girl," the ersatz rancher commented. "You have been more than patient through our Oktoberfest adventures—I truly appreciate your understanding."

"Otto—how long have we been together? Four, five years? During all that time Sofie has constantly been in your thoughts, and finally you had the chance to see her up close as a woman and as a star performer. It was important for me, too, you know. I never had a child, but I can understand how parents never let go of that role, and I am happiest when you are smiling."

"So, how do you imagine Sofie as a mother, Branka?"

"Well, they say that different hormones take over when a mother first holds her baby, and all other concerns become secondary. Nature builds that into females."

"You didn't answer my question."

"Sofie didn't really have a role-model mother; Lilka's devotion to her nation and government responsibilities always came first with her. And then, Sofie went to live with you in Berlin at what? Fifteen or sixteen? Just when girls begin to be young women. You were involved in your career, too, and suddenly you were both immersed in wartime. I'm not certain how she evolved from a shy little Polska to a celebrated chanteuse while fleeing across occupied Europe with a homosexual piano player. Perhaps she got her motherhood training caring for that Dieter chap?"

"No, it hasn't been easy, and I think that she has navigated the cross-currents well—but sometimes a bit selfishly, too."

"That must be hard for you to say, Otto. I have thought it, but would never have said it to you if you hadn't opened the door. It happens to attractive and talented people, you know. Others want to be with them and recognized by them, and in their eagerness they sometimes foster a sense of entitlement in those special people.

"With a talented, beautiful young woman, it can take the form of gifts or preference, and her expectations grow with each flattering act. I know that you designated Sofie as your hostess while she was still a student, and that put her into the company of very important people in Germany. You invited her to sing when you entertained, and I'm sure some of your celebrated guests went out of their way to encourage her—even to help her. No?"

"Of course, but she has remained gracious and thankful. She's considerate, and much of her success has resulted from her own effort—not from being moved ahead of the queue by others."

"How did she first get to sing with Django and Grappelli, Otto? Remember, you told me about it."

"The King of the Gypsies, Janusz Kwiek, called them to the table where she was sitting, and they humored him by letting her do a number. But … but she surprised the group and captivated the audience by herself once she was on the stage. The audience asked for song after song, based upon her performance."

"Yes, Schatzi—but an important Gypsy leader convinced a popular Gypsy musician to let her sing in a major showplace. She could not have opened that door for herself, don't you see? But we are getting away from your question now. You are concerned about whether she will be able to balance her career ambitions with the less glamorous responsibilities of a mother—dealing with dirty nappies, late-night feedings, crying—all those things we missed, Otto!"

❧

Otto raised his hand, interrupting the conversation, and pointed at a dust trail rolling up the long driveway toward the fazenda. No one had called from the little guardhouse, which was quite unusual, unless the car's driver was expected by Gerda and Kurt Hahn. Then he saw the distinctive yellow color of the small Willys which belonged to their language instructor.

"Do we have any more language lessons? I thought we completed our course last month. Why would our professora be coming here now?"

"I suppose we'll know in a minute. Relax. Be sure to greet her in Portuguese. Ha!"

"Boa tarde, professora—coma vai?" It brought a quick response as the little vehicle came to a halt and its door opened.

"Olá, Gerda and Kurt—my car seems to know the way here and we both have missed seeing you. May I join you for a few minutes? It's so beautiful at this time of day."

"Join us in enjoying our afternoon caipirinhas," Gerda insisted as her husband moved a third chair to the front of the porch. "It is so nice of you to come this way—but aren't you a long distance from your university?"

"I had a midday appointment in Florianópolis and am on my way back to Joinville. The best roads take me near here, and I wanted to speak with you two, so . . . well, here I am."

"So this doesn't have to do with our language lessons? What then?"

"Well, *queridos amigos*—this has to do with something for which I first owe you an apology. You have graciously invited me to join you for *refeição noturna* on many occasions—lovely dinners with you in your home, following our language sessions. And, when I've needed to visit a *banheiro*, you have directed me down a hallway past your private living quarters, and my curiosity has drawn me to a photograph and a wall poster within your master suite, which is a room I should not have presumed to enter—but I did."

"Likenesses of a young, blonde woman. Yes?"

"Exactly. And I became curious about her relationship to you. The prominence of the two likenesses made it clear that she was, or is, very important in this fazenda. But you never referred to having a child or other relationship which would account for the placement— where you would see her as you began each morning and again in the evenings before dropping off to sleep. "

"And why was that important to you?"

"Just a part of my instinctive interest in the people I greatly enjoy. Nothing sinister. But then, my curiosity grew much stronger when I saw that same young woman's face on Oktoberfest posters and I learned that she would be in Blumenau performing. When I asked if you were planning to attend, I expected an enthusiastic answer and possibly even some confirmation of your relationship to the singer. But that didn't happen. You passed over it with no hint of interest."

"But you continued to be intrigued. So what did you do?"

"Well, I attended the three concerts featuring the singer Sophia and, observing her, I felt certain that she was the same person. So, I walked among the couples seated on the lawn, thinking I might recognize you in folding chairs or on a blanket near the stage. Then I saw the presentation of flowers to the singer through the intermediary of a policeman—and suddenly I understood that she is important to you and that you went to great lengths to be near her but to avoid being seen."

"So, what more do you want to know?"

"Wait—I already know more, and my purpose in coming here is to inform you, not me. Please hear me out, Kurt. I later asked the Blumenau police chief about the excellent control of that large number of revelers. I told him I was preparing a report for publication. He told me about augmenting Blumenau with police from other regional forces, but he added that a unit of US FBI men from Florianópolis came here, too—looking for a particular military officer.

"Earlier today I met with a Mr. Jerome Doyle in Florianópolis, interviewing him regarding the final days of FBI presence in Brazil. He wasn't sure how I knew his people were in our community in the first place, but he said that his group's mission had uncovered many spies and sabotage plots while Brazil was a wartime ally of the USA. I asked about future pursuit of former Axis leaders who have come to live in Brazil, and he said that his people have no jurisdiction to pursue them, and that if they are tracked down at all, the thrust of that effort might come from Jewish survivors of Nazi internment camps in Europe. Either he was telling me that there is no current American effort to search among the German-Brazilian community for such fugitives, or he is actively looking and wants to keep the effort secret. Why would he send twenty-four agents to Oktoberfest if there is no assignment to find one or more of those people?"

"And why have you come here to tell us about your research and conclusion?"

"Because I'm reasonably certain that you are Sophia's German father, who disappeared from Europe in 1943. And I'm guessing that she is being followed in hopes of encountering you. And finally, based upon my friendship with you, I believe that you deserve the chance to re-start your life in this young nation—much as my own family has done."

"Thank you. I believe I understand," Kurt responded. "Please stay and partake of refeição noturna with us; we are having Gerd's delicious Oktoberfest schnitzel with some of my best '39 Gruner Veltliner. You won't find that anywhere else in Brazil, professora. What say?"

❧

Four hours later, an inebriated young woman guided her Willys slowly down the hill from the fazenda. Gerda and Kurt Hahn waved to her from their porch and watched until the glow from the little car's headlights blended into the Brazilian night sky.

Gerda raised her eyebrow quizzically and asked, "So, what do you think, General?"

The stolid man beside her flicked away a small piece of the crust from schnitzel, which had adhered to his soft shirt. "It is dangerous having so much personal information moving about our community, Branka."

51

❧

The Tour Moves to São Paulo

São Paulo had long been the center of a prime Brazilian agricultural region, and the crops of coffee and other foods which originated near there were moved to the proximate seaport of Santos, from which they could sail over the Atlantic Ocean to waiting world markets.

However, late in the nineteenth century, immigrants from Italy and Germany began the city's transformation into an industrial and financial center. A principal mover among those entrepreneurial newcomers was one Count Francisco Matarazzo, who emigrated to the area from Sicily and created a business empire and an impressive family, aggregating fourteen children.

Before World War I broke out, a favorite Matarazzo daughter named Lydia married a prominent Doctor Pignatari in Naples, Italy, and in 1917 she delivered a strapping son there. He was named Francisco Matarazzo Pignatari, but he was called Baby from his earliest years, when his parents moved from Italy to Brazil. His two formidable family names gave Baby a running start in Brazil, and by age twenty, he was already managing a large metal products company. Baby became one of the wealthiest men in South America at an early age, but he was better known for his flamboyant style and insatiable appetite for beautiful and talented women.

Baby had first noticed the international singer named Sophia when she auditioned with the Buca Pittman Orchestra at the Copacabana Palace Hotel in Rio de Janeiro, and on that occasion he had conveyed his appreciation in the form of an armload of white roses handed to her by a smiling street vendor, in front of a full house of sophisticated diners and music lovers. A few weeks later, in Buenos Aires, he had encouraged the inclusion of the Pittman Orchestra and their new featured vocalist in a huge benefit performance celebrated at the venerable Teatro Colón. The newspapers had lavished attention on the event because of its sponsorship by Argentina's presumed next president, Juan Domingo Perón, but the prized tabloid photos from the event had been those of Colonel and Señora Perón huddled with Baby and the voluptuous vocalist Sophia.

It had set off ripples of conjecture about yet another Pignatari conquest, but only Baby knew that the evening had ended with him assisting the vomiting beauty to her room and helping her to remove her gown before she collapsed into bed. It had not been so much chivalry as pride that ended that long evening with a naked woman asleep alone in her bed and her tall, handsome escort dabbing at food stains on his formalwear before leaving. It had indeed been a late evening of intimacy, but not the variety Baby wanted to project.

A lot had transpired since that encounter in BA, and normally it would have been filed away in some neglected corner of Baby's memory bank, but something about the combination of Sophia's innocent vulnerability with her physical perfection continued to torment him. He knew that the Pittman Orchestra would be ending its current tour in São Paulo, the center of his sphere of influence, and he constructed an important event which could collaterally bring him into contact with Sophia again.

For fifteen years Brazil's direction had been overseen by President Getúlio Vargas, and the country had inched toward prosperity until it could not avoid becoming embroiled in World War II. During the first eight months of 1942, "neutral" Brazil lost thirteen merchant ships to the marauding German U-boats, and on August 22 of that year, the country finally entered the war on the Allied side. But quickly there were charges that the Vargas government was secretly aligned with the Nazis, even as Brazilian troops were fighting with the Allies in Italy. Under pressure, President Vargas resigned and Brazil's war minister, Eurico Gaspar Dutra, emerged as the probable new leader for the country. Baby knew that Dutra was opposed to communism and in favor of national capitalism, and he became an early supporter of the new leader. He understood that support of Dutra could give a significant boost to his growing industrial complex.

❧

The 600-kilometer drive from Blumenau to São Paulo passed through some of the continent's most engaging scenery, but it also meant diesel smoke, rough roads, and cramped seats for over ten hours, which was not an attractive scenario for the already uncomfortable Sophia. When Buca indicated that she take a seat next to him, her patience for the trip became even thinner.

"I have some good news to share with you, Sofie," he began, "but it's not totally arranged yet, so it must be just between us for now."

"I'm fascinated, boss," she replied, with one raised eyebrow making it clear that Buca's surprises were not always received as golden nuggets. "What is it that's brightening your morning?"

"Well, you know that President Vargas has stepped down, and we're going to have a new president before long. Our friend Baby Pignatari is close to the probable successor, and he's planning an elaborate gathering at his seaside house in Guarujá just about the time we complete our gig in São Paulo. He has invited the Pittman Orchestra to provide the music for a dinner dance, and he is picking up the tab for us to spend three days in Guarujá."

"Where in hell is Guarujá, Buca? Halfway up the damned Amazon River?"

"Now settle down, *mi amor*. It is just north of Santos on the seacoast. A little more than an hour's drive from São Paulo and a beautiful place to rest and relax at the end of our tour before we return to Rio. Only one evening of work and the chance to become the favorite musicians of some of the country's most prominent people. If we do well, it will virtually assure a full schedule for us."

"You're telling me that the tour is going to continue for three additional days, and that Baby may be stalking me in his own enclave during part of that time, right? You know I'll do it for you and the guys, Buca, but I don't want any headline photos like the ones in BA. I understand that was mainly my fault, but this has all been new to me, and there has been a lot to learn."

"Sofie, look at it this way: In only about ten weeks you will have visited some of the most famous cities on this continent and sung for two men who will soon be the presidents of their countries. Large, sophisticated audiences have learned your name, and you have earned as much money as you'd see in a year of working a small room in the Copa. Lola would have sacrificed her firstborn for a gig like that, and we made it pretty easy for you."

"I'm sorry, Booker. I'm just tired, I guess. Do you mind if I sleep for a while? Bus rides don't agree with me. I'll be ready to give it my best in São Paulo—and in that little place by the ocean, too."

"Guarujá."

She hoped that she could camouflage her pregnancy in performance gowns for another week and that Baby wouldn't be expecting his guests to participate in a pool party during their command performance for Brazil's future president. Sofie fell asleep smiling at the thought of reviewing these little stories with Dieter, back on their sun-washed terrace.

52

—————

✤

End of the Blues

"Two months!" Dieter exclaimed. "We've been out there forty nights, exploring a new musical form together. Would you have believed it possible when we began? I wasn't sure we could find enough material or enough interested people for a week's work, but the audiences have gotten larger and more enthusiastic. And, it's been great for the Copa."

"I know, querido. I had the feeling that we were getting more creative every time we set up, and it required fewer and fewer prompts. You seemed to know where I was going as soon as I did, so it took all the fear out of improvising. Like you could read my mind. That hasn't happened for me often, but it made all the difference working with our blues format."

"Y'know what I'd like to have if we do this again? I'd like a mobile microphone so you could move out among the tables. Increase the feeling of intimacy, like those violinists who move among the tables in Paris. You could even sing to an individual guest for a few bars when that seems appropriate—make it really intimate. What do you think?"

"I think I'd better wait until I'm not pregnant before I venture away from a spotlight concentrated only on my face and shoulders. I'd be like a cow that slipped out of the barnyard if I got close to those little tables now. You don't know how awkward it is to move a protruding belly and big caboose among close tables in the dark while trying to remember the melody we're working. It could be like a slapstick comedy, Dieter."

"Well, you've never tripped over me in the dark, Lola. Light as a ballet dancer."

"Ha—you're easy for a naked lady to find in the dark, Piano Man!"

"Devil woman."

It was the final night of a partnership that had gone well beyond the goals either had contemplated two months earlier. Since neither had foreseen it, neither had prepared for the painful feelings that came with the last chorus. Lola chose a closing song recently featured in a popular American movie and sung by the dancer Fred Astaire. It was called "One for My Baby and One More for the Road," and she worked its forty-eight bars and a soulful key change like a natural professional blues singer. When she and Dieter finished and extended their hands toward the appreciative Copa audience, each had tear-brimmed eyes and a twinge of regret for what had transpired.

✍

Back at his Ipanema apartment, they moved about silently while Lola tossed together a plate of *picadinho*—Brazilian hash—and Dieter relaxed with a cigarette in his favorite chaise. Neither wanted to break the silence first, but both knew that they were at the end of a comfortable and productive relationship. It would require exploration, conversation, and regrets. Finally it was Dieter who cleared his throat and began to speak.

"Lola, you and I never expected any of this to happen, and now we're at a point where we can't just ignore it and proceed along the same road. You understand that, no? Where one door closes another always opens. Our 'Blues Nights' have opened a door we didn't know was there ten weeks ago. I think you'll be in a good position to build that format into your own business on the beach, and I'm going to try to give you my full support when you launch it."

"What does that 'support' mean, Dieter? Would you appear with me or help me to get the money needed to start the business? Or would you point others in my direction to be my patrons? Or would you just wish me well in your Sunday prayers? There are so many levels of 'support,' and just that word alone doesn't do much to make up for my loss."

"Loss?"

"You! I'm losing you, Dieter. Our time together has been the center of my life for weeks now. We have created music together; discussed myriad subjects, and made love under the absurd condition I'm in. It's the most intimate relationship I've ever had, and in one snap of the fingers it will disappear. Your promise of support—whatever that means to you—is no substitute for yourself. Got it?"

"I'm so very sorry, Lola. You had needs and I did, too. We moved from mutual loneliness to new feelings of belonging in just hours, and it made everything better for a while. But I thought we both understood that it was more like a holiday trip than moving to a new home. If I had no other obligation, I would be celebrating with you tonight—but I have a deep relationship which began in 1938 and sustained me through years in Theresienstadt and has helped me to emerge from that ordeal. My feelings for Sofie and for you are totally different—and each is important to me. It's complicated, but most emotional attachments are complicated. Would it have been better had I just refused to be a part of your life? I don't think so, do you?"

"No, I don't, Dieter. But understand that when I walk out of here for the last time, I'll be totally alone; you'll be celebrating the resumption of a precious love story. It's not the same. It's really not!"

"We'll share the same memories, and they'll be uniquely ours forever, Lola. Cherish what has been and don't lament what might have been."

53

Guarujá

As promised, the drive down the hills from São Paulo to the roadway along the Atlantic coast took less than ninety minutes, and soon their bus was passing through small groupings of houses adjacent to broad, white, sandy beaches and the long, rolling waves which washed onto them. Sofie could see several well-kept villas behind lush floral hedges and imagined that soon they would be turning into one of the larger ones. Instead they continued through a small village and then turned onto a long, white pier, which extended outward for at least fifty meters, where it resolved into a large boat mooring.

Waiting there was a covered barge with abundant deck capacity and a crew of eight men in matching white uniforms. Within minutes they had helped the musicians of the Buca Pittman Orchestra into individual seats and pushed off, with powerful twin diesel engines growling and a white bow wave leaping outward on each side.

Sofie shrugged her shoulders at Buca and shouted over the engine noise. "Where are we going? Guarujá was back there."

"Baby has his own island," was the smiling reply. "You'll be able to see it ahead in another few minutes." And soon it hove into view—a patch of tropical green trees etched across the blue waters with a palatial white building on the highest point of land. Once again, Baby's extravagance had exceeded her expectations, and she knew there would be more surprises after she stepped from the barge and entered the uniquely beautiful structure above.

The orchestra's first performance was to be in the ballroom of the mansion after dinner that evening, and Buca and Sophia had been invited to dine with Baby's guests on a terrace overlooking the water. Dinner was four hours away and she had free time until then. Her room had a small walled balcony with comfortable seating, and in minutes Sofie had fallen asleep in the warm sunlight with the sound of waves lapping at the little island's seawall.

She hadn't realized how tired the long tour had left her, but, stretched on her back with free time, she resolved not to undertake any more commitments like this one, no matter the lure of luxury and fame.

She might have remained asleep in the sunlight much longer had not a knock on her door wakened her. In response to her acknowledgment, she was informed in Portuguese that dinner would be served in forty-five minutes—not very long for a performer to squeeze into her glamorous gown, pile her hair into a cascade of summer curls, and add a touch of rouge to her tanned face. Sofie realized that creating Sophia so far into her pregnancy had become very time-consuming, so she quickly returned the sequined sheath dress to her suitcase and instead slipped into a more comfortable long white cotton pullover which gave no hint of her amplifying body. Its only concession to glamour was the deep neckline, where viewers would be drawn to the contrast between her skin color and the creamy fabric. She stepped into her most elevating shoes and descended the curving stairway to the dining terrace below with renewed confidence in her wholesome good looks.

Whatever her apprehensions about Baby's pursuit might have been, the seating chart for the forty-eight-place dining table gave her immediate relief. Baby was, naturally, at the head of the table, in a chair that looked shamelessly like some royal throne, with a seat level two inches higher than those of his dinner guests. To Baby's right, his guest of honor was, appropriately, the new president of the country, Gaspar Dutra, a smallish man who seemed embarrassed by all of the attention he was receiving.

Of more interest to Sofie was the lady seated at Baby's left—one Marina Parodi Delfino, a pretty enough Italian woman with delicate features and a genuine smile. When she inquired, Sofie was shocked to learn that Marina had married Baby when he was only twenty-three, and that he limited his philandering to his time away from her. Sofie immediately concluded that Marina would be getting most of her handsome host's attention over the weekend, and with that assurance, she relaxed and looked forward to what would be her final appearance on the tour as vocalist with the Pittman Orchestra. Perhaps the additional three days really was the good news Buca had celebrated.

Sofie's place card was near the middle of the long table. A grizzled Brazilian naval officer was seated to her left, and he began providing a running account to all those in his vicinity of how the anemic Brazilian Navy had been integrated into the US Navy as a part of their futile effort to keep merchant ships safe from the marauding German U-boats in the South Atlantic. She wasn't certain whether naval warfare or international business would be less interesting over dinner; the American to her right extended his hand and said, "Jerry Doyle, Importers and Exporters Service Company from New York City. How are you, Miss Sophia?"

"Delighted to meet you, Mr. Doyle; I hope my English won't be too hard for you to understand. I've been shuttling between Portuguese and Spanish on this tour, so please feel free to correct me if I make an error. What brings you to this beautiful little island?"

"I'm sure there won't be any language problem—but don't you and Booker communicate in English? He's an American, I believe."

"Usually we use Portuguese—Buca's been here since thirty-seven, and most of the boys in his orchestra are Latinos. When he talks about the great musicians he played with up north, he sometimes switches to English, because that's the way the good stories were—how do you say—concocted? How do you know Baby, Mr. Doyle? Does your company supply something for his steel mill?"

"No, no. We're not in manufacturing. We're more of a wartime consulting firm, trying to keep hostile activity to a minimum in friendly, neighboring countries. I've been back and forth between the States and here all through the war. You know, there are lots of Axis agents and sympathizers in Brazil and Argentina, and we try to keep a lid on their effectiveness—do a pretty good job, too."

"Well, with the war ended, are you finished with your work, or are there still some matters to require your attention here?"

"Loose ends—yeah, that's it—loose ends. How about you, Miss Sophia—all music?"

"That's what I do. I never was interested in politics and I was able to work in my profession through the war. I moved to Brazil in forty-three and have made my home here, that is until Buca offered me the chance to be his vocalist on this wonderful tour. I hadn't been outside Rio until two months ago, and now I have seen other places. I'm ready to get back to Rio."

"Where was your home in Europe?"

"Oh. I was born in Kraków; went to college in Berlin; lived for a while in Prague; lived in occupied France, and finally sang with an orchestra in London. Pretty much all over the place. My passport is Swiss, because of family origins there. The same music is popular in all those places, so I'm a bit of an international diplomat. Does that make sense, Mr. Doyle?"

He was being too inquisitive, so she excused herself for an extended visit to the banheiro, and when she returned to the table she quickly engaged the old sailor in conversation about the waters surrounding Baby's island. She shifted her position just enough to expose ample cleavage to assure his undivided attention. Who indeed was Mr. Jerry Doyle from America? Could he be one more of the trackers with little cameras trying to catch her meeting with her father?

Somehow music always sounded better to Sofie outside under the stars. It didn't have to deflect off hard surfaces or risk being swallowed into soft ones; instead it floated away in the moist air and joined the growl of distant thunder and cries of seabirds bedding down for the night. She was scheduled to offer three solos and had already delivered five when Buca signaled that it was time for the orchestra to begin its medley of "good night" standards.

There were no vocals in the mix, so she stepped to the side and closed her eyes to better hear the skillfully blended instruments begin with "Good Night, Sweetheart."

A large hand grasped hers and a deep masculine voice inquired, "May I have this dance, Sophia?" When she opened her eyes, they were only inches from those of Francisco Matarazzo Pignatari, the consensus-perfect blend of masculine adventure, elegance, and raw lust.

"Why not, Baby?" she responded with a smile of surrender as she placed her free hand on his right hip and raised his left hand to the level of her shoulder while transitioning into the first graceful steps of the last dance. Somehow she knew that Baby would be a superb dancer, and their movement together was flawless. They floated past a blur of his guests' faces and Sofie knew that she saw Buca, Brazil's new president, Baby's wife, and the enigmatic Jerry all smiling in the crowd. When the medley finally ended, they were outside in the moonlight, and no one had the temerity to interrupt the moment.

"I had to speak with you, Sophia," he began. "So much was wrong when I left you in the Alvear in BA, and I'm not good at putting things into writing. I can imagine that you awoke at some point and couldn't remember how or with whom you had gotten to your room."

"Or why I was totally naked in my bed with the draperies pulled and my clothes folded on a chair and why the room attendant told me that the gentleman had departed some time ago."

"Well, I was the gentleman. After we were photographed with Perón and Evita, you said you thought you might faint—but before you could do that, you gagged and threw up, mostly on me. I found your room key in your purse and got two waiters to help me move you to the elevator. For a few minutes you were violently sick, and then you were totally passed out, but breathing well. I cleaned your face and hair with a wet towel, but you were still covered with foul liquid—so I pulled all your clothes off and finished cleaning you. I was able to lower you into the bed and surround you with pillows until I was sure you were past the vomiting spells. After an hour, I made myself presentable and left—but I engaged the housekeeping lady on duty to check on you regularly. Next day she assured me that you got started again. I'm so sorry that I didn't tell you this earlier, but I thought you would know that 'nothing happened' during the night."

Sofie stood on her toes and planted a kiss on Baby's cheek, then stepped back. "That is so sweet of you, Francisco; and I am very relieved. You see, I'm well into my first pregnancy, and it would bother me forever if I thought I had . . . " She wiped away a tear and continued, "Nobody here knows that, and I think I can keep it a secret until we are back in Rio. Will you do me that one additional favor?"

"That plus one more. Your dinner companion, Mr. Doyle, is only posing as a businessman. It's a cover for his work with the American FBI, which has been with us in Brazil throughout the war. When he learned that the Pittman Orchestra was playing for this gathering of business leaders with President Dutra, he asked officially to be invited and to be seated by you. Be careful—you apparently have some knowledge he is trying to obtain."

"Don't say any more, Francisco. I know the matter, and you should not be burdened with the knowledge. But thank you once again. I'm deeply indebted. Now go dance with your wife—she's a lucky lady."

54

─────────

❧

After the Fox

Chefe Suarez arrived at the Delegacia do Pólicia building in Blumenau a few minutes after eight o'clock on a Friday morning, and he moved quickly to his office with only a few mumbled words to the night sergeant and his secretary, who quickly fell in behind the Chefe, carrying a steaming cup and a small stack of papers.

"Anything that won't wait? I need time for a haircut and massage this morning to work out some kinks."

His secretary knew that on Fridays the Chefe often enjoyed the company of his favorite masseuse at a nearby hotel. It was his reward to himself after the rigors of a week in his rolling armchair. "There are a couple of things for you to sign—on the top of the pile, boss— and a petition from the Marian Society of the Paróquia Santo Antonio to investigate charges of prostitution in Himmelblau Palace Hotel."

"Please let them know that I'm going personally to follow up on those allegations today."

They both chuckled for a moment, but then she resumed her dour expression. "You know that we had a fatal automobile accident north of here last night, don't you? Up near Massaranduba, where the road is so close to the river."

"What did he do—miss that sharp curve and go over the edge? Some drunk *menino* does that every few months. Any passengers?"

"Fortunately not, but it wasn't a young boy; it was a woman who appeared to have been about thirty, and she might have been struck by a larger vehicle. She was driving a little yellow Willys and it did tumble off that high ledge, as you guessed."

"Aw, that's so sad. What do we know about her?"

"Well, I think you may have known her. Remember the attractive lady who came in shortly after Oktoberfest and talked to you about crowd control during the festival?"

He filled his mouth with a huge bite from his rosquinha, drowned in the coffee, then blurted, "'Course I remember her—a sweetheart; was gonna write something nice about me for some school publication, wasn't she?"

"Exactly, Chefe. She was from the university in Joinville and you told her how we got extra crowd control people on the streets during that week. She was really interested in the FBI people who came up from the coast. I was, too."

"Lookin' for spies, they were. Germans and Italians who slipped in here to avoid capture or reprisal back in Europe. But they were looking for a particular guy that week—Nazi general who stole a fortune. Yeah, I remember her. What was the cause of death?"

"Blunt object—blow to the back of her head. Probably the roof of the car."

"Awful! Had an Italian name, I think—didn't she?"

"DeSimone, Chefe. Lucia DeSimone. Single. Language teacher. Family in the area—we're contacting them now. Can I tell them we're investigating the accident? They'll want to know."

"What'd you say about being struck by a larger vehicle?"

"Oh—the officer's report said there was impact with painted metal high up on the driver's side door. There's no painted metal at the spot where she left the road. It left a deep dent. Could have been enough velocity to drive the little car sideways—sideways off the road, that is."

"Anything unusual in the little car?"

"Let's see. An overnight case with clothes; a roadmap of Santa Catarina state; a *maleta* with several pages of handwriting; *bolsa* with some money; small hand towel with something which might be vomit on it; more of the same substance on the front of her clothing; car keys and what looks like house keys; and—"

"Anybody look at the contents of the maleta?"

"Don't think so, Chefe—you wanna take a look at it? We have it in the lockup."

"I do. Can you get it here by early afternoon? I'm going out for a couple hours now."

❧

By midafternoon Chefe Suarez had picked through all the materials in the briefcase and had focused upon a handwritten account titled, *On the trail of General Otto von Seigler.* It contained the deceased teacher's description of a German couple living on a fazenda near Blumenau and it linked a photograph and a poster in their dwelling to the singer Sophia, thought to be General von Seigler's daughter. She had added to her account the FBI agents' futile monitoring of Sophia's performances during Oktoberfest, where they hoped to interrupt a meeting of the general and his daughter. Her final entry in the brief account mentioned her drive to the US consulate in Florianópolis, where she was able to confirm with FBI agent Jerome Doyle that the US War Department had enlisted the FBI's assistance in their ongoing search for the elusive general.

Suarez thought to himself that the young woman had done some excellent investigative work, even though there was no indication whether she intended to assist in the general's apprehension or was merely satisfying her own curiosity. When the Florianópolis FBI office had contacted Suarez about monitoring attendees at the Oktoberfest musical events, there had been little mention to the Chefe of the reason for their interest, and he hadn't been made aware of any reward for information leading to capture of the German general. Nevertheless, he instructed his secretary to try to reach Agent Doyle by telephone that afternoon. He sensed that someone out there was eager to find the fugitive, and usually that meant some form of compensation for valuable information.

❧

"Good afternoon, Chefe Suarez. This is Jerome Doyle of Importers and Exporters Service Company calling you from the US consulate in Florianópolis. I received a message that you might have some information regarding a person we have been seeking."

"Good afternoon to you, Mister Doyle. Yes, early in September, we were asked by your office if you could add twenty-four American FBI operatives to our Blumenau Police Battalion during the Oktoberfest concerts, and quite naturally we accommodated that request. It was my understanding then that the daughter of a fugitive German military officer—a professional singer—would be here, and that he might try to contact her during the time she was in our city. Is that essentially correct?"

"Yes, it is. But, why the call now after the celebrants and entertainers have all left?"

"Well—sometimes pertinent information doesn't surface exactly when we want or need it. That's the case here. If there is still an active interest in finding that individual, and if there's a meaningful reward from some interested party, it might be timely for you to come over to Blumenau and take a ride in the countryside with me."

"You're saying that you have some new information on his whereabouts?"

"Could be—but who's interested in finding him? This is a heavily German community and a Brazilian police chief shouldn't risk public disapproval for trivial reasons. Has some government authority indicted him or offered a reward for his capture? I have no authority to arrest him myself. Do you understand the delicacy of my position?"

"Chefe, the United States and Brazil are allies. Our War Department has received complaints against this individual from a European organization of Jewish survivors of Nazi aggression. Our OSS began an investigation in Europe and our FBI units in Brazil have been continuing the search. If you can facilitate his capture, I would use my best efforts to recognize your help appropriately."

"When can you come to Blumenau, Mister Doyle? We could drive to the location where he might be living within an hour and you'll know fairly quickly whether the resident there could be a Nazi general in hiding. If so, I'm always authorized to hold any suspect for two days while proper extradition routines are followed. It's your decision—I wouldn't be comfortable doing this on my own."

"That's understandable, Chefe. How about I come to your office next Tuesday—about ten—and we can talk this over in private and then take a look at the lead you've gotten. This has proven to be an enigma so far; I hope you are onto something."

55

―

Chicago

Her supervisor at Sears Roebuck appeared suddenly at Gretchen Hasse's work station and told her that "a man from the War Department" was in the reception room on the first floor, requesting to speak with Gretchen. "I've checked his identification and he seems to be the real thing. Nice-looking fellow named Joseph English—called Assistant Director of Investigations—from Washington DC," she asserted. "If you want to talk with him, we can go down now and I'll put you in a private office with a telephone. But if you'd rather not, I'll get his number and tell him you'll call when you're free to do so."

"Did he tell you what it's about?" the slightly flustered clerk queried. "My papers are all in order and I don't have anything to do with the War Department."

"Nope. Seemed to think you'd know the subject matter."

"Well, I guess I should talk to him while he's here, rather than having to go someplace else and waste time. But, does the phone in that office have a call button? If he gets obnoxious I want to be able to get away from him—fast!"

"We'll cover you, Gretchen. But he doesn't look like a

threatening type. It's probably some technicality or request for info on somebody you know. I'll tell him you're coming down in the next ten minutes."

❧

"Good afternoon, Miss Hasse. I'm Joe English. I was Bill Carney's associate at OSS in London when we first got the information on General von Seigler from Simon Wiesenthal. We already knew that OSS would soon be disbanded, but Bill was intrigued by Wiesenthal's account of currency and bullion 'liberated' from Poland's national banks. He championed the idea that we should investigate the accusation and find the general. I believe Bill contacted you as a part of his search?"

"He did. In Prague, where I was living. A mutual friend arranged for us to meet."

"That friend was Lilka Rudovska from the Polish Intelligence Service?"

"The SWW, yes."

"And you helped Mr. Carney in his search?"

"Oh, you'd have to ask him whether I was helpful. We met for dinner and talked about that matter but also discussed my availability to work for whatever intelligence service your country might assemble within Europe after OSS was closed. I had spent several years in Czechoslovakia during the war years, and the knowledge I acquired had the potential to be useful to the U.S., but on balance, I thought it better not to make that association."

"But you acquainted Bill with the relationship among the General, his daughter, Sofie, and a German named Dieter Meister, who was her companion?"

"Not intentionally—he came into possession of a letter from Mr. Meister to me, which he read without my permission. From the contents, it was clear to Mr. Carney that Dieter Meister had been captured and imprisoned by the Nazis, and that I had a minor role in his escape. It also placed Dieter in Brazil currently, which was useful information for Mr. Carney's search."

"And, after that, are you aware that Bill was able to involve the FBI's people in South America, and that they were actively observing Sofie—or 'Sophia,' as she calls herself professionally—with the assumption that she would make contact with the general at some time?"

"That would be logical."

"Did you tell Dieter that this pursuit was going on wherever Sofie moved?"

"Mr. English, I haven't seen Dieter in four years, and I have only fragmentary knowledge of the FBI and its efforts to follow the daughter. They are very perspicacious people and not likely to overlook clumsy Americans following them in foreign countries. They would know anything I might be able to tell them. Is there anything else? I should be back at work."

"There is. Have you seen Mr. Carney recently?"

"Mr. Carney apparently went to lots of trouble to find me here, and we saw one another on a couple of occasions."

"And you gave him more information about the general and the others?"

"No—I don't believe he asked, and I didn't know as much as he. I'm employed in Chicago and trying to advance. He spoke about his new responsibilities with the War Department and the fact that a successor intelligence activity will be started in the future. Good to know if I ever want to work in that area again. I've probably forgotten more about Czechoslovakia than your desk huggers have ever learned."

"Did you know that Bill Carney perished in the LaSalle Hotel fire?"

"I looked for his name in the published casualty lists but haven't seen it. How sad that he died—he was a capable and interesting man, and probably had worked in much more dangerous surroundings than the LaSalle. Very ironic and very sad, Mr. English."

"Bill and I were close friends as well as teammates. I know that he wanted to see you again—even though, as you indicated, there was nothing more he could learn from you about our quarry in South America. I knew that you did see one another here in Chicago, and his desk book indicated he was having dinner with you on the night of he fire. Did he?"

"You know that he did. We were together for about four hours—but I was back in my room before midnight and knew nothing about the fire until the following day. Since he was on a high floor, I was afraid he might have had trouble getting out—and when I didn't hear from him, I was even more worried. You're confirming that he was a casualty?"

"Probably—smoke inhalation. Of the sixty-one deaths we are aware of, most were caused by that. It must be an awful thing to experience. Several of the people were burned so badly that they couldn't be identified. He's still in that category."

"Why have I not seen his name in the victim lists?"

"The name by which you knew him wasn't his real name—just as Gretchen Hasse isn't yours. We all seem to hide behind pseudonyms for one reason or another. Bill did it in England to protect his wife and daughter. Oh—I can see you didn't know about them. He married a Brit who worked in our London office about five years ago. She was pregnant at the time—with his child. Cute little thing. We're having a memorial service for him in Bethesda next week, and the wife is being flown over by the War Department. They live with her parents in Surrey now, and she'll stay there, but she wanted to attend the service.

"Bill was the moving force behind the effort to locate the general, and without him, that folder will be shelved. There's no US effort to track down any Nazis not indicted for the Nuremberg trials. I think that eventually Wiesenthal and his associates will get organized and probably receive some national backing—from the Allied countries or somebody. If so, we'll have a file to contribute to their background. But, for now it's inactive.

"Miss Hasse, I know that Bill and you hit it off personally and that his loss will weigh heavily for a while. I'm really sorry, and as his friend I wanted to wrap this up privately with you."

Gretchen extended her hand and gripped his firmly but didn't want to encourage a consoling embrace or even a peck on her cheek. There was too much raw emotion being sorted out in her head, and she couldn't expose it to anyone.

56

⁘

The Investigators

Jerome Doyle's driver huddled with Chefe Suarez, examining a road map of the area to the northwest of Blumenau. They traced State Road 416 as it wound north through Pomerode—another enclave of German culture—and found an unpaved side road that wandered off toward the west into a hilly sector with no named settlements. "Our fazenda is in that area. It has a long cattle fence and is identified only by a sign announcing 'Propriedade—Nao Entre,' to discourage uninvited visitors."

"That would be us, eh, Chefe?" quipped the faux American businessman. He had arrived from Florianópolis early for their meeting and was eager to move on toward the possible hiding place of the fugitive General von Seigler.

Chefe Suarez's unsmiling secretary brought three brown paper lunch bags plus some chilled cola bottles to the travelers and then waved as they pulled away from the curb in a dusty sedan with unreadable diplomatic license plates. It would be three or four hours at the earliest before their return, so she walked to her favorite *salão de beleza* and picked up three movie magazines from a table in the waiting area. It promised to be a rare day without conflict and confusion at the office, and she intended to take full advantage of it.

As soon as they were settled into their seats, Jerry Doyle began to speak excitedly. "Chefe, I have a real surprise for you; since we spoke last I have actually had the pleasure of meeting and speaking with our chanteuse 'Sophia' at a reception for Brazil's new president!"

"Accidentally?"

"Oh no—not at all. The Pittman Orchestra's tour moved on to São Paulo from here, and once again our agents were posted there to watch for anyone resembling a fugitive general trying to contact his daughter. Even though that stakeout was unproductive, the duty officer learned that the Orchestra had recently been contracted to play at an exclusive reception for Presidente Dutra. The US emissary to Brazil, Mr. Henry Wise, made a direct request that I, as representative of American businessmen, be among the invitees. The gathering was up the coast a little bit from Santos, on a private island—gorgeous spot! Once I saw the table setup, it only took a few greenbacks to get my place card moved alongside hers at dinner."

"I'm impressed, Mr. Doyle; that was creative! I saw her only at a distance during Oktoberfest—is she attractive up close?"

"A knockout. Tall, tan, and full bodied with a whale of a voice. She also speaks very good English and even better Portuguese."

"Did you learn anything additional about her father?"

"Oh, not at all. She didn't even mention having parents—only the places where she had lived and worked in Europe before coming to Brazil. Very guarded. Very guarded. And that makes me suspicious that she knows where he is and won't give us a clue— unless we see them together. So, how did you find out about this fazenda we're looking for?"

"Just a lucky break, Mr. Doyle. A young woman got curious

about a German couple and then put together the fact that their daughter is probably the singer, Sophia, who was coming here to perform during Oktoberfest. She couldn't understand why they weren't looking forward to it and even boasting about their daughter. Eventually she concluded that the parents were deliberately hiding the relationship.

"She learned from a conversation with me that the FBI had added some of their agents to our Oktoberfest surveillance and she was smart enough to make the connection—those people are hiding here! We know there are lots of Germans and others 'of interest' living secretly in this region, but this particular one seems to have a price on his head. The sad part is that she didn't disclose all of this intentionally; it was only because she died and I read her notes and observations that I learned so much. For all I know, she might have intended to protect them because they were friends, and would never have purposely shared her conclusions."

Half an hour later the driver stopped and pointed to a driveway leading off the lonely road with the only identification of its occupants being their warning not to enter the private property. "This fits the description. Should we continue inside?"

"Why the hell do you think we came all this distance? Of course we enter and drive up the hill to the house. Let's go!"

Along the way they arrived at a gate, paused in the raised position, next to a small building, which appeared empty. They continued on until the fazenda building became visible on a ridge above them. They could see a flock of chickens feeding in the open range grass and some Charolais cattle grazing near a stream. A small woman was intent upon moving the chickens toward a fenced area while an attentive collie nipped at any cows that moved too far away from their barn. On the porch of the dwelling, a thick-bodied young farmer was sharpening his machete with a whetstone laid across a small table. He looked up and asked "Kann ich Dir helfen?" which Doyle recognized as a pleasant German greeting, much like "How can I help you?" He decided to test the man's English.

"We're looking for Senhor Kurt Hahn."

"I'm Senhor Hahn," was the quick reply. How can I help you?"

"We are looking for Gerda and Kurt Hahn, who own this fazenda; I thought they were older. Is the lady walking at the side of the house your wife—Gerda Hahn?"

"Yes—and you may also see our children coming from school soon. The four of us live here and we have owned this house and land for several years. I don't know any other Hahn family in the area, so we must be the people you're seeking."

Chefe Suarez showed the farmer his badge and papers. He identified himself as the chief of Blumenau's police force, then told the man that a young woman had been killed nearby in an automobile accident a week earlier, after dining with friends in this area. Had he heard about that accident? By then the woman had walked to the porch, and she offered, "We are very secluded up here, Chefe—don't have many social friends who join us for dinner. The last time was six or seven weeks ago, wouldn't you say, Kurt?"

He agreed immediately. Then she continued, "Please come inside; I'm preparing dinner now for when our girls arrive home from school. Let's share some coffee while I finish. We'll try to help you any way we can. But, in about twenty minutes Kurt will have to drive down to the highway to meet the school bus."

Both visitors were quick to accept the invitation, and they motioned to their driver to join them inside the house. Doyle and Suarez were eager to view the poster of Sophia, which the girl's notes had described. It could confirm that they had arrived at the right fazenda.

That opportunity was delayed until her husband had departed to meet the school bus, then Chefe Suarez finally spoke up. "We left Blumenau over two hours ago. Senhora Hahn—might I visit your banheiro? Too much coffee, you know." She nodded her approval and pointed him down the hall past two closed doors. Doyle understood that he was supposed to provide diversion, so he entered the kitchen and began assessing the contents of a large cooking pot.

"*Feijoada*—Brazilian beef stew," Gerda announced proudly. "Would you like to taste some? It's made from our own ingredients." She dished out a small sample and handed it to the American, who rolled it around appreciatively in his mouth and then flashed a broad smile of approval. He reckoned that the chief should by now have had time to check the poster of Sophia.

"Chefe, you must come here! You've gotta try this feijoada. Best I've had since I came to Brazil." Then, turning toward the woman, he added, "May I use your bathroom, too?" Without waiting for her response, the two switched roles, and Doyle was able to hurry down the hall where he expected to view the confirming poster of Sophia. As he looked inside the room he had to stifle his voice. He was looking at the only wall art anywhere in the building—a framed photograph of a smiling grey fox!

They had indeed been outfoxed by General von Seigler, who from the time of his arrival had anticipated the eventual need to move on. The fugitive general and his companion had temporarily assumed the identities of family members already settled in Santa Catarina, who had then joined the wealthy fugitives as household staff. Now they had their reward—owners of an attractive, secluded fazenda, probably with comfortable savings tucked away somewhere safe. The quarry had moved on to another part of the huge, friendly continent, with new identities.

The return drive to Blumenau seemed much longer, and the fragments of conversation were about the lapse of time that had facilitated von Seigler's escape and the conundrum of whether the deceased young woman had been the victim of drunken driving or something more sinister.

57

℞

End of the Tour

There was talk of establishing regular air service between São Paulo and Rio, but for now the normal way to traverse that 500-kilometer distance was by bus, over chippy roads for anywhere between ten and twelve dusty hours. The Pittman Orchestra had chartered one of the best buses available, but there wasn't much to distinguish it from the regular junkers in public service. Buca and Sofie shared a seat with extra legroom, aft of the central door.

"Glad to be heading back to Rio?" the suave orchestra leader asked.

"Well . . . yes and no. It has been exciting to sing to such distinguished audiences and get to know new places. And there's no question that excellent musicians and arrangements allow a singer to project a more finished product. All of that was good. Probably my most exciting time as a performer since I sang with Django in Europe."

"But?"

"But, I've missed Rio and Dieter and my apartment—and I've got some business to attend back there."

"Would you think about working with the Pittman Orchestra

again in the future?"

"Will you be offering that opportunity? Unless there is an opportunity, I can't clutter my time with 'what if.'"

"You're the best singer we've had. Audiences have called you out for encores in each place we've performed. And, I think your voice and delivery improved at each session; you learned to rely on your accompaniment as a partner. And, most of all, except for that first little episode in BA, you were a 'good citizen'—never gave me any trouble. I noticed that you really cut back on the cognac after Argentina."

"I guess that's as good a cue as any for something I have to tell you, Buca. I'm expecting a child, and I know that healthy babies and heavy drinking aren't compatible. But I wasn't really fair to you. I knew that Lola's spot was going to be open because of your feeling about singers in maternity garb, and I found out about my condition before the tour launched. My decision to keep it to myself was selfish, Buca. If I had lapsed into morning sickness and lassitude, I could have been a heavy anchor on the tour's buoyancy. But the tour was an opportunity I wanted to grasp—so, in a way, I lied to you, boss."

Buca stared at his star vocalist for several long moments before speaking. "I'm . . . I'm stunned, Sofie. First, because you were willing to put the tour in jeopardy for all of us, but also because you pulled it off completely. I was going to use this trip to introduce the subject of an expanded role with us, but I guess that's moot for now. Well—I'm happy for you and Dieter—and when I have this digested, I still want to look down-line with you and see whether we should be putting together a letter of understanding. "

Sofie let out a relieved sigh. "Thanks for not throwing things at me, boss. You have my sincere apologies. By the way—no mention to Dieter or anyone right now. I have to break this to him first, and I don't want anyone else beating me to that. Hope you understand—

do you?"

The next eight hours were very quiet, with both the singer and the bandleader feigning sleep but really reviewing options and thinking about the sixty days they had spent together on the road—and what their future association might be.

❧

Dieter arrived early at the bus station in Rua Jango Pádua, where large, noisy carriers from São Paulo regularly nosed into the high curb and discharged stretching travelers. Finally, he saw the private bus that had been hired to carry the Pittman Orchestra on the last leg of its long tour, and he squinted to see long blonde hair through the dusty windows. He was still moving unproductively from window to window when strong hands spun him around and pulled him into a pleasantly perfumed hug. He realized that he had forgotten how tall and full-bodied Sofie was during her absence, and instinctively, he drew her even closer. There were no words from either as the embrace morphed into a full kiss, and finally they drew back just enough to stare into one another's eyes.

"I'm feeling that I'm meeting someone brand new," Dieter blurted, not knowing how prophetic the greeting sounded to Sofie. "You look fabulous, my diva! I'm so happy to have you back in Rio." They instinctively stepped back into their embrace, then rubbed noses and kissed again. This time there was no FBI agent watching from the shadows, but instead, a dark-haired woman concealing her bloated stomach watched and then turned away without being noticed.

Sofie had already taken her leave of Buca and each of the orchestra members during the last hour of their long trip, so she only waved in the direction of the parked bus and helped Dieter to load her trunk into a waiting cab. Soon they were speeding toward

Ipanema, their apartment, and the most momentous development in their lives since their first meeting in Berlin in 1938.

⁓

Sofie had chosen a soft, comfortable cotton pants suit, in the style of current Hollywood stars, for her long bus trip, and she wore a belted raincoat over it, which didn't seem necessary in the warm early-evening Rio air. When they stepped into their apartment, she was quick to drape the coat casually over her shoulder, hooking it with two long fingers, again mimicking popular actresses. "Well—how do I look after so long away, Schatz?"

"Schön, my love! Never better. You look as if you've been on a beach vacation."

"Can you tell that I gained a little weight?"

"Not really. Maybe just a little. I'm sure that the food was superb in all of those famous hotels. Wasn't it?"

"You know I'm not a Fleischfresser, Dieter. No, I ate lightly most of the time, and didn't drink any of the wine after my first appearance in BA. Mostly fishes and vegetables. And I cut 'way back on desserts, too. Look again." She turned her left side toward him and opened the top enough to expose her breasts and dorsal curves, then asked, "See anything?"

"Oh, Jesus!" the stunned man blurted as he looked even closer at the small protrusion. "You're . . . you're. Oh, my—you're going to have a baby, aren't you!"

"No, Liebling. *We* are going to have a baby! This little *Maus* is yours as much as mine. Surprised?"

"I never expected . . . you never said anything about . . . oh, God, yes, I have never been so surprised since I realized I was still alive outside Theresienstadt. Here—sit down. What can I get for you?"

"Just get used to it, Liebling. This seems to go on eternally once it starts. And the changes come in millimeters, but they keep coming. I've been able to conceal it all through the tour—except from one observant person. I'll tell you about that later. And, I guess I'm one of the lucky expectant mothers—no nausea or pain—just some things I can't wear any more. Are you okay with this? It will change plans for both of us, you know."

"I do, Sofie. Remember, I've made forty appearances with Lola, and I can see how being pregnant has affected her movements and limited the performance clothes she can wear. But it hasn't hurt her singing—not at all. If anything, she seems smoother in her delivery. But when, how did you find out? Where were you? BA?"

"Dieter, I was still right here, and I was seeing my doctor for shots before I went off on the trip. He checked my vital signs, weight, etc. just as a routine matter, and he said I was doing well, near the end of my first trimester. I was shocked, but I left the office an hour later with a whole new perspective—and an ethics issue. Should I tell you and Buca? I decided that I could do the singing and save you two some worry. Lucky for me, I never missed a performance or blew a note. As with your Lola, I was focused when I stepped on stage, and I stayed within myself. Did she say she was nervous?"

"We both were. New material; different audience; new partner. But it went well, and over the ten weeks we got very confident. The manager was helpful, too, and because the take was good, he was our third partner. There are already a couple of copycat shows along the beach, but ours was first and it remained the pace-setter. Sorry you couldn't have heard us—I'd like to have had your input on the whole idea."

"So, where's she now? Does she have anything to do?"

"Don't know. She talked about opening her own music cafe for younger audiences down the beach a few kilometers. That area is less expensive for anything starting up. And there seems to be demand for something affordable. No question it is beginning to grow, but I didn't have any time to check it out."

"Did she ask you to help her with it?"

"Not exactly, but I'm sure that would be of interest to her. We've already gotten past the learning stage, and it's comfortable together on stage."

"More than with me?"

Dieter didn't answer. The conversation had already veered away from Sofie's return and her exciting news to his activity with Lola during Sofie's absence, and that already weighed too heavily upon him. He lighted a cigarette and walked out into the twilight to the terrace where so many secrets had been incubated. A cool breeze penetrated the last of the afternoon heat, and the evening star materialized to the east over Ipanema's beach.

Half an hour later, Sofie tiptoed barefoot onto the terrace, wearing one of her favorite silk robes, and planted a light kiss on Dieter's forehead as she eased into the space beside him on the soft cushion. "You know, I love you, Piano Man—and I don't demand that you always be perfect; only that you love me, too."

A shadow materialized in the street below for just a moment before it dissolved into the darkness. If anyone had been watching, they might have described a huddled woman who had been watching the fading lights on the terrace above.

58

————

The Changing Landscape

It had been—what?—over four months since she last walked down Rua Francisco Otaviano to the point where it intersected with the beach and the beautiful Atlantic Ocean. Today it was cooler, and Sofie pulled her light windbreaker together and buttoned it over the little person inside, who was daily becoming more obvious. She removed her walking shoes and allowed bare feet the undeniable pleasure of "mushing" in the soft sand—that little process of pushing them through the sun-warmed top level and discovering the remains of rain which had fallen overnight. Once she and the beach had become reacquainted, Sofie set off in the direction of the Copacabana Palace Hotel, where she had been a fixture so recently, yet so long ago.

The scaffolding had been removed from the beach side of the new building where workers had greeted her on many mornings, and a new occupant standing on his sunny balcony didn't seem inclined to return her wave. A food vendor had set up his rickety establishment where her favorite sand sculptor had produced daily miracles and spread a sheet to collect coins. She thought about trying some of the aromatic cafezinho the *fornecedor* had just brewed, but knew instinctively that she would never get to her destination without having to relieve herself if she did so. Long walks along the beach would have to be planned better for now—*make a mental note, Sofie.*

At the reception desk, she learned that Carlos had been replaced by a recent hotel-school graduate from America, who greeted her with an overly practiced smile and European-accented Portuguese. Sofie responded in English. "I'm Sophia—Sophia Havlik—and I've been the singer in the Bar do Copa for quite a while, but I've been performing on the road recently."

"Oh, you were the partner of 'the Piano Man' before Lola, right?"

"I guess you could say that; I hadn't quite thought of it that way. I'm not sure whether my mail has been picked up lately and wanted to check with you—what's your name?"

"I'm Cordell, ma'am. Sounds like 'Cornell' with a head cold—that's where I went to school. They placed me here after graduation. Isn't this just the coolest hotel ever?"

"My mail, Cornell?"

"Cordell. Yeah, there's some stuff in a container in the back. Let me get it for you, and you can sort through it over in that corner of the lobby—there's a little desk with a good light. Would you like me to send a waiter from the Lounge? Coffee or something?"

Sofie ignored the question with just a smile and carried the box to the indicated desk, where she was pleased to see a large, empty waste paper basket available to receive the collected contents. Separating the wheat from the chaff took no time, and she was left with five items she deemed important.

First was a check from the Booker Pittman Orchestra for 8,000 US dollars, representing her agreed salary of $500 per week plus a share of the tour's profits. It was a lot of money in postwar Brazil, but she knew that she had earned it. Put another way, it was probably one hundred dollars per song, and everything else was a free tour of South America's most intriguing cities, plus the priceless opportunity to see her father.

Next there was a curt, written message from the manager of the Copacabana Palace Hotel that the upcoming season's demand for accommodations appeared to exceed the Hotel's capacity, and consequently they would be refurbishing several unused rooms, among them, Room 626. She quipped to herself, "Well, I'll have to rent it someday just to show my child where her life began." Then she realized she had assumed that her baby would be a girl. Was that a sign?

The third letter bore a local postmark from five weeks earlier and the return address of her doctor's office. Inside was a notice that she had missed her follow-up examination and scolding her with a reminder that those periodic visits are essential to assure a healthy mother and child. By now she had probably missed yet another essential visit, and so she scribbled the telephone number on a page of the Hotel's courtesy notepad and stuffed it into her windbreaker pocket.

That brought Sofie to an envelope embossed with the name "Paramount Pictures" and the name Stuart Heisler written above the logo. Neither meant anything, but the content was exciting. It announced that there would be a motion picture starring Bing Crosby and Fred Astaire, showcasing the music of Irving Berlin. Mr. Heisler had been in the audience at the Copa when Sophia had first sung with the Pittman Orchestra, and he invited her to audition for a role in *Blue Skies*, as the film was being titled. It was dated three months earlier. And for now, Sofie would be auditioning for a delivery room. But, she decided to write at once to Mr. Heisler to thank him for his interest and to tell him she would like to be considered if something appropriate was being cast in the future. Did she mean that? Sofie didn't know, but "keep your options open, girl" had been one of her father's frequent reminders.

The final item spared from the waste basket was a postcard. It pictured a lake with mountains behind, and beneath the photo was the identifying legend "Laguna Mar Chiquita," which she translated as "Little Ocean Lake." On the obverse side, familiar handwriting said simply, "Grandmother passed away, and after the fire we have moved from her home. All is now well." The card bore Argentine airmail postage.

In the seldom-used Encyclopedia Britannica on a high shelf of the hotel's library, Sofie was able to learn that the salty lake was located among the mountains of Argentina's Cordoba Province, near the center of the country. The description also noted that the Province had a heavy concentration of immigrants from Germany. Sofie planted a kiss on the handwriting, then tore the card into multiple pieces, about half of which she dropped into the heaping basket and the remainder she placed in her pocket to drop in another receptacle in the lobby. With Juan Domingo Perón now in the Casa Rosada, there would probably be a period of time during which immigrant Germans in Argentina would be safe from their pursuers.

As she walked past the reception desk, Sofie smiled and said, "Obrigado, Cornell" to the young man, who returned her smile and responded, "De nada, Senhora Hablick." Sofie patted her stomach lightly and mused, "It's a whole new day, little girl. I think we can handle it."

◈

At the doctor's office, she was again scolded for missing her follow-up appointments, but desisted from offering the excuse of being in other countries. The doctor remembered his attractive patient and carefully examined her from head to toe; it was the most extensive exploration of her body parts with the lights on that she could remember. When he had finished and invited her to get dressed, the doctor said that she looked exceptionally well, but in view of the passage of time, he would like to have blood, urine, and stool samples and schedule a follow-up in four weeks.

"And, how long until the baby comes?" Sofie inquired.

"Since we don't have a precise starting point, it appears to me that it will be at least another ten weeks before you deliver.

"And the sex of my baby? Any guess on that?"

"Your added weight is well distributed—much of it in your hips, breasts, and upper legs. Less in your belly. That's more frequent in female babies, but no assurance. Don't have your heart set on the sex—be happy that it seems strong and healthy. Are you feeling movements? I detected some."

"I surely am—little protests, then a sort of change in position."

"That does sound like a female, Sofie. I'll see you in four weeks. Easy on the cognac!"

All in all, it had been a good day, but she decided to take a cab rather than walking again. When she arrived at the apartment, she thought she saw Lola walking down the street.

59

Phoenix

Elsa—or "Gretchen," as she regularly reminded herself, decided it might be a welcome diversion to attend a movie and then have a light dinner alone near her hotel. The recent LaSalle Hotel fire still weighed heavily on all of her hours, even including the troubled sleep she was experiencing.

The current offering in her local Balaban & Katz movie house was Alfred Hitchcock's *Notorious*, starring the handsome Cary Grant as an American agent and Ingrid Bergman portraying a promiscuous woman being recruited to infiltrate escaped Nazis living in Brazil. The contrived Hollywood plot contained so many similarities to her own enigma that she wanted to follow it to its conclusion, which—with Hollywood—would have to be a happy one. Before she was halfway through her box of buttered popcorn, poor Bergman's character was getting married to an evil Nazi, ably portrayed by the always-evil actor Claude Raines. When Grant finally carried poisoned Bergman from the Nazi lair, where uranium was hidden in wine bottles, Elsa had been thoroughly entertained and was even able to smile slightly at her own situation. The movie had delivered the desired palliative effect, and she walked with keen anticipation toward a quiet restaurant on a side street near her hotel.

"Why not begin with a small glass of Dubonnet, and then sample one of Chicago's famous steaks?" she suggested to herself as she settled into a corner table near the window. "Get back onto the horse you've fallen from and conquer the fear." As she lifted the fragrant glass, she saw the man enter and seem to inspect all of the diners within sight, then proceed purposefully toward her table.

"Gretchen, you should not be eating alone tonight. May I sit down?"

Heavy-rimmed glasses and a mustache couldn't camouflage a voice—even that of a dead man. William Carney, or whatever his name was, pulled a chair back and sat there, to the amazement of Gretchen Hasse, or whatever her name was.

"What the hell, Carney! What's going on? Two hours after I left you that goddamned hotel fire killed or injured about two hundred people and everything since has suggested you were dead. Even your pal Joe came to see me, with black crepe draped over his face, and he left me to cry over something that hadn't happened. Yes, sit down! And start with an apology, and then an explanation. If you weren't dead, I could kill you myself. What the hell is this—some goddamned Alfred Hitchcock movie I'm living?"

"Okay, lower your voice, Gretchen—or just shut up for a minute. After you left I had to get some fresh air, so I took a walk and then sat on a park bench thinking about you, us, the new agency, the Nazi in Brazil, the mess in Europe—everything going on in my life. By the time I got back, the first fire alarm had sounded and nobody was allowed to enter the building so that the engines and men could do their job. But, it got out of hand very quickly and I could see that it might turn into a tragedy, because so many people were asleep above the visible level of the flames. That's what happened. It got so blistering hot that metal melted and many remains are beyond identification. I hate to say this—but for me it was a dream scenario."

"Explain that, please."

"Well, strangely, an ideal intelligence agent is one with no history at all. No parents, no family, no residence, no school records or medical records. I had nothing to do with the fire, but it allows me to create a new person who can't be traced because he died. And you're nearly the same thing. New identity in a new country with no obvious links back to Danzig or Prague. Think about it, Gretchen— think about it!"

"All right—what do I think about your wife and daughter in Surrey? You were all ready to bed down with me in Prague and never said a damned word about them, even when we were getting close to . . . oh, you know, close to acknowledging that there might be . . . you know what I'm trying to say, dammit."

"Brigit and Aimee are fine. We had already trashed the marriage and they had gone to her parents' place, which is gorgeous. They never approved of her marrying a Yank, but they had no choice after she was pregnant. Aimee is too little to remember me; I was hardly ever there. And, for them, the best part may be that she doesn't have to go through the ignominy of a divorce, and the USA will pay her a very large death benefit. That's already in the works, and I've agreed on the number with the War Department.

"Look, there's going to be a new intelligence service and I'm going to be a part of it. I'd like to have you by my side—on salary, of course, but truly on my side—because I think we may be able to understand one another better than most couples can. What we do is unique, Gretchen. You can't just explain it in a normal relationship, and if it's not understood it will sooner or later come between two people.

"Now, I've already said too much—but I haven't told you my new name or anything, so I can walk away and this can just be a dream you had after a movie."

"How did you know I went to a movie?"

"I followed you there and sat three rows behind. Good, wasn't it?"

"Not when she had to marry that creepy Claude Raines, it wasn't. I've had to romance a few creepy guys, but they all departed before breakfast. What would you like to have for dinner, mystery man? Or may I still call you William?"

"Let's keep it Gretchen and William for now. That's a good starting point."

❧

Carney didn't even walk her to her hotel. He followed at a distance and turned away when she stepped inside the door. It had all gone well, and more than ever he found her to be intelligent and interesting. General von Seigler had deftly slipped away from the FBI and was now able to hide almost anywhere within the seven million square miles of the South American continent. That was about twice as big as the entire USA, and with no supportive police or agencies to help search. The only way to find his new hiding place would be his own outward communications, and the one person to whom he might send them was his own daughter, Sofie.

Somehow he must get Elsa back into contact with Dieter, and hopefully Dieter and Sofie would remain devoted to one another. It was a long shot, but there could be a very large payday for the general's captor.

❧

At the War Department's small Chicago office the next day, Bill and Joe shared coffee and donuts and the story of the previous evening's meeting.

"Can you believe the fucking movie she chose to see! It was all about Nazis in Brazil and a cache of uranium in wine bottles and a notorious woman being used by a government guy to learn the Nazis' secrets. So on point! Wow. It set you up, Bill."

"Well, you set me up, too, Joe. That fabrication about a wife and daughter gave credibility to my Phoenix-rises-from-the-ashes story. Everybody gives a thought to starting over at some time—leave all the troubles behind, isn't that a song lyric? But a guy with a bad marriage leaving a government insurance policy and getting a new identity? That's good stuff. Next we have to get Elsa—or 'Gretchen'—to get back in touch with Dieter, and see if there's any clue as to the general's new whereabouts. He sure outfoxed the FBI. Gotta hand it to him."

"Yeah. The fly in the ointment may be the other singer Dieter was shagging while Sophia was off singing on tour. If she finds out and throws him out, she won't be telling Dieter any family secrets for sure. Our Rio guys followed them pretty closely and they had no doubt that it was more than a duet in the Copa. They were pretty hot an' heavy, Bill. I guess you'll be seeing Gretchen again soon, huh?"

"I'll give it a couple of days, just to whet her appetite. Then we can see if it's a real lead."

60

Picking Up the Pieces

Sofie had been back in Rio for several days, but they had been consumed with her medical matters, cleanout of Room 626, handling accumulated mail, and acquiring the clothing and other things needed by a first-time expectant mother. At the conclusion of each day she had been happy to eat a full meal and fall asleep. She and Dieter both understood that a longer conversation was necessary to fill in the gaps of their separation, and on a warm, starlit Rio night they finally pulled two chairs close together on their terrace and broached the avoided subjects.

"What was the high point of your tour, Schatz? Was there any one day better than all the rest?"

"Yes, Dieter—there was one in Porto Alegre that I'll never forget. I wasn't expecting it at all, and suddenly I was having dinner in a little German restaurant with Poppy and Branka. As he sometimes does, Poppy 'materialized' with no warning, and we were just a small family unit discussing things like having a baby and enjoying life with loved ones."

"Does he live near Porto Alegre?"

"I really don't know. They came from somewhere by auto that

day, but I didn't want to know the starting point. I saw him again in Blumenau, where I was singing at Oktoberfest, but that was not a place for conversation—only an opportunity for him to watch my public performance. We couldn't speak."

"Is it a long way from Porto Alegre to Blumenau? I don't know much about that part of Brazil."

"Well, I learned that Brazil and Argentina are both huge—not like the small nations in Europe, all huddled together. I think the drive between those points would be ten hours, at least, and some of the roads are pretty basic. Why?"

"'I was just trying to get an idea of the area those people looking for him would have to filter. Now I'm seeing better why they followed you, hoping to catch sight of him rather than going to all the German settlements in the country and searching for clues."

Sofie remembered the postcard fragments still in the pocket of her windbreaker and decided not to reveal that her father's location a few weeks prior was no longer of any value. She resolved to dump the torn pieces into a refuse container near the beach and not mention the card to anyone—even Dieter. She changed the subject of their conversation.

"Liebling, I noticed that you still have that awful newspaper photo of me with the Peróns and Francisco Pignatari on the board in our kitchen. Why on earth did you keep it? It was in an Argentine tabloid and I was hoping it would escape notice here in Rio when I mailed it to you."

"Hmmm. I believe Buca also sent it to Lola and Lola shared it with me. I was amused but also curious that you and Baby were linked in the caption."

"Well, we were standing there just like that—and a few minutes later I apparently threw up all over Baby. I was nervous—my first night on the tour and in the Teatro Colón in front of some really uppity people. I had consumed enough cognac to calm my nerves and loosen my vocal cords, but perhaps a bit more than I should have. Actually, my singing was good that night, and the acoustics are superb, but I blacked out sometime later and slept well into the next day. Before you ask, I'll tell you. Baby got me to my room and into my bed for the night, but he was a gentleman. We talked about it in a place near Santos where the tour ended."

"You saw him again?"

"Yes, he hosted a big dinner party for President Dutra and a gathering of Brazilian businessmen and their wives. Buca was invited to provide the music; it was important exposure for the orchestra, so the tour was extended. Baby sought me out there and provided details of that earlier night in BA to put me at ease. I felt better knowing all about it, and I was also happy to meet Baby's wife, who is a very cultured lady."

"A blind and deaf woman, perhaps?"

"Dieter, there are hundreds of variations among successful marriages. I'm not going to become an arbiter of others' relationships until I understand my own. Right now I'm dealing with a dozen dark hairpins scattered through our apartment and my identity at the Copa being described as 'Lola's predecessor with the Piano Man.' Can we put a little sunlight onto that so I am not consumed with jealousy and worry?"

Dieter felt a wave of guilt engulfing him. He had long anticipated an eventual need to delve deeply into his ill-advised infidelity, but when there was no longer a way to delay the conversation, his mouth became dry and his lips seemed nearly paralyzed. He reached instinctively for a nearby coffee carafe and clumsily tipped it onto its side, sending the dark contents washing across the little serving table and onto the floor. His efforts to absorb the spilled liquid were equally inept, and his sweeping motion with a table napkin launched a coffee cup onto the floor, where it fragmented into dozens of sharp edges. When he finally looked up from the small disaster he had caused, it was with the fear that he was about to embark on something much more embarrassing and destructive.

He began with both hands pressed against his temples and then moved his head from side to side as if that could somehow erase the events he was about to disclose.

"You are entitled to it. The night you flew away, I was miserable and went back to the Copa rather than to an empty apartment filled with your things. I ran into Lola there—I was playing a few tunes and a lady in the audience started singing. She was good, and I didn't recognize her until she reminded me. She laid out the idea of an "improvised blues" program, and we got several guests listening immediately. The manager encouraged us to continue, and the format caught on. We did forty nights of it, and working together in the hotel evolved into a sort of, well, a friendship of need, I guess."

"What did each of you 'need,' Dieter?"

"Initially, I think she needed to tell her story to a sympathetic listener. She's all alone and pregnant and can't even identify the father. She needed someone to tell her that doesn't render her valueless. She has musical talent, and she identified an opportunity to create some value from her talent. As she became convinced of that, her creativity gained and her whole outlook brightened."

"And you?"

"It's more an excuse than an explanation. Hundreds of days and nights in a place like Theresienstadt can change a person. I was accustomed to eating good, regular meals at the Fischerstube, where I worked in Berlin, and at the Havlik Clinic in Prague where we lived—and almost overnight I was reduced to dining on the cold scraps from plates I was washing. When that happened, I reverted to being an animal when I ate. My companionship in Theresienstadt was with dying men, and each cold night we huddled under a thick, old coat and shared its warmth. Intimacy with them allowed me to sleep.

"The hairpins are here because Lola was here—often. We talked, ate, and were intimate sometimes. It was selfish and inconsiderate of me—totally unfair to you, but possibly vital to Lola, and at least another 'warm coat' for me. The strange thing is that there was never a moment in those weeks when I wasn't totally in love with you, but then, I never passed up a scrap of chewed gristle stuck on an officer's plate, even if I wasn't hungry at that moment. Does that make any sense to you, Sofie?"

She stood facing away from Dieter and then walked to the window, looking out toward the Atlantic Ocean, as if there might be an answer etched on the horizon. When she envisioned being in the apartment for an endless procession of nights and days, alone except for a small child in a crib, Sofie winced. However disappointed she might be by his infidelity during her prolonged absence, Sofie knew that she would need Dieter at her side as they tried to master the skills of responsible parenthood. Finally she turned back, and with a faint smile in Dieter's direction, she emptied her own regrets.

"I'll have to think about it, Dieter. There were nights during the war when I drank too much and in the morning couldn't remember how I got to bed with some guy lying there asleep. And there was that morning I woke up naked in the Alvear Palace in BA and the housekeeper handed me that newspaper picture. I wasn't sure what had transpired and I wished fervently that I could erase it all and never have to explain it to you. It's a mess, isn't it? We've both been given so much and have treated our good fortune so carelessly. And now, in just weeks, we are going to bring our child into the world. How fair are we being to her?"

"To her? You didn't tell me . . . "

"I haven't any idea. I get little hints that it's a girl, and after a while it just continues."

"You're right. Our whole conversation has been about us in the past, and this should be about our child in the future. That's something we can do together and agree upon."

"I love you, Dieter, and that's what I want most for us and our daughter. Two parents who are honest and loving and smart. We've already gotten through the 'honest' part tonight. Are you still interested in the 'loving'? Because I'm starved after nearly three months away. This may be a little awkward for a pregnant lady, but . . . "

"If you take the top position it's easier—and we can even watch," he laughed. "I learned that from a friend while you were on tour."

"You *bastardo*—I love you."

61

The Changing World

While Dieter and Sofie were busying themselves "normalizing" their lives in Rio de Janeiro after the conclusion of her tour, there was an inescapable realization that the end of the war had by no means heralded a new era of world stability. In February of 1946, Juan Domingo Perón had cemented his control of the Argentine government; he had been elected president, and his party had won control of both houses of Argentina's legislature. With those political bodies firmly in hand, Perón transformed rapidly from popularly elected president to absolute dictator.

A second postal card to Sofie from Cordoba reaffirmed that the senders were happy with their new location and living in a community heavily populated by German-speaking immigrants, who were accepted enthusiastically by the new Argentine administration. In the concluding sentence, the unidentified sender expressed the hope that news of a new Havlik arrival would be appearing in newspapers before long. Sofie understood the reminder and made a note to do so but did not share the agreed conduit and code with Dieter. No need to burden him with that small scrap of information about her father's current location. Once again, the fragments of the torn card were deposited into an oceanside refuse basket.

A month later, Britain's wartime leader, Winston Churchill, summed up the divided political face of postwar Europe while delivering a speech in the United States. The heart of his message observed "from Stettin in the Baltic to Trieste in the Adriatic, an iron curtain has descended across the Continent." Dieter and Sofie both understood that returning to the separated country they had left was no longer an option for them, nor for Sofie's father and his companion. It was time to optimize their Brazilian lifestyle.

Sofie was the first to make the suggestion, which lifted a large burden from Dieter's shoulders. "Have you ever given consideration to Lola's idea of a music-themed bistro in one of the new beach communities?"

"Bistro? Interesting choice. How did you come up with that, liebling?"

"When I was singing with Django, in Paris during the war, we were around the corner from a little spot on Place du Tertre which had a plaque identifying it as 'the world's first bistro,' so named in 1814. That was when the Russians occupied Paris and drove Napoleon into exile. The owners said that the occupying troops liked the music and ready meals they could enjoy there. They called it a 'bistro,' which was some kind of description from the Russian language, I think. Lola could have Rio's first bistro. Don't you think that would get attention?"

"I'm afraid it will be a long time before Lola can afford to start a business. She just had her baby and is still living upstairs over a gift store on Castilhos. She's paying a little girl from the *favelas* to help her. That's a long way from starting a bistro in Leblon, even though it's a good idea. I'm afraid someone else will beat her to it."

"Dieter, we are going to have a baby soon, too. And we should probably be living in a small house rather than this elevated apartment. And we should also be looking for a business, even though we are anything but poor. What if we found a building on Leblon where there could be a bistro with some parking and an apartment for a full-time manager? Lola could have the occupation she wants, and we could share ownership—and perhaps even perform there together from time to time, as a catalyst for other performers to come by. We could buy a little house nearby in Leblon, and still be only a few miles from the Copacabana."

"You've really been thinking about this! I must admit, I've had some of the same thoughts, but I couldn't have broken the ice. It's your money and it has to be your decision. Let's take a taxi over to Leblon on Saturday and just drive around with something like this in mind. I think we'll be able to decide better if it is a viable plan or only a crazy dream."

They were in the process of looking at available real estate in the nascent beach communities to the south from Copacabana and Ipanema when Sofie went into labor unexpectedly, and Otto Juraslav Havlik announced his noisy entrance into the sunny Brazilian afternoon only twenty minutes after his parents had raced into nearby Hospital Samaritano Barra. It had lived up to its name of Good Samaritan by being on the spot when needed.

☙

Hans and Ursula Purm were relatively new to the Cordoba community, which spread across a hillside above the salty Argentine lake. They had found a modest, empty house favored with an excellent vista and had furnished it in elegant local furniture, fashioned from a unique cebil wood called "Patagonian Rosewood." Hans had told the *ebanista* who had designed and built the furniture that its dark, rich cherry hue reminded him of the best pieces from cabinetmakers in his home area of Germany. But when asked about his European origins, the handsome middle-aged man had retreated from the subject totally. Now he sat on the wide porch of their new home, enjoying the visual panorama to the east while thumbing his way through a stack of recently delivered newspapers.

"Himmel, Gerda! I think this is it—look."

"That's Ursula—or Ushie, in the familiar, Hans. We left Gerda back in Brazil. Remember?" "You're right—but look at this. Right here in *O Globo,*" he blurted. "I'm an opa, Ushie!" The personal notice read:

Otto Juraslav Havlick, 2.7 kilos/ 51 cm was delivered
on Saturday at Hospital Samaritano Barra near Leblon
Beach to parents Zofia y Dieter Havlik of Rio de Janeiro.
All are well and happy. Isolde.

"He has my name, Ushie! Can you imagine—I have a grandson. Now we must find a way to see him and to provide some appropriate gift. What do you think we can do?"

"We can thank God for this miracle and put a brief acknowledgment in *Floha do Norte* saying that *Tristan* is thrilled with *Isolde's* good news. But we can't use any real names. We just moved from our comfortable fazenda in Brazil to a community in another country, and we had to dash away or be caught there. As soon as those FBI people know that Sophia has a baby, they will be looking for you to come and see him. They are smart professionals, and we must be smart also, or bad things will happen."

❧

A week after Baby Otto had been delivered, Sofie returned to the apartment with him, while Dieter was playing for the noonday diners at the Bar do Copa. She was not expecting any callers, but the building's *porteiro* called up from the entry to inform her that a senhora with a baby wished to visit her. Sofie told him to bring her up himself so that she could be assured that it is a friend, although she knew instinctively that she and Lola were going to have their first conversation.

When she confirmed her intuition, Sofie extended her hand and said, "Welcome, Lola. We haven't met before, but I believe that a conversation between us is overdue. Please sit—would you like some coffee, or perhaps something stronger?"

"You are very kind to receive me so cordially, Senhora Sophia—I am here to give you my explanation of events during the time you were away from Rio and to beg your forgiveness, although I understand that my behavior may be unforgiveable. Will you hear me out?"

"Lola, I believe that I know already as much as I need to about the relationship between you and Dieter during those weeks. Hearing it again will only make it more painful, and I have already accepted the reality of human weakness, because I have also been susceptible at times. Dieter and I have been blessed with a wonderful new son, and we are both devoted to his well-being and his future opportunity for happiness. These last few years have tested many people, and just about everyone has done a few things which might have been avoided but weren't. If it is of any comfort to you, I imposed myself on Dieter back in 1938 when we first came into contact in a basement bar where he was the piano player. I don't think Dieter even knew when our relationship crystallized, but I did, because it was my invention. Then the war separated us for more than three years, and when we were reunited here in Brazil, a new learning phase began."

Lola was moved by Sofie's sincerity and understanding. "Thank you, Sophia. I am envious of you on so many levels—your beauty, your talent, your success, and your intelligence are all so far above the norm. When you took 'my job' with the Pittman Band, you can understand that I wanted something of yours in return. What could be more appropriate than your man? I'm ashamed at how satisfying it was to have his exclusive attention as a performer and then as an intimate."

"And, at that same time I was singing to the audiences you might have entertained under other circumstances. How strange, Lola! Anyhow, it is a new day and perhaps we can build from here to our mutual advantage. When I went into labor, we were passing through Leblon looking for a safe house and also for a location for a bistro, where audiences can meet tomorrow's new talents and enjoy good food and beverages. We even have a name for the spot—it could be "Lola's Bistro Leblon." Can you envision that?"

"I've thought about it often. I assume that Dieter has mentioned my dream. But being able to imagine something and to actually accomplish it can be far removed from one another."

"What if Dieter and I had a source of the funding needed? Do you think that, among us, we have the capability to organize and run it?"

"Of course—but that's like asking whether I could reach the highest shelf if I were two meters tall. I'm not two meters tall, so the question is flawed."

"But that's what I'm saying, Lola. We believe that we could acquire the funding if there is a viable plan. One which tells how many employees, what equipment, what furnishings, what advertising . . . can you put meat on the bones of your idea? Can you manage the business with some ongoing help from us? I believe that I know an investor who could bring others with him."

"Baby Pignatari?"

"We are very good friends."

62

Red Tape

When President Truman hastily disbanded the wartime OSS in 1945, it was with tacit recognition that the nation was weary of war and that the tangle of wartime agencies should be unwound quickly and "normal life" re-established in the United States. His decision was hastened by the urging of FBI Director J. Edgar Hoover, who viewed OSS as a competitor in the investigative areas where his FBI had dominated. But others—particularly some leaders of the nation's armed forces—saw that the rising tide of Communism in Europe and Asia would soon necessitate creation of a centralized intelligence source operating in all the world's trouble spots. Some assets of the OSS had been shelved, for safekeeping, within the State Department and others in the War Department, and both those units awaited creation of a single, unifying intelligence agency.

In January of 1946, the first step in this evolution took place when a small inter-military unit called the Central Intelligence Group (CIG) was assembled and placed under the guidance of Admiral Sidney Souers. For the next two years, CIG held onto the slack reins of national intelligence and worked to preserve leftover assets from the halcyon years of OSS. William Carney and Joseph

English were plucked from the discard pile and assigned with others to create the infrastructure for a Central Intelligence Agency, which would become reality only two years later.

Those two wartime friends sat together in Bethesda comparing notes. Joe brightened and said, "Have you noticed that our old buddy Whatsisname Wiesenthal has started running something called the Jewish Central Committee, and they're still looking for important escaped Nazis?"

"You mean like our General von Seigler? Living a cushy life somewhere in South America and spending the savings of some old Jews struggling in Europe? Seems as if we got close to finding him a few times, but got outfoxed. His trail has gone cold, but it could get warm again. The guys at our consulate in Rio have reported that his daughter, the singer, has had a baby boy, and we can assume that at some point the general is going to want to see his grandson. Sophia and her piano guy, Dieter, and the baby are still in Rio—in plain sight.

"Trouble is, there's no manpower to devote to watching them.

"If Wiesenthal and his people would fund me, I'd go down there myself for a couple of months. But if there were eventual recovery from him, we would be entitled to get a share of it, and I'm not sure if that is part of Wiesenthal's program.

"Remember the Polish girl, Elsa, who provided our first link to Sophia and Dieter in Rio?"

"Sure—the lady you were seeing the night of the LaSalle fire, when you got 'killed.' What about her?"

"I was able to place her temporarily at the War Department Office in DC. She's a fount of information for them about Czechoslovakia. The Soviets are moving quickly to take control of all the public services there and they're moving their comrades into government buildings in Prague as they throw the Germans and

Czechs out. She's really an asset in making sense of those moves, but she may yet become useful in fingering General von Seigler for us, too."

"Do you still see her . . . ah . . . 'romantically,' Bill? None of my business, but I thought you found her intriguing on a personal level as well as a professional one."

"Geez—that fabrication about me having a wife and daughter in England had a chilling effect on her, and I can't turn around now and tell her it was all made up. That would just add another layer of suspicion. I was even thinking of printing a phony marriage announcement from some little news rag in England—you know, 'Lord and Lady Whoosit announce the marriage blah, blah'—then quietly adding that the bride's first marriage ended with the tragic death of her first husband in a Chicago hotel fire. Whatta you think?"

"Well, at least the fire part is real."

"Right. Well, I got her out of Sears, Roebuck and out of Chicago and into a government job. That earns me some points with her, and I'll continue to nibble at the edges once in awhile. But. I'd like her to initiate any resumption of our social contact, and I kinda think she will do that at some point. Catching those ex-Nazis in South America will take years and will require infinite patience, believe me."

At the War Department's intelligence office, two assistant undersecretaries filled their coffee cups from the percolator, which was always in play in the tiny office kitchenette. One pointed with his nodding forehead at a slim woman working at a desk across the adjacent office bullpen. "Have you met that Gretchen yet? Amazing lady!"

"Amazing how? Kinda pretty, but not centerfold material

for *Esquire.*"

"No, I meant her language skills and grasp of European nuances. She translated a little Russian publication for me, and then a German document. Then I hear she's fluent in Polish and Slavic, and I'm talking to her in English and she gets it all. Where'd they find her? She's a human Rosetta Stone!"

"Somebody said she was SWW—Polish Intelligence. Got out of Prague ahead of the Reds moving in and found work—for Sears, Roebuck in Chicago."

"Probably also plays the violin, cooks like Chef Vatel, and screws like a rabbit, huh?"

"And memorized the Sears, Roebuck catalogue in an afternoon. Wanna give her a try?"

"Definitely not. I hear somebody upstairs brought her in from Chicago and she's private property."

"Oooh, interesting! I guess she bears watching, huh? She might be spying on us right now!"

63

Restless in Cordoba

Joseph Kingsbury-Smith was one of the finest correspondents of his time; he was the first American writer to be granted an interview with Stalin after the war in Europe was over, and he was one of those privileged to be in attendance at the Nuremberg trials of alleged World War II criminals. Not only did he attend the trials, but on October 16, 1946, he also witnessed the hanging executions of ten leaders of Nazi Germany. There were thirteen Nuremburg trials, and in the aggregate they adjudged the guilt of one hundred eighty-five indicted individuals, ranging from political leaders to military, industrial, and medical figures who served the Third Reich. Kingsbury-Smith's observations were published and read around the world. One interested reader studied the materials on a porch high above a salt lake in Cordoba, Argentina.

Hans Purm also read the published observations of the Chief Justice of the United States Supreme Court, Harlan Stone, that, in his opinion, the proceedings at Nuremberg amounted to "a sanctimonious fraud." The wizened Chief Justice went even further and described the Nuremberg trials as "a high-grade lynching party." Then Associate Justice William O. Douglas piled on and agreed with his chief. Obviously, the thirst for justice had not been universally popular among America's judicial elite.

Hans grumbled to Ursula that it was a strange thing for them to be saying, given the fact that the chief prosecutor at Nuremberg was another of the associate justices of the US Supreme Court, Robert Jackson.

"What troubles you so much?" his companion queried. "Hasn't it always been that way at the conclusion of wars? The victors write history the way they want it to be recorded, and the vanquished are disposed of before they can regain strength. Remember the example of Napoleon, where he was sent into exile and came thundering back to torment Europe again? If they had just stood him against a wall after the surrender, think of the misery that could have been avoided. Nuremberg is much less Draconian than that."

"Consider this then, liebling. In 1940 or '41 the Soviets murdered more than twenty thousand of Poland's most elite military and intellectual leaders and dumped them unceremoniously into trenches in Katyn Forest. They said that Germany had done it, and the Americans and British let it pass. Now, at Nuremberg, they are again trying to assign that atrocity to the German general staff. I was a participant in the Polish Campaign and am acutely aware of what we did and did not do. We did not have anything to do with the Katyn Forest Massacre, but the former Allies will be more comfortable if they don't have to acknowledge the truth.

"And, please also reflect upon this. The first Nuremberg trial is focused upon twenty-two men who were at the controls of the Third Reich—they are rightly responsible for the direction it took. The remaining twelve trials are adjudicating the guilt of citizens who were ordered to support the mandates of their government—probably under penalty of death if they did not do so. Imagine if the war had resulted differently and Germany was seeking to punish the

Americans against whom it fought. Certainly General Eisenhower and his commanders would be the first to stand trial. But then at the second level we would be prosecuting Henry Ford and Henry Kaiser and Albert Einstein and all of the industrialists, scientists, and others who worked in support of the American war effort. Where would that leave the country in its attempt at postwar recovery?

"Certainly I was a part of the war effort of the Third Reich. I was a professional military officer long before they came to power, and I participated in two wars on behalf of my country, always obeying orders faithfully. When the National Socialist direction became repugnant to me, I had three choices. I could continue to follow orders with which I disagreed fundamentally; I could try to change the direction of the leadership; or I could leave my post in wartime and be a deserter. After the failure of the Oster Conspiracy—of which I was mistakenly suspected—there was little probability of overthrowing the leadership, so I chose to walk away."

"And here you are on a hillside in Argentina, living comfortably with an old Polish spy who was tired of the prostitution, drugs, and murders which became a part of gathering intelligence, much as you became sick of wartime atrocities. It's not ideal, Otto—but it is far better than swinging at the end of a rope in some cold courtyard, surrounded by morbid, vindictive people. Accept the fact that in Argentina in 1946 we are not pursued on a daily basis and can read about those ugly things in newspapers from abroad. This old spy appreciates and loves you and cherishes each day we have together."

"So then, would you consider attending Carnival in Rio with me, when we can be invisible in the crowd of visitors, while police and military are overwhelmed with problems to attend and are partially inebriated for at least two weeks?"

"It would be my pleasure, general!"

64

⌘

1947 in Rio

The highlight of Brazil's year 1947 was the state visit of US President Harry S. Truman, his chief advisors, and his immediate family to the Brazilian capital, Rio de Janeiro. President Truman had already decreed that the Western Hemisphere would remain within the exclusive postwar domain of the United States, and this visit was designed to cement that relationship with South America's largest and potentially richest nation.

It was decided that President and Mrs. Truman, together with their daughter, Margaret, would fly from Washington to Rio in the President's swift new aircraft, *Independence*, an Army Air Force Douglas VC-118, the military version of the manufacturer's new DC-6. The trip would require stops in Jamaica and in Belem for refueling the aircraft and its passengers. A large contingent of advisors, plus members of the working press, were to fly separately on an aircraft leased from the pioneering air carrier Pan American. Because the new *Independence*, with its top speed of 390 mph, was considerably faster than the commercial carrier's planes, the entourage had to depart ahead of the president on each leg of the journey in order to record his historic arrivals at each stage.

Once in Brazil, the Americans were accorded the most lavish receptions and ceremonies President Dutra and the Brazilian Congress could devise. Brazil's classically beautiful Palácio Laranjeiras became the Trumans' home, and many of the highest-ranking officials accompanying the president filled the best suites in the Copacabana Palace Hotel. Secretary of State George Marshall and his wife were housed at the American Embassy. President Truman gave a rousing speech to a cheering Brazilian Congress at Palácio Tiradentes, and his Brazilian hosts threw a festive dinner party with entertainment and dancing for more than a thousand guests at Palácio Itamaraty.

Not to be outdone, the Americans brought their famous battleship USS *Missouri* into Rio's harbor. It had been launched by Margaret Truman, the president's daughter, in January 1944, and later had served as the location where on September 2, 1945, America accepted the surrender of Japan. Eighteen hundred naval personnel from the *Missouri* joined twenty-five thousand Brazilian troops in an exciting parade through the capital city. Brazil's press declared that the week-long celebration was the most joyful and elaborate affair in the nation's history. At the conclusion of the state visit, President and Mrs. Truman and their daughter were to sail back to the United States aboard the *Missouri*.

On Avenida Vieira Souto, not far from the Rio de Janeiro Country Club and just off Leblon's dazzling white beach, Lola's Bistro Leblon had opened for business a month before the American president's visit to Brazil. *Jornal do Brasil,* the capital's leading newspaper, had covered the opening and focused its lens on the attendance of a group of opening-night luminaries who were guests of the bombastic thirty-year-old industrialist Baby Pignatari. The article also mentioned an array of young musicians and their variations on traditional samba and jazz standards. It finally praised the vocal offerings of its namesake, Lola, and of part-owner Sophia, a former standout performer at the Copacabana Palace. "Even though the bistro's atmosphere is informal," warned the reviewer, "reservations are strongly recommended if you don't want to be disappointed."

The Booker Pittman Orchestra had been contracted to provide dance music for the hundreds of invitees to the Palácio Itamaraty affair, and Buca drove to Leblon with the specific purpose of engaging his former tour vocalist for that evening. Sofie was reluctant. Since the conclusion of the tour she had been fully occupied with her new son, the move to a rented house in Leblon, and funding and opening the bistro with Lola. Once the bistro was operating, she had concentrated upon learning the popular local beach sambas, accompanied by guitars, rather than singing the more complex standards performed by larger bands. But, as he often did, Buca persisted, appealing to her artistic appetite and reminding her that it would be an opportunity to perform for a third national president.

With that in mind, Sofie set out to learn anything she could about the musical tastes of the American president and quickly found that he was an accomplished pianist with wide-ranging interests. However, his strongest musical efforts in recent years had been directed toward advancing the singing career of his daughter, Margaret, who was accompanying the president on this current trip. With another inquiry, Sofie learned that Margaret had quite recently recorded the soprano aria from *Pearl of Brazil*, singing with the Detroit Symphony. What if Buca could find an arrangement of that composition and invite Margaret to sing it for the distinguished gathering at the Palácio Itamaraty? It was worth a try.

The evening produced an unexpected result. After hearing her, Radio Globo, Rio's foremost radio station, offered Miss Truman the highest salary ever paid to a performer in Brazil if she would sing one evening radio show for a sponsor. She gracefully declined the offer, thinking that it might take away from the seriousness of purpose of the president's trip, but it brought the biggest smiles of their trip to the president and his wife.

Sofie was, of course, delighted to perform again before a large and appreciative audience, and she wished only that her father could have watched as his daughter sang for the president of the United States, only two years after the conclusion of World War II. There was an irony in the situation that brought a touch of sadness to Dieter and Sofie, even as they celebrated the recent positive events in their lives. A week later, on a hillside in Cordoba, Argentina, Hans Purm waved to Ursula and shouted, "Ushie—come and see the newspaper photos of President Truman's visit to Rio. There's one where I think I can see Sofie in the background with the Pittman Band!"

US President Harry S. Truman and his daughter Margaret sailed past Rio's Sugarloaf Mountain as a part of the president's three-week friendship visit to Brazil in September 1947.

Photo: Courtesy of the Harry S. Truman Presidential Library & Museum

65

⸙

Happy Anniversary

Friday, March 6, 1948, was to be the busiest day ever at Lola's Bistro Leblon. It was the first day of Rio's six-day Carnival, leading up to Ash Wednesday. The parade of celebrants would proceed from Ipanema's Rua Presidente Morais directly into Leblon's Avenida General San Martín and then double back along the beachfront. In both directions, thousands of people would pass near the bistro, and table reservations had been accepted for double the building's legal capacity, beginning in mid afternoon and extending past midnight.

On the previous Thursday night, Dieter and Sofie ate alone on the terrace of their new Leblon house, which faced southeast over the placid Atlantic Ocean. Sofie poured a glass of champagne for each of them and then raised hers in a salute to her partner.

"What's the occasion, querida?" he questioned.

"Aha—you'll never guess, but it is a very important anniversary. March 5, 1938—ten years ago tonight—fell on a Saturday. That evening, I went with school friends to the Fischerstube in Berlin and was so impressed with the handsome piano player that on the way out I tore his photo from the poster at the entrance. I took it back to my room at the university. A year later that photo was what Poppy and I used to produce your military identification papers for our hurried escape from Germany and into Czechoslovakia. So, Dieter, as of this evening, I have been in love with you for ten years. *Prost*, my sweet man!"

Dieter was, as often, amazed at the complexity of this beautiful woman. He stepped to her side and eased her upward from the chair, then embraced her softly for a tellingly long time. "You are so much more than I deserve, Sofie. I don't know of a way to tell you all the things you are to me."

"With more than a song lyric, I hope," she quipped, recognizing the words from his favorite Jerome Kern composition. "Given the number of obstacles we faced, I really believe that we have squeezed all that was possible from our first decade. We've survived Gestapo pursuit, a cruel war, your incarceration, the deaths of dear ones, escape to another part of the world, new languages and customs, pursuit by spies, and the arrival of our child."

"You're right—and you're leaving out a few things that could have brought it crashing down. But here we are with our own house, a promising business, and some good friends, too. What else could we ask for?"

"Well, that's the other part of the toast. I have a couple of things to tell you."

"Oh, my—let me sit down again. Okay, go ahead."

"Yes—that's it. Another baby. I just found out today, and it's going well. Maybe this time I can have a daughter named Astrid, to balance with Otto. She'll be born before his second birthday, so it won't be long before they can team up on us and get whatever they want."

"And?"

"And . . . Poppy and Branka are going to be among the revelers in Carnival this week. They are booked at a hotel in Ipanema and have made dinner reservations for two nights in our bistro. Their names are now Hans and Ursula Purm, and they have Chilean passports—but that's not where they live."

"You *are* filled with surprises! I was suspicious about the baby, and I am over-the-moon happy for us and for Otto. I'm also happy that your Poppy and Branka are going to see their grandson, but, as always, we want to be sure that occurs privately. They are going to want to spend some time with little Otto. How do you propose to arrange that?"

"Easy. I'll bring him to work with me and he can be upstairs in Lola's apartment playing with her baby, Diego. They do well together, and Lola's *enfermeira do bebe* is Otto's favorite. She knows lots of games and has good songs and stories for little people. We can even take their meals up there."

"Shall we finish the champagne?"

"I can't—at least for the next six months. But I thought that a sip or two today was a proper salute for two such important announcements."

"I agree. Let's make sure it all goes well."

At the Copacabana Palace Hotel, Security Director Octavio Oliveira followed his normal practice and examined the daily list of new guests being registered. He was curious about one of them—a Mr. William Carney with a diplomatic passport identifying him as an employee of the US government in Washington DC. Why wouldn't he be staying at the consulate or the embassy—except, of course, if he were here on vacation like any other of the swarm of Carnival tourists. But then, if he were here on vacation, would he have traveled alone to the world's best party? Men who came without wives or sweethearts rarely opted to stay alone in the most expensive hotel on the beach. He reexamined the list to see if there were any obvious names who might be under US surveillance—or protection. Nothing he saw suggested that, and Octavio sat at his table in the Bar do Copa trying to make some logical connection for Mr. Carney's presence.

Octavio thought back to the young ex-military fellow, Samson, and then to himself, watching for a "shadow" moving behind Sophia. He decided to call the Piano Man to see if the name William Carney meant anything to him. Probably not, but that whole thing of following and filming Sophia had been too dedicated to just go away, and they should be warned about this fellow from Washington at the Copacabana during Carnival.

Dieter's first response was that he didn't know anyone from Washington, but somehow the name sparked a memory, and finally it materialized. In Elsa's apologetic note after she had mishandled his letter to her, she mentioned the name of the man she had greeted in Prague. Dieter sorted through his box of correspondence until he found it, and there it was: "The trail of money . . . may be too appetizing for Mr. William Carney to ignore . . . !" And now someone with that name, working with the American government, had checked into the Copacabana Palace where both he and Sofie were well known. If he was any good at gathering intelligence, Mr. Carney could quickly learn where they now resided and worked. Worst of all, Dieter knew that the target of all that earlier pursuit was also coming here during Carnival Week, and he was seeing flashing danger lights in the whole situation.

❧

At the War Department's intelligence office, Gretchen Hasse picked through a pile of daily dispatches from Czechoslovakia, some of which had been intercepted from the occupying Soviets and others smuggled past censors by loyal Czech citizens. She also read the latest available copy of *Lidové Noviny,* the Czech language daily "people's news," and a smaller paper called *Russkiy Yazyk,* literally a Slavic "Russia Speaks" publication. Buried in the back pages of each, there appeared a small story about the mysterious disappearance of Swiss banker Maxmilian Ullrich, who had headed the Prague offices of a prestigious private Swiss bank. It was the infamous "Two-Minute Max" she had visited to withdraw Dieter's generous gift to her, and probably also the intimate who oversaw a substantial part of General von Seigler's wealth. This could only mean that once again the heat was being turned up on the search for the general, and she knew that posed danger for Dieter and his Sofie.

Gretchen called the private CIA number of the risen William Carney, only to learn that he would be out of the office for several days—destination undisclosed. She wondered whether he was in Prague driving bamboo wedges under the fingernails of Two-Minute Max, or perhaps in Rio hoping to catch General von Seigler stealing a few minutes with his daughter during Carnival.

After thinking for a few minutes, she sent a wire to "The Piano Man" at the Copacabana Palace Hotel reading, "Medical authorities in Washington are warning of infestations of leeches in your waters, which may attach to your body and suck blood. Be generally careful and especially aware of genus Carneis, species Williamis, which is very dangerous during this season. Signed: Dr. Elsa Danzig, MD." She wished she could call Dieter, but she was afraid he might already be under surveillance.

66

Carney's in Town

"How much does Lola know about all of this, Dieter?" Sofie had listened to his warning from their friend Octavio at the hotel and reviewed with Dieter the wire from the ubiquitous Elsa, both alerting them to the presence of someone named William Carney in their city this week. Now she was wearing her general's no-nonsense face and determined to know all of the elements of their potential threat. Her new role as mother wiped away any pretense of moderation; Sofie was angry and determined.

"I can't really remember all of what I told her. We had conversations that rambled on, and sometimes they were more like confessionals. Of course, she knew that your father was an important military officer and that you had spent your formative years as his intimate in Berlin. I suppose I referred to your strong identity with him, and his generosity toward both you and me. But I never quantified that, because I don't even know those details."

"Don't you imagine that our Ipanema apartment gave her some idea that we had resources? And don't you think that our role in funding the bistro confirmed that impression?" Sofie didn't give him an opportunity to respond, but continued. "You included her in some very personal facts about us, Dieter. And if we are facing another of those damned spies or whatever they are, we have to know whether she's on our side. Now! Get serious about this. It's not just you and me anymore—we're protecting two babies and two older people, right?"

"Of course, of course. What do you think our next step should be, Liebling?"

"I think we should take the initiative away from Mr. Carney and not just be reacting to what he might do or where he might show up. If he's at the damned Copacabana Palace, let's go there and introduce ourselves. This is our city, Dieter—and we have friends here. A threat only harms you when you accept it, and I'm bloody tired of being intimidated."

❧

Two hours later, with Dieter in her wake, Sofie walked swiftly to the reception desk and called out, "Cornell, come over here. I need to talk to you."

"Cordell, Miss Sophia—like saying Cornell with a head cold. Remember? How can I help you? You seem disturbed."

"You have a guest named William Carney—an American from Washington, DC—and I need to talk with him. Is he in his room? What room is he in?"

"Let me see. Okay, his key is not in the box, so he's in the building. He might be in his room or he could be in one of the public rooms. Would you like me to call his room?"

"Please do it. And if you reach him, tell him that two friends are in the lobby and would like to see him."

"His room doesn't answer, Miss Sophia. Let me check to see if he is in the spa or perhaps the Bar do Copa having a libation." After making a pair of inquiries, the visibly annoyed Cordell squeezed out a practiced smile and said, "Okay. He's in the Bar do Copa, sitting alone near the south window, looking at a stack of papers, and drinking a *cervija 'Bohemia.'* You won't have trouble identifying him; he's a large black man and probably the only person drinking alone in the room."

Cordell's description had been accurate, and soon after that, they stood beside the table and addressed the lone man intent upon a small pile of papers. This time, Dieter spoke first.

"Mr. Carney? Mr. William Carney?"

"Yes, can I help you?"

"You're from Washington?"

"Yes—US Department of Agriculture. Assistant Secretary for Latin America. And you?"

"We're locals. My wife and I both perform here at the hotel, and we have a new bistro on Leblon Beach called Lola's Bistro Leblon. It's about five kilometers from here. We'd like to invite you to be our guest for dinner some night during your stay in Rio."

"Well, how nice! May I assume that you are 'Lola,' young lady?"

"No, I'm Sophia. You can see my picture in the main lobby. I sing here with the Booker Pittman Orchestra once each week. My husband, Dieter, is called 'the Piano Man' here in the Bar do Copa. Lola is our business partner in the bistro. It's a new venture for us and we want visitors like you to know that there is more to Rio than just Copacabana and Ipanema."

"What's the format of your bistro, Sophia—mmm, pretty name. What kind of music?"

"We are showcasing young Brazilian talents and the new music being created in our beach communities. It takes something from the samba rhythms and a little from American jazz and even some classical guitar, and puts them together in what they call a 'new thing'—a *bossa nova.* This week we have a twenty-year-old from

Ipanema named Tom Jobin who plays piano and guitar. Our audiences love him."

"Well—maybe when I come back. Tomorrow I'm going to Mata Grosso, where we're experimenting with some hybrid corn. Could change eating habits in the interior if it is successful. One of those ideas Rockefeller got all hepped up about while he was here. Secretary Anderson is really behind it now, and I've got two weeks to put together an evaluation."

"Rockefeller? The oil guy?"

"His grandson—Nelson. FDR made him Undersecretary of State for Latin America, and he really got into the nuts and bolts of these countries. Hey, thanks for coming over to my table. Sorry I'm so busy, but if I can I'll hit Lola's Bistro on my way back. Boa sorte, my friends!"

"And good luck to you, Mr. Carney."

❧

"What do you think, Dieter?" Sofie asked as soon as they were out of earshot. "I looked at the papers and folders he was reading and they were all about agriculture. But that could just be cover, too."

"It could, but if they are covering, they did a good job. Did you notice the dirt under his fingernails? That was real. So were the calluses in his hands. I shook one just to check. Like leather! And he handed me his card—it was just what he said. I think we've been paranoid about this one. But it's good to have the reminder. Like a fire drill, huh?"

"I guess so. Remember, we also got a red flag from the fat Polish girl, Elsa. Can you find out what was rattling her?"

"The telegraph company can probably identify the sender's number, but I don't know what name she uses. Can we just forget this misadventure and enjoy Carnival together?"

"I'm all for that, Liebling. I'm tighter than a treble-note piano wire right now."

❧

The lifeless body of Maximilian Ullrich was found in a tangle of weeds in the Vltava River, downstream from Prague, by a cattle farmer. His wallet contained a healthy amount of cash, and his Rolex watch was still in place and working. There were no signs of violence inconsistent with the official conclusion that Herr Ullrich had fallen accidentally from a pedestrian bridge while relieving himself into the swift river. His pants were unbuttoned, which further supported that finding.

William Carney returned Elsa's unanswered call four days later and said he was sorry to have missed it while he was vacationing in Miami with a member of his office staff. Elsa said she had been calling to get the name of the very old restaurant where they had dined in Prague—for a friend who was going to Czechoslovakia while tourism is still permitted.

Every element in these two scenarios was a pure fabrication, but they gave Sofie and Dieter 'permission' to retreat from their worry and enjoy introducing Poppy and Branka to little Otto and to share the good news that Astrid would be joining the family early in March.

67

1948

William Carney asked Gretchen Hasse to marry him in Washington DC during the early summer of 1948. At the ceremony, Joseph English served as best man for his fellow CIA trainee, and Magda Kruboski of Chicago was matron of honor for her wartime SWW colleague. Magda's two daughters served as flower girls. The newlyweds honeymooned in San Diego, California, where Mr. Carney's mother was living in a retirement home. Among the vows the couple exchanged was a mutual promise not to engage in further pursuit of escaped World War II participants living in Latin America.

In Buenos Aires, dentist-turned-motion-picture-director León Klimovsky contracted to film *La Guitarra de Gardel* in Argentina beginning late in 1948, and he travelled north to Rio's beaches in search of talented new guitar virtuosos. After visiting multiple clubs, Klimovsky settled upon Lola's Bistro Leblon as the area's richest source of original musicians. He signed two of them to appear in the motion picture and incidentally asked the bistro's proprietress, Lola, to return to Argentina with him to assist in the production. She consented and departed for Buenos Aires with her son, Diego, and his baby nurse—with no fixed date for her return.

The new nation of Israel was launched in May 1948 and accorded instant authenticity by US President Harry Truman's formal recognition. Concentration camp survivor Simon Wiesenthal had worked with the moribund OSS for over a year, but that effort had floundered when the wartime intelligence agency was summarily closed. Wiesenthal then transferred his ongoing effort to collect depositions from other concentration camp survivors to the new Jewish Documentation Center in Linz, Austria. They identified over three thousand such Nazis, but their pursuit was again frustrated as the wartime Allied nations refocused their efforts onto restructuring and financing postwar Europe. Wiesenthal's pursuit was narrowed to only half a dozen notorious war criminals and, collaborating with the new Jewish nation, those efforts eventually bore fruit. General Otto von Seigler was not considered a prime suspect, and like thousands of other former Axis officials and collaborators, he was free to establish a new lifestyle in the friendly political atmosphere of South America.

Sofie gave birth to a healthy baby girl, who arrived two weeks early and was named Astrid, with no dissenting voices. Sofie and Dieter Havlik assumed full-time management of Lola's Bistro Leblon, and from time to time diners were rewarded with one of their piano-and-voice duets, reminiscent of many earlier performances in the Copacabana Palace Hotel. The bistro continued to be an incubator of the bossa nova genre of music, which became Brazil's musical signature a short time later. Hans and Ursula Purm from Santiago de Chile visited the bistro a month after Astrid's birth and stayed for a week at their favorite Ipanema hotel, where they enjoyed practicing their excellent Portuguese in conversations with the staff.

In June 1948, the Soviet Union and their puppet government in East Germany imposed a blockade on the city of Berlin, which lay within East Germany's boundaries. The blockade effectively stopped roadway, railway, and canal transportation of essential supplies and foodstuffs into the Allied sectors of the city. Under the command of US Air Force General William Tunner, a heroic airlift aggregating more than two hundred thousand individual flights by Douglas C-54 "Skymasters" kept the people of Berlin supplied for the next year.

With the reality of the Berlin Blockade staring them down, twelve nations drafted an alliance, to be called the North Atlantic Treaty Organization (NATO), with the purpose of providing collective security against the perceived threat of further aggression from the Soviet Union. When the NATO model was approved and implemented a few months later, Lilka Rudovska moved from her retirement apartment in London to a hotel in Brussels, Belgium, where she helped to design the new organization's Intelligence, Surveillance and Reconnaissance function. One of her first unofficial tasks was to trace her only daughter's current location in Brazil and dispatch a long, handwritten letter. A reply, filled with baby photos, was airmailed back to Brussels within a few days.

❧

Sofie and Dieter enjoyed the quiet early-evening air of a Leblon Sunday, sipping caipirinha cocktails on the wide beach near their home. Quiet times together were usually limited to the wee hours after the bistro closed its doors and before their children opened their eyes. But this evening they had felt confident that their new Assistant Manager Cordell and Security Director Octavio would oversee the enthusiastic weekend diners ably at the bistro.

"I can't believe we're doing this," Sofie laughed. "It's almost like when we used to drive up to Poppy's house at Muggelsee to be alone together. Do you remember how we used to cuddle on that thick Alpine rug in front of the fire?"

"If I ever forget those nights you will probably be helping me to get my shoes onto the correct feet, Liebling. You were the most beautiful thing I had ever seen, in that firelight—and there were times when I was convinced I was crazy and dreaming the whole thing. I had to touch you often to reassure myself."

"How lucky that I'm tactile! I could hardly wait for those touches. I'm glad we got past some bumps in the road and took advantage of our good fortune—this all feels so good now. Should we just sit back and enjoy it, or should we be putting together a five-year plan like those Soviets do?"

"What would you like to add or do by they time you're forty that you haven't got now? Anything special beckoning to you?"

"Oh, I'd like to visit some of the places we always hear about in the United States. They seem to be setting the pace in many things, and it would be fun to see them where they start. Like New York and Hollywood, maybe. And I'd like to go back to Berlin and Prague and Paris and London where I learned so much about myself. Maybe even sing a little while with Stéphane and Django if they still have a group over there. And, I guess I want to find something special to do with a part of my money from Poppy. I know that at least some of it belongs to someone else, but that's like trying to put an egg back inside its shell. But, maybe some charity or scholarship which helps some people who fell behind during the war."

"I like that. Are we happy with two little Havliks? Or do you want to have another? You're thirty-three years old, so that's not an option forever—and you have had the first two without really any problems."

"Easy for you to say, Piano Man, but I was the one looking like the Hindenburg and getting kicked in the belly late at night. I'm not sure that at thirty-five I can put the parts back together as well as I did the first two times. I'm already a lot curvier than I was on that rug in front of the fire, in case you haven't noticed. Have you?"

"I've noticed that every man who walks into the bistro takes a little extra time to look at you, and when you sing there, even the chattiest people turn their chairs and quiet down."

"Thank you, sweetheart. But what about you, Dieter? What's in your five-year plan?"

"Be a hero to Otto and Astrid, first of all. Get them reading good books and make sure they hear good music sometime during each day. Make sure they know how to survive in any kind of storm, and assure them they're loved unconditionally. Teach them to win, but not at any cost—and to be graceful winners when they do beat their competitors. And—if the time and circumstances permit—I want to go back to Theresienstadt and plant some flowers just outside the gate, where Elsa picked me up in a garbage can filled with fish entrails."

Their conversation gave way to the sound of soft waves washing on hard-packed sand near the water's edge, and Sofie remembered a Keats poem from her university studies which described "the moving waters at their priestlike task of pure ablution round earth's human shores." Hadn't they both worked through personal challenges and emerged cleansed and ready to face the future confidently together? It was time to reconfirm their wonderful partnership and make that commitment a part of every future decision.

Sofie tousled Dieter's sun-bleached hair and smiled. "Are you ready for dinner, sir? I hear there's a great little bistro a short way down the beach from here, and I think we might get a table there if we hurry. After all, it has been a busy day."

AUTHOR'S NOTES

When the Axis powers surrendered and the fighting stopped, the United States was both militarily and economically the mightiest nation on earth. Nevertheless, challenges began to arise immediately, mostly from aggressive Communism. On March 12, 1947, President Harry Truman, in a speech to the US Congress, first set forth a policy of containment which was known as "the Truman Doctrine" and was understood to contain the commitment of the United States to come to the aid of free nations whose independence was threatened by such "outside pressures." There was no paucity of challenges to the Doctrine, leading to the formation of NATO and to the continuing involvement of America in the affairs of Europe, the Middle East, and the Far East.

Perhaps it was this refocusing which sidetracked what had promised to be a natural postwar partnership between North and South America—one continent having every technological advantage and the other with extravagant, unexploited natural and human resources. Had that played out as expected, there might have been an ongoing, parallel effort to pursue and root out escaped former Axis functionaries then living in South America. Instead, the U.S. became involved in the civil strife of Greece and Turkey; the birth pains of nascent Israel; the administration and funding of the Marshall Plan throughout Europe; the recovery and recasting of Imperial Japan; and the enigmatic clash of communism and nationalism in Asia.

Exiled Germans (much like our hypothetical General Otto von Seigler) were soon able to blend into their new nations, whose leaderships often welcomed—or at least overlooked—their presence. President Juan Peron and First Lady Eva Duarte de Peron assumed almost dictatorial powers in Argentina, and prominent Italian and German families thrived there after the war years. Evita (who had lamented the early deaths of Gershwin and Mozart in conversation with Sophia in our story) lived an even briefer life, dying at age 33 in 1952. Over the following quarter-century, her corpse was moved secretly among several locations in South America and Europe before final burial in Argentina in 1976.

Booker "Buca" Pittman was known to the author during his working years in South America, and, as portrayed herein, Buca's big band was considered the finest on the continent. He performed in several countries but always based his band in Brazil, where he died in 1969. His stepdaughter, Eliana, became a popular vocalist in the style of Ella Fitzgerald, and she later gained notoriety as an actress in Rio de Janeiro, where she makes her home.

Francisco "Baby" Matarazzo Pignatari was probably the most charismatic Brazilian of his time. He was bigger than life, incredibly good-looking, and flamboyant in his interactions with people who interested him. He married four times but somehow managed to accommodate and maneuver through scores of public relationships with some of the most beautiful women of the postwar years. All the while, he remained an attentive and successful businessman. If you were in Rio in the late 1950s or early '60s, chances are you got to be a walk-in guest at one of his incredible parties in the Copacabana neighborhood—or at least to see the people rushing in and hear the music blasting out. Baby continued to amaze with his energy and imagination until his death in 1977, in Sao Paulo. Brazil.

Simon Wiesenthal was the patron saint of the pursuit of escaped Nazis. As described in this story, he sought assistance from the western Allies, but after receiving insufficient support, he created the Documentation Center of the Association of Jewish Victims of the Nazi Regime. It was a major repository of the personal stories of persecution recounted by thousands of Europe's surviving Jews, and it was helpful in keeping the pressure on major Nazi offenders scattered throughout the world. Mr. Wiesenthal's name became synonymous with that pursuit, which he continued until his death at age 96 in Vienna.

I have included cameo references to two friends, who played important roles during the postwar period covered by this novel. The first, USAF Lieutenant General William Tunner, directed the miraculous Berlin Airlift, which defied the Soviet Union's bold attempt to swallow Germany after the war and thereby kept alive the hope for European survival and independence. Gen. Tunner was my commander during my Air Force active-duty years, and he later became a fellow director of Seaboard World Airlines, which company was my working identity for sixteen wonderful years.

There is also a brief reference to Nelson A. Rockefeller, New York State governor and vice president of the United States. Mr. Rockefeller was an early advocate of US partnership with the South American countries, and he made strong personal commitments to the economic and social advancement of that continent. I was privileged to work with the Rockefeller interests in South America and to live there for several years, which yielded some personal insights helpful in writing this novel.

Finally, please allow me to add a personal note to my readers. This sequel was written in large part to respond to requests from readers of *Über Alles*. Many of them expressed their appreciation of the characters I had created for inclusion in that earlier novel, and felt I should follow those characters deeper into their lives in a sequel. In so doing, I have allowed each to make some mistakes or to exhibit traits that may dull some of their luster for those readers. Dieter, Sofie, Elsa, Lilka, and Otto von Seigler would not be "real" if they didn't stumble occasionally—just as you and I. Life is not about maintaining perfection, but about dealing with imperfection when we recognize it or are guilty of it.

My characters and I thank you for your interest in us, and we wish you well until we meet again.

—ROBERT ARTHUR NEFF
Pinehurst, NC 2019

THE COVER ILLUSTRATION

Sophia On Tour

In 2016, prominent artist Kathleen Ericson read a manuscript draft of author Robert Arthur Neff's historical novel *Über Alles*. From the mental images it inspired, she sketched likenesses of the book's principal characters, Dieter Meister and Sofie von Seigler, as she imagined them. At that time, Ms. Ericson expressed the hope that there would be a sequel to *Über Alles*, and that she might again have the opportunity to read the manuscript.

Kathleen Ericson did get to read an early draft of the

sequel *After All* in 2018, and it summoned up images of Sophia singing on tour in South America during the immediate postwar years. Author Robert Arthur Neff agreed that Ms. Ericson's oil painting of what she had visualized effectively captured important elements of *After All*'s message, and he requested the artist's permission to incorporate her original work in the book's cover.

Illustrator Daniel J. Middleton has adapted Ms. Ericson's painting of *Sophia On Tour* in creating the cover of *After All*.

ABOUT THE AUTHOR

From his early years, Robert Arthur Neff has thrived on international involvement. Military service, business responsibilities, and personal travels have familiarized him with the locations and events entwined in his sequential historical novels, *Über Alles* and *After All*. He describes both books as "either a history lesson wrapped in a love story, or the reverse of that."

The author visiting the infamous Theresienstadt detention facility in today's Czech Republic in November 2017. Approximately 165,000 Nazi prisoners were sent to Theresienstadt during World War II. Of those, some 88,000 were deported to Auschwitz for extermination, and 17,247 survived and were liberated on May 5, 1945. The rest were either transferred to other concentration camps or died at Theresienstadt during the war years.

Photo: Robert Arthur Neff.

Mr. Neff studied engineering, political science, and law at Cornell University, then he "entered the real world" as a JAG officer in the US Air Force. He was assigned to the 63rd Troop Carrier Wing of MATS, which aggregated squadrons deployed to overseas locations ranging from North Africa to Europe to Canada's DEW Line to New Zealand and Antarctica. These became a new kind of classroom for the itinerant lawyer.

After his military service, Mr. Neff knew that he wanted a business career that would continue expanding his knowledge of many cultures and countries. He had the good fortune to find just such a job with the Rockefeller Brothers' International Basic Economy Corporation, headquartered at "30 Rock." Initially his assignments were focused upon Western Europe and the Middle East, but later they shifted to the management of various South American businesses, and that continent became Mr. Neff's home for several years.

Prominent international businessmen were demanding more efficient, affordable air cargo services to accommodate the exploding growth of high-value international commerce. A leader in the movement was Mr. Laurance Rockefeller, whose participation in the airline industry collaterally yielded a welcome opportunity for Mr. Neff. He became an officer and director of Seaboard World Airlines, a major all-cargo airline which was pioneering international carriage innovations and also performing world-wide contract carriage for the US Department of Defense. Seaboard and the Flying Tiger Line later merged, and their combined activity eventually became an integral part of the contemporary Federal Express Corporation, from which Mr. Neff is a retiree.

Mr. Neff now resides with his wife, Julie, in Pinehurst, NC, and on Beaver Island, MI. They continue to visit other parts of the world frequently, and Mr. Neff has formalized his lifelong interest in writing, drawing extensively upon themes suggested by his work and travels. Favored leisure activities include playing jazz standards on his oversized grand piano, watching and playing tennis, and enjoying the uncomplicated attractions of Nicaragua's Pacific Coast, where he does much of his serious writing.